Deborah Carr lives on the island of Jersey in the Channel Islands with her husband, two children and three rescue dogs. She became interested in books set in WW1 when researching her grandfather's time as a cavalryman in the 17th 21st Lancers.

She is part of 'The Blonde Plotters' writing group and was Deputy Editor on the online review site, Novelicious.com. Her debut historical romance, *Broken Faces*, is set in WW1 and was runner-up in the 2012 Good Housekeeping Novel Writing Competition and given a 'special commendation' in the Harry Bowling Prize that year.

🐦 @DebsCarr
📘 DeborahCarrAuthor/
www.deborahcarr.org

Also by Deborah Carr

Broken Faces
The Poppy Field

Mrs Boots

Deborah Carr

OneMoreChapter

One More Chapter
a division of HarperCollins*Publishers*
The News Building
1 London Bridge Street
London SE1 9GF

www.harpercollins.co.uk

This paperback edition 2020

First published in Great Britain in ebook format by
HarperCollins*Publishers* 2020

A catalogue record for this book
is available from the British Library

ISBN: 9780008363314

Set in Birka by Palimpsest Book Production Ltd, Falkirk
Stirlingshire

Printed and bound by CPI Group (UK) Ltd,
Croydon, CR0 4YY

I'd like to dedicate this book to Florence Boot and to all strong women who help others to recognise the best in themselves.

Chapter 1

August 1885 – 27 Queen Street, St Helier, Jersey

Florence Rowe waved at Emile, the boarder from the chemist at number 29 who had raised his hat in a friendly salute. As usual at this time of day, Queen Street was bustling with shoppers and shop assistants out on their errands. She didn't mind waiting for her good friend, Albert, to finish wrapping the packet of tea she had been sent to buy for her father's stationer's shop, which was situated between the chemist and the tea merchants. She loved her job in her father's shop, on the bustling street, but it was always nice to step away for a few minutes to catch up with Albert's news and share her own with him.

'I had a customer in here yesterday,' he said, tidying away the small weights he had used to calculate the correct amount of tea leaves. 'He's an artist from Birmingham. He came to the island last week to stay with relatives for the rest of the summer. He was telling me that it was reported in his local newspapers about a poor young woman on a roof.'

'Sorry,' Florence asked, confused. She was used to Albert's

1

catastrophising, but this story was a little odd. 'What did you say?'

'Someone heard screams in the middle of the night.'

'Where, here?'

'No, in Kidderminster.'

Florence realised she had no idea what Albert was talking about. 'Maybe you should start again. From the beginning.'

'The artist told me that just before he came to the island he read about a local woman, a young lady somnambulist, dressed only in her night clothes. She was still asleep when she climbed out of an upstairs window and onto the roof of her family home.'

'How do your customers come to share such stories with you.' She was struggling not to giggle. 'They only come in to buy tea.'

'Maybe they can see that I need a little drama in my life.' A customer entered the shop just then and Albert lowered his voice and added, 'We've been friends since we were children, Florence; can you remember a time when we had something worth being excited about?'

'Apart from going to the theatre, or such like?' she asked, not wishing him to become maudlin, which he could, if she ever let him.

'Yes, those outings are fun, but not like the story the artist told me.'

Florence was always fascinated by Albert's latest intrigue. Her father wouldn't entertain the newspapers being read in their home. His only connection to them was caused by necessity when he advertised his stationer's, W. H. Rowe. Albert was her connection to the sensational stories printed in them. He loved discovering the latest dramas occurring on the island and she loved that he took time to share them with her. She wasn't sure though if it was the stories themselves, or his dramatised account of them.

'Was she all right?' she asked.

'Yes, thankfully,' Albert continued. 'The girl's father and a police constable threw a rope up to her. They managed to rescue her before she fell headlong to her death.'

Florence focused her attention on her purse so that he couldn't see her amusement at his dramatics. 'That's a relief. Poor thing, waking up in such a predicament.' She wondered how much longer he was going to spend wrapping up her tea.

'That's what I thought.' He patted the neat package. 'There you go.'

'Thank you,' she said, paying him and taking her tea.

'It's such a relief that the weather has improved, don't you think?'

'Yes. Father has been fretting about the stock not being delivered on time, as the ferries were cancelled due to the summer storms last week.'

Albert nodded, happy to have another drama to focus on. 'We've had the same problem here,' he said, putting her money in the till and giving her change. He folded his arms across his chest. 'Thankfully we had a delivery brought in this morning. Now everyone is panicking that the weather will change again, so they're all rushing to stock up on their favourite tea mixture before it does.'

'That's one of the downsides of living on an island, my father always says.' Florence knew the problem well. Her own mother was always concerning herself with the boats' arrivals at the harbour. 'Hopefully it'll stay nice and hot for a while now. It is supposed to be summer, after all.'

She went to say something else, but, as she glanced out the window, all thoughts of what it was disappeared as she noticed one particular lady marching up the pavement on the opposite side of the street, her lady's maid at her side laden with various bags and boxes. Florence could not help feeling sorry for the young woman scuttling along slightly behind her mistress, who was, by the determined expression on her lined face, on her way to give some poor soul a scolding.

Florence groaned.

'Whatever is the matter?' Albert asked. 'Are you unwell?'

She shook her head. 'No, look.' She pointed out of the window. 'She's paused. I think she's about to cross over to this side.'

He stepped forward, peered out at the focus of her concern and shivered theatrically. 'I hope she doesn't come in here. She's a monstrous woman. She always has something, or someone, to complain about.'

Florence doubted that Mrs Wolstenholm would be buying her own tea. She probably left that job to one of her servants. Her heart dipped as she realised that the route the woman was taking was to W.H. Rowe next door.

'Oh, no. She's going into Father's shop. I'd better hurry back. Thanks, Albert,' she shouted over her shoulder.

She ran out of the shop, following the lady's maid in through

4

the open shop door, the jangling of the brass alerting her father and sister Amy to their arrival. She closed the door quietly behind them, Mrs Wolstenholm oblivious to Florence coming in behind her. The lady tapped her silver-topped walking stick noisily on the wooden floorboards.

Dropping the packet of tea quickly behind the counter, Florence skirted around the woman and her servant, a smile she did not feel fixed firmly on her face.

'Mrs Wolstenholm, how delightful to see you today.'

The woman waited for Florence to come directly in front of her before looking her slowly up and down as if she had never seen a specimen quite like her before. 'I don't take to modern women,' she sniffed, glancing at Florence's bustle. 'All those ruffles and draping material, it's too fanciful if you ask me. I believe unmarried women should wear plainer clothing.'

Florence had not asked her. She hid her irritation, determined not to give the woman satisfaction of knowing she had annoyed her. Florence liked wearing a larger bustle, despite the discomfort it brought to her. She loved fashion and was not going to be dictated to about her clothing by anyone else, especially not this rude woman.

'Is there anything I can help you with today, Mrs Wolstenholm?' Florence asked, ignoring the insults being thrown at her; she knew better than to annoy her father's best, but rudest, customer or give her any cause to be angered further.

Mrs Wolstenholm waved her gloved hand as if swatting an annoying fly. 'Where is your father? I wish to speak with him.'

'Are you certain I will be unable to assist you?' Florence

asked, aware that she knew all there was to know about the workings of this shop.

Mrs Wolstenholm rested both hands on the top of her walking stick and glowered at Florence. 'I will not be served by a girl. I have asked for your father; he always serves me.'

Frustrated by the woman's rudeness, Florence forced a smile. 'Would you like to take a seat while I fetch him for you?' she asked, indicating the smart cushioned chair her father had brought into the shop for his less than sturdy customers.

'I shall not be waiting long enough to take a seat,' she barked. 'Hurry now, girl. I do not have time to dawdle.'

Florence heard footsteps and turned her attention to the storeroom door, relieved to see her father's arrival. He was wearing a similar forced smile to the one she felt sure she had on her face.

'I'm most dreadfully sorry to have kept you waiting,' her father said, hurrying in to join them. He glanced at Florence and tilted his head briefly indicating that she take his place unpacking the latest delivery. 'We've only a moment ago been delivered of an order that was delayed.'

'Yes, yes, man,' she snapped. 'I am not here to discuss your business. You sent word that you had several books you believed might suit my taste.'

Florence reached the doorway at the back of the shop leading to the small room they referred to as the storeroom, although it really was not much bigger than a large cupboard. She couldn't help feeling angry on her father's behalf to hear the dragon of a woman address him so rudely. She turned to watch him.

'I do.' He hurried over to behind the counter from where Florence saw him take a bundle of five books.

He raised his right hand to catch Florence's attention. 'Fetch one of the new books by Mr Thomas Hardy that I asked you to put aside for Mrs Wolstenholm.'

Wanting the grumpy customer out of their shop as soon as possible, Florence hurried to do as he asked. She leant into the trunk and took out one of the immaculate copies of *The Mayor of Casterbridge* that she and many of their customers had been waiting weeks to read. She could not help thinking how unfair it was that someone as horrible as this woman was always first in line for everything she wanted, simply because of her wealth.

She pictured some of the young women who entered the shop, like poor Nelly Cooper, so desperate to be able to enjoy books, but having neither the time nor the money to do so. She would appreciate the book so much more and she deserved to read it more than this woman too, thought Florence, hearing Mrs Wolstenholm's grumbling coming from the shop. She picked up one of the pristine copies and hastily took the book to the shop and placed it onto the counter.

Leaving her father to serve the woman, Florence returned to the storeroom just as her sister Amy arrived from the family's flat above the shop. Florence was older by just one year and enjoyed working with her sister who was also a shop assistant. Many times, she had dreamt aloud to Amy about owning her own shop one day, but they both knew that it would take many years for either of them to be able to afford to do such a thing, if indeed they could ever find a way to save up enough money to do so.

'Did I hear Mrs Wolstenholm's dulcet moaning?' Amy whispered.

Florence covered her mouth to stifle her giggles. 'You did. I can't fathom how that poor maid of hers can stand hearing her constant insults to everyone she meets.'

'We're very lucky to be shop assistants for someone as dear as Father.' Amy peered around Florence at the offensive woman. 'I overheard our parents speaking the other evening when I passed the living room. They were saying how that woman in there is only a shopkeeper's daughter. She's no better than we are.'

Florence widened her eyes, stunned. 'You'd never know it to watch the way she treats people of a lower station than her own, would you?'

'No. She's from the same background as we are. Her father was a shopkeeper too, so you would think she wouldn't speak down to Father like she does.'

Florence mulled over her sister's words. Somehow it seemed even more appalling that this woman who spoke to their father so abruptly had come from a similar background. What right did that woman think she had to talk down to decent people like her father? Somehow, this woman's rudeness seemed worse coming from someone who, Florence assumed, must have also been on the receiving end of another's patronising behaviour. She surely must remember how it felt to have less than others and have to silently accept their ill manners simply because she was not in a position to put them in their place.

'Do you know, Amy,' Florence said, having to remember to keep her voice down despite her anger, 'when I get my own shop, I'm going to remember this particular customer and how she makes me feel when she addresses our father in the way that she does. It's shameful the way she is putting him down. How dare she?' Florence knew full well that the woman dared because she could afford to go elsewhere to spend her money, whereas their father could not afford to lose his best client. 'I'll never forget where I'm from. I'll also never speak down to people like her. Ever!'

Chapter 2

'Florence, where are you? Mr Boot will be here at any moment.'

She could hear her mother calling but didn't answer immediately. She only had half an hour before the end of her lunch break when she was expected back at her father's shop below their flat. Why couldn't her mother leave her in peace to read? Just this once.

Florence flicked through the pages of her book in frustration, forgetting momentarily that she had only borrowed the book from her father's shop. There were only a couple of pages left until the end of the chapter. Desperate to discover what happened next, Florence read on, entranced by the new book from Mr Thomas Hardy. She couldn't bear to wait a moment longer to absorb this book.

Biting the side of her fingernail, she read on, shocked by the unforgiveable behaviour of Michael Henchard drunkenly selling his wife and baby daughter for five guineas at a country fair.

'Horrible man,' she mumbled, gasping in shock and almost

dropping the book when her bedroom door burst open and her sister Amy walked in.

'I might have guessed you were hiding in here with a book,' she said with a knowing smile on her face. 'Didn't you hear Mother calling for you? Father's guest is arriving soon, and he wants us to meet him.'

Florence closed her book slowly and sighed. 'I don't know why he wants us to meet the man. Isn't he a chemist? What could we possibly have to say to him?'

Amy snatched the book from Florence's hands and read the description. 'Actually, he's a druggist.'

Florence was surprised her sister knew this about Mr Boot, but, determined to distract her sister from telling her off about borrowing the book, she asked, 'That's as maybe, but I still don't see why we need to spend time with him. Anyway, how do you know this about him?'

Amy stared at her and Florence could see she was amused to have surprised her in this way. 'I heard Father speaking about him to Mother earlier.'

'What's the difference between the two jobs then?' she asked, intrigued.

'Apparently a druggist manufactures and sells drugs and medicines, whereas a chemist specialises in the science behind the chemistry.' She thought for a moment. 'I think that's what Father meant.'

'I heard he owns shops,' Florence said, trying to work out why this man was so important to their father. 'Maybe that's why he wants us to meet him when he arrives.'

Amy stared down at the cover of the book in her hand before

glaring at Florence. 'Father will be furious if he discovers you've taken this from the new stock. You know we are forbidden to read the new stock. And there's a long waiting list for this title.'

Typical Amy not to allow her to get away with doing something she shouldn't.

Florence couldn't help feeling embarrassed. She hated being caught out borrowing the books. Her father didn't mind too much if they were from old stock but insisted that she and Amy never bought the new books to read, at least until the rush from their customers had ended.

'I'm aware of that,' she said trying to defend herself, 'but I've heard so much about *The Mayor of Casterbridge* and I simply couldn't wait any longer to read it.'

Amy closed the bedroom door and leant against it, lowering her voice. 'That's as maybe, but we can't spare any copies of this one. You know only half the shipment arrived and we need every spare copy for those who've been waiting to read it.' She shook her head. 'I thought I'd spotted you taking a peek at the beginning of the story earlier when you were supposed to be unpacking the delivery.'

Florence felt her face reddening. 'I had intended returning it by tomorrow.'

'You shouldn't have borrowed it in the first place. It won't be new if it's already been read.'

'Yes, I know,' Florence replied, irritated. 'Stop being so pious. We both know you've done the same thing, many times. Anyway, I can't see that I'll have the opportunity to read it by tomorrow now. I'm meeting friends to see a play at the Theatre Royal later this evening.'

Amy narrowed her eyes. 'And will Albert be one of those friends?'

Florence hated it when her sister teased her Albert. Amy knew well enough that they were merely friends and had been since childhood. He was fun to be with and made her laugh. She knew her mother suspected they were secretly courting, or maybe she simply hoped it was the case. Florence hated deception, but on this occasion if it kept her mother happy and also from trying to persuade her to find someone to marry, then it was worth it.

And Albert was fun to be with. He treated her as an equal and she knew they both enjoyed their mini debates on current events and novels. How many of her friends' husbands could she honestly say that about, she mused. None, she was certain of that.

She thought of the downtrodden women of her age and younger that she'd seen coming into Rowes. Initially unmarried, then excited to be courted by a man they had hopes for. Florence thought of the many of them with fake smiles, hiding their disappointment of the future they had hoped to enjoy. Or she was being cynical, as Amy had hinted she might be.

She loved her father very much, but he was definitely the head of the household, as he should be, but the older she became the harder it was to be told what she could and could not do each day. Why would she swap one man controlling her life for another? It didn't make any sense. As far as she was concerned, marriage was not a state to which she aspired.

She realised her sister had been speaking. 'Sorry, what did you say?'

'Will Albert be attending the play with you at the Theatre Royal tonight?'

She suspected she had missed something else her sister had said, but didn't say so. 'Yes, he will be.'

Amy handed the book back to her. 'I think you and Albert are well suited. I know Mother is secretly pleased that you've finally seen sense about your intention to stay a spinster.'

Florence narrowed her eyes at her sister. 'Stop it. You know there's nothing of the kind going on between us.'

'I do. However, you two shouldn't forget that his mother is one of our mother's oldest friends,' she said, her tone one of warning. 'When either of them do finally discover that there's less to your friendship than they imagine . . . well, you'll probably be facing a bit of trouble.'

She didn't like to think of her mother being upset due to something she had done, but, as her mother kept reminding her, at twenty-three she was at risk of 'being left on the shelf'. It was somewhere that did not concern Florence; the prospect of being married and dictated to by a man horrified her far more than an unmarried status.

'You know full well that I have no intention of ever marrying.' She scowled. 'The thought of being any man's chattel is too dreadful.' She stared at her unmarried sister only one year younger than herself. 'Why doesn't Mother make such a fuss about you? It's always me she seems to worry herself about. I don't understand it.'

'Because I wouldn't mind finding a beau and she knows that. She simply worries about your need for independence.'

Florence couldn't help feeling a little guilty for the concern she gave her mother, but she had made up her mind long ago that marriage wasn't for her. The thought of asking permission from a man in order to make decisions was too ghastly. It was bad enough having to be told what to do by her parents.

'Come along,' Amy said, handing the book back to her and opening the bedroom door; 'I can hear Mother's voice getting more irate.'

Florence knew when she was beaten. She raised the book to her nose and breathed in the familiar scent. Surely there was no smell more heavenly than that of a book? Hearing her sister mumble something under her breath, she picked up the new bookmark that she had treated herself to from her previous week's wages and slipped it between the pages. *The Mayor of Casterbridge* would have to wait.

'Florence, answer me,' her mother shouted, sounding, Florence thought, more het up than usual. She stood up and went to check her hair in the mirror.

'Sorry, Mother.' Florence stood up and went to lean over the banister. She gave her mother an apologetic look. 'Amy and I are on our way down now.'

'This is Mr Boot,' her father said, one hand holding the lapel of his waistcoat and the other indicating a man with a friendly smile that reached his eyes. 'He'll be staying in Jersey for a few weeks.'

Florence watched her parents greet the new guest. He was handsome in his own way, she mused, with his greying hair and piercing hazel eyes. She presumed him to be about ten or fifteen years older than her. There was something about him that she couldn't help liking, which seemed odd as he hadn't even opened his mouth to say anything yet.

He took her sister's hand and gave a slight bow before coming to Florence.

'This is my daughter, Florence. She and Amy assist me at Rowe's, our stationer's downstairs.' He regarded his family. 'Please, take a seat everyone. Mr Boot is also in retail,' he explained. 'He has several shops of his own. Mainly in Nottingham, I believe?'

Mr Boot smiled. 'That's correct. I ran them with my mother up until last year when she sadly passed.'

It dawned on Florence who this man was and why the name seemed familiar. 'You're Jane's brother?'

He nodded, his smile widening.

Her father gave her a questioning look. 'You know Mr Boot's sister?'

'Yes, Father. We met last year when she was on the island. We attended functions together. I introduced you and Mother to her.'

'I met her, too,' Amy said. 'Several times. She came to the shop and bought—' she thought for a moment '—an artist's pad, some watercolours and brushes, if I remember correctly.'

Mr Boot laughed. 'Yes, that'll be Jane. She was most upset to have left her paints behind when she travelled. She wrote to me during her stay here recounting visits to Rowes. She insisted that if I visit Jersey, I must look up your family and introduce myself to her good friend, Miss Florence Rowe.' He stared at Florence thoughtfully for a brief time, as if recalling his sister's words. 'She told me that you showed her much of the island and ensured her time here was thoroughly enjoyable.'

Florence recalled the friendly, charming woman who she'd befriended and how well they had got along. 'She told me about your mother's passing,' she said, unsure whether she should be mentioning it, but aware that Mr Boot and his mother had worked closely together in their shops since his father's death when he was only ten. 'I was sorry to hear of your loss.'

His expression darkened and for a moment she thought she'd been too personal. Then, he cleared his throat. 'It was. I think it was doubly difficult as we'd also worked together. Jane insisted I take time away from the business to visit Jersey for a holiday. She thought the sea air would do me good.' He laughed. 'I've only been here a couple of hours and already I feel somewhat refreshed.'

'You haven't been to Jersey before, Mr Boot?' Amy asked.

'This is my first time. I haven't thought to take time away from my business before now.' He smiled. 'I'm told the weather is always sunny in Jersey, and the milk and new potatoes are the best in the world.'

Everyone laughed. She thought back to the stormy weather they had experienced for the previous few days, which had cut the island off from the mainland and France when the ferries to Southampton and St Malo had to be cancelled.

'And you wouldn't be wrong thinking that, most of the time,' her father said. 'Although, maybe not so much about the weather. I believe it's slightly warmer than on the mainland but it can rain here just as much when it chooses to.'

'Usually when you least wish it,' Florence added.

Mr Boot smiled at her. It was a friendly smile; she noticed something more behind his eyes than she had expected. Then her father began discussing aspects of Mr Boot's visit and Florence listened as their guest chatted to her parents. She liked the sound of his voice. She recalled Jane explaining that her accent was an East Midland's one. It was gentle and different to the voices she usually heard each day. Although, she mused, a lot of those were French, or the locals speaking Jèrriais. It wasn't surprising, therefore, that they did sound different.

If what her father was saying were true, which she assumed it was, she had never met anyone as successful as Mr Boot. She liked that he wasn't boastful or arrogant. He seemed very matter-of-fact, and, by what Jane had said, he didn't take much time to do anything other than work very hard. Her thoughts were interrupted hearing her father mentioning her name.

'. . . day off tomorrow and I'm certain she would be delighted to show you some of the sights here on the island. Wouldn't you, Florence?'

All thoughts of finishing *The Mayor of Casterbridge* vanished; however, she found that she didn't mind nearly as much as she would have expected.

'Yes, that would be lovely,' she said, smiling at Mr Boot. 'We could, um—' she thought quickly, recalling how Jane had mentioned that her brother was sometimes troubled by an ailment, which she believed might be rheumatoid arthritis. If that was the case, then she assumed that walking far would not be something he would wish to do '—take the Jersey

Railway to St Aubin, if you wish? Or, maybe the Jersey Eastern Railway to Gorey. Whichever you prefer.'

He rested his hands on his legs and nodded. 'I will leave the choice to you. Maybe we could do one trip tomorrow and the other on another day?'

Florence had hoped for some time alone after such a busy early summer at the shop, but expected that time with Mr Boot could also be enjoyable. She did like showing friends who were new to the island the places that she particularly liked.

'I would enjoy that,' she said. It was only a slight fib, because she would rather have been alone, and she instantly felt mean for her thoughts.

The mantel clock chimed the hour and Florence and Amy stood. 'We should return to the shop,' Amy suggested.

Mr Boot winced slightly as he stood up. 'I apologise. I have taken up more of your time that I intended. When would be convenient for me to call on you tomorrow, Miss Rowe?'

Hoping to make his day as relaxed as possible, Florence said. 'If you call on me at ten o'clock, then we could make our way the short distance up the road to Snow Hill and catch the train from there to Gorey.'

The eastern terminus was so much closer than the one for the westbound train. Let the poor man rest as much as possible on his first days here, she thought; after all, it was what he had come to the island to do.

He gave a slight bow with his head. 'I shall look forward to our adventure, Miss Rowe. Thank you.'

Florence stared at him thoughtfully. There was something

different about this man, but she couldn't work out what it might be. She was surprised to realise that she was looking forward to their outing, too. 'As am I, Mr Boot.'

She followed Amy from the living room and down to the shop. Father rarely permitted the shop to be closed during the daytime and already Florence could see five disconcerted customers waiting anxiously by the front door.

Amy rushed over and unlocked it, turning over the closed sign to mark the place open, once again. 'My apologies for making you wait,' she said sweetly.

'Anything wrong?' one of their regular customers – a short, sour-faced elderly woman with an overly large hat – had grumbled.

'Father has an unexpected guest,' Amy explained, widening her eyes over the woman's head as the lady marched past her to the display of postcards Florence had put together that morning.

'I hope this isn't going to be a regular occurrence; I've been waiting ten minutes to buy a map from you. This really won't do.'

Florence was tempted to give the woman a snappy retort. Their father never let his clients down and would be mortified to think he had upset anyone by his actions. Without having known about Mr Boot's arrival prior to his appearance, even Florence could tell, simply by her father's temporary closure of the shop, that he had thought him important.

She opened her mouth to speak, and just then Amy said, 'I doubt it will happen again any time soon.' Her sister looked at the brown wrapping in the lady's basket. 'I suspect you were able to choose some nice material from the haberdashers while you waited?'

The lady beamed at Amy, her complaint forgotten. 'I did, as a matter of interest. I spotted a fine fabric in their window display and simply had to have it.'

'All is well then,' Florence said, wanting to be sure the woman didn't take her complaint to their father when he returned to the shop. She would hate for his day to be ruined by someone else's criticism.

'It is.' The woman held up a copy of *The Mayor of Casterbridge* in her gloved hand. 'My daughter tells me this book might be something I'd enjoy. What do you think?'

Florence's thoughts had been consumed by the unusual man she had met earlier. Hurriedly thinking of a reply, she wondered if the daughter had yet read the book, not minding so much that she had been held back from being able to read more of it by now. 'I've read a little,' she admitted, 'and I enjoyed it very much. I'm afraid I'll need to check we have your name on the list of customers who have ordered the book.'

She hoped the woman was on the list; the thought that she would have something else to grumble about worried Florence. She took the lady's name and went to check.

Movement by the store-front window caught her eye. The front door to their flat was open and she could see her father and Mr Boot speaking outside. She stepped forward into the shadows behind the counter, hoping to watch Mr Boot unobserved. There was a kindness about him that emanated from him as he chatted to her father. For someone who had come to the island to recover from the loss of his mother and overwork, he still displayed a positivity about him that made her smile.

Mr Boot turned to walk away and, spotting her, waved.

Mortified, Florence waved back, before lifting her father's order book diverted her attention back to checking for the customer's name.

Florence couldn't understand why she was acting so strangely. She was usually so contained and sure of herself. There was something about him that intrigued her though. Was it because he was so successful? No, she was never impressed by that sort of thing. Or simply, she wondered, could it be that he came from a different background to any of the men she had previously come across in her social life? Most of the men she knew worked for a living, and most of them were around her age. Mr Boot had already done very well for himself and was over a decade older than her. Could it be that he was more interesting than the men she knew? Possibly. She wasn't certain. Either way, she realised she was looking forward to her outing with him the next day, very much so.

Chapter 3

They sat opposite one another on the train. Florence was relieved the weather had remained warm and sunny and she had been able to wear her new straw hat for the outing. Not that she expected Mr Boot to have any interest in the latest fashions like she did. Or, maybe the fashions were different in Nottingham; it was a city, after all and not a small island whose connections were mostly closer to France than England.

Mr Boot seemed more relaxed today, she decided happily. The train slowed to a halt at the Georgetown stop. She realised he was staring at her, and as he smiled at her she couldn't help thinking what kind eyes he had.

He cleared his throat. 'How long does the journey take to Gorey?' he asked, turning his attention out of the window to the passengers waiting for others to alight before stepping onto the carriage.

'About twenty minutes,' Florence replied. 'To be honest it's a few months since I came this way.' As she admitted this fact, she couldn't help wondering why she hadn't made the effort before now. 'If I want to walk to the sea front, it's only a couple of minutes from our flat to Havres des Pas. My father doesn't like me walking alone by the shipyards along that way though, so I temper my outings there, too.'

'I had never thought what it must be like to have daughters before, but I can imagine it must be worrisome for a father when they are independently minded.'

For a second she wasn't sure if he was criticising her, then saw the gentle twinkle in his eyes and knew that he was merely thinking of something that had just occurred to him.

'Yes, Father does worry about me and Amy sometimes. Our older sister Adelaide is married now. She's a teacher. However, I don't think Amy and I are probably as compliant as the daughters of some of his friends.'

He looked confused. 'In what way, may I ask?'

'I suppose in that—' she considered her words, delighted with his interest '—we aren't as timid as maybe most of them are. We have opinions and share them more openly than Father would like.'

He frowned. 'Opinions about what?'

She didn't want to offend him; he was older than her, after all, and she suspected slightly more old-fashioned than her friends. He had asked though, and she wanted to be honest with him. 'Mrs Beeton says in her *Book of Household Management* that the mistress of the house should consider herself as "the commander of an army". She believes that women running their homes should feel as important as men do going out to work.'

'Is there anything wrong with that sentiment?'

She shook her head. 'No. It's just that it is not my ambition to simply run a household.'

He thought for a moment. 'Surely, though, a well-run house is extremely important.'

She was enjoying herself immensely. It was fun being able to debate with this man in such a way. 'Yes, it is very important, and I would love to keep my own home at some point; however, I hope to have more for myself.'

'Such as what, may I ask?'

She spotted a twinkling in his hazel eyes but knew it wasn't due to amusement, but she suspected that he was enjoying their conversation as much as she. 'I would like to run my own business. I don't believe that being in charge of a home will be enough for me.'

His eyes widened. 'Do you know something, Miss Rowe? I believe you will find a way to achieve your ambition.' He tilted his head. 'What's more, I feel certain you will be successful at it.'

She was taken aback by his confidence in her. 'Do you really think so?'

'I do. You have intelligence, you work hard, and you seem very determined. There is no reason why you should fail.'

She smiled at him, delighted with his reassurances. 'People do fail though, and maybe I could be one of them.'

'That is always a possibility. I've failed at some of the things I've attempted to do, quite a few times,' he said, surprising her with his honesty, 'but to me, a successful person is not someone who falls at the first hurdle, but who dusts themselves off, rethinks their strategy and tries again. And sometimes has to keep on trying until they find a way of achieving what they set out to do.'

She gazed at him in awe of his open-mindedness and frankness. 'You make a lot of sense. Thank you for sharing your thoughts with me.'

'It is my pleasure. For now, though, you assist your father at Rowe's. He must enjoy having you and your sister working for him?'

Florence agreed. 'He does. I think he would have preferred my brother to work for him, so that he could train him to take over from him when he retires, but Willie hasn't never been interested in the shop.'

'That's a shame,' he said, looking a little unsure. 'Although I don't see why you and your sister wouldn't be any less successful at running the business. My mother took over from my father when he passed when I was ten years old. She was a good business-woman too, and I learnt everything I know from her.'

Florence liked his attitude to women and business. It gave her hope that in this world where man was king of all he possessed, that maybe Mr Boot wasn't the only man to believe women were capable of much more than was usually expected of them.

The train moved off once again. 'I don't know why but I hadn't realised there would be so many stops on such a small island,' he said.

'We'll reach Pontac soon and you can see the coast from there. It's one of my favourite stops,' Florence explained. 'When I do come this way, I love to look out at the rocks in the bay.

I'm told it can be very dangerous for the fishermen's boats, but the bay is very pretty for those of us looking out from a carriage window.'

'My sister tells me that this island is blessed with many bays worthy of inspection.' He laughed. 'She also said that she believes you and she visited most of them during her time here.'

He had a wonderful laugh. Deep and rumbling, infectious.

'We did visit a few.' Florence recalled only too well those pleasant, sunny days with Jane. It wasn't hard to imagine her and her brother getting along well; both seemed such friendly people. 'But there are many more we didn't explore.'

'You're very lucky to live on such a beautiful island,' he said, as they passed several pretty gardens with the glistening sea in the background.

'What's Nottingham like? I've never been.' She wanted to know more about this man and where he came from.

'It also has its beauty, but a different one to this place. I particularly admire the red-brick buildings in the town. I enjoy the hustle and bustle of the streets. I find it inspirational.' He gazed at her for a moment. 'There's a lot of green open space around the city, and if I'm not working, I'll go for a ride in my carriage to take in the air.'

'It sounds wonderful,' she said, trying to picture the place. The largest town she had ever experienced was St Helier and she doubted that was anything like the size of Nottingham. 'And of course, Nottingham is where such beautiful lace mostly comes from. We have a customer who will only wear lace sourced from there.' She recalled the last time Mrs

Wolstenholm had boasted about the fine lace on the sleeves of one of her dresses.

'It is a thriving industry,' he said thoughtfully. 'However, with that comes its own issues and pitfalls. On the one hand the industry provides work for many of the populous, but the hours are long, and a lot of the factories provide little in the way of benefit for their staff. We have a lot of poverty in many areas and the poorer people of Nottingham suffer as all do who have very little.'

She had witnessed the slums in St Helier a few times when her father took her and her siblings to deliver food from their church a couple of times around Christmas time. He believed it was a valuable part of their education and had wanted them to see how sheltered their lives were. She had never forgotten it and was grateful to live with her family in their little flat above their shop. She had so much compared to those with very little.

'I feel rather ungrateful to have moaned about being a shop assistant after hearing about these poor workers in the factories.'

'You shouldn't. You're ambitious, and, as I've said, there is nothing at all wrong with that. I don't want you to form the wrong idea about Nottingham; it does have its slums and overcrowding and occasionally there have been riots.' Florence gasped at the thought. 'However, it is a vibrant place, and I do enjoy living there.' He hurriedly added, 'That's not to say I think any less of your island. I only wish I had thought to visit here before now.'

'At least you've discovered it now.'

A silence descended on them and, surprised to be caught without any idea what to say next, Florence stared out of the window. It was disconcerting to not feel in control for once. Wasn't she the one who always knew what to say? The person her friends relied upon to take the lead when conversation dried up? What was wrong with her that she felt so empty-headed now?

'It really was very kind of you to come out with me today on your day off,' he said, breaking the silence and putting her at her ease once more. 'I hope I didn't disrupt any other plans you might have had.'

She shook her head. 'No.' She usually spent her days off going for a walk to the sea and finding somewhere peaceful to read the latest novel she had chosen from W. H. Rowe. The thought reminded her of the book she must now return to the shop display before her father discovered it was missing.

The train came to a halt and several passengers exited. Florence spotted one of congregation from their Wesleyan chapel stepping onto their carriage and suppressed a groan. She was a particularly nosy woman and Florence suspected that she would stay in their carriage just to find out more about her companion.

'Good morning, Miss Rowe,' she said, not looking at her, but at Mr Boot instead. 'And you're with a friend today, I see. Sir, I'm Mrs Bisson. We attend the same church in Grove Street.'

Mr Boot stood and doffed his hat. 'Good morning, Mrs Bisson,' he said, his tone friendly.

'Do you mind if I take this seat?'

Florence quickly scanned the rows of empty seats nearby. She wasn't surprised that the woman was so insensitive, merely disappointed to have their journey interrupted.

'No, please,' Mr Boot said politely, giving Florence an apologetic glance. He sat back down, his breath catching slightly as he did so, Florence noticed. 'Let me introduce myself.' He took Mrs Bisson's hand. 'My name is Mr Jesse Boot. I'm on holiday on the island and Mrs Rowe has kindly offered to show me some of the sights you're lucky to enjoy here in Jersey.'

She seemed charmed by his friendly way. 'We are particularly lucky, I'm told. Although I've never left the island. Never felt the need.' She studied him for a few seconds. 'Will we see you at chapel on Sunday then, Mr Boot? As a guest of Mr and Mrs Rowe?' she added pointedly. 'Miss Rowe's family and mine are practising Wesleyans, which is how we are acquainted.'

His look of surprise when he stared at Florence concerned her. Did he have negative views about their faith? She hoped not.

'My faith is important to me,' she said. 'I know we're seen as non-conformists in the Protestant church, but it's all I've known, and I believe it's the right way to worship. I see no reason to change my views.'

'I hadn't realised, Miss Rowe,' he said. 'I would love to accompany your family on Sunday, if I may, for I, too, am a practising Wesleyan.'

Stunned, Florence opened her mouth to speak, but failed to produce any words. She pressed her lips together, trying to gather herself. 'Yes, we would be delighted if you would join us,' she said eventually.

This man was becoming more intriguing and appealing by the minute, she decided. It was confusing to feel such affinity with a man she barely knew. It unnerved her slightly.

'That is good news,' Mrs Bisson said. 'How long are you planning to stay here?'

Florence could see he could not have heard the woman's question as his eyes were still locked on hers. 'Mr Boot?'

He blinked several times. 'Sorry? I, um, was thinking.'

'I asked—' Mrs Bisson's irritation was barely veiled '—how long you were planning to stay on the island?'

'I had initially planned on a fortnight. However, I can see that there is much more to see here than I had assumed on such a small island. I may therefore delay my departure a little.'

Florence could tell Mrs Bisson's interest had been piqued, so decided to distract her. 'How is your daughter now?' Florence asked, aware that by asking this question, the woman would give them chapter and verse about her daughter's new marriage to a wealthy farmer in St Mary. Hopefully Mrs Bisson's chatter would last the entire length of her journey, so Mr Boot and she could be left to their own thoughts.

As the woman told her things she had already heard several times, Florence watched the rolling waves as the train moved on. Her instincts told her that meeting the man sitting opposite her had been an important occurrence in her life. She wasn't sure exactly how it would manifest itself, but something in her changed. For the first time in her life she liked the idea of spending time with someone over the thought of being alone with her books. The thought stunned her . . . excited her.

Florence realised Mrs Bisson was standing up and that the train had come to a halt. 'This is my stop,' the lady said. 'Well, it has been very pleasant speaking with you, Mr Boot. I do hope you enjoy your time on the island.'

They waved to Miss Bisson through the window as the train moved on.

'I'm not certain she learnt much about me at all,' Mr Boot said, smiling.

'I know, but she's happy to chatter and tell us all about her family.'

'You're a Wesleyan too?' he asked after a moment's silence. 'Jane never mentioned that to me.'

Florence smoothed down a non-existent crease in her skirt. 'I don't think it was something we ever discussed,' she said, thinking it strange that if Jane had been a Methodist, she had not thought to ask Florence which chapel she might attend on Sundays. 'We were more interested in visiting the library, taking tea at some of the hotels and taking strolls in the countryside.'

'That sounds like Jane,' he said thoughtfully.

They sank again into a comfortable silence. It seemed strange to Florence not to feel the need to find something to discuss, but she felt that simply being in each other's company was pleasant enough. This really was a new experience in many ways.

The train pulled into the station at Grouville. Florence

followed Mr Boot, taking his proffered hand as she stepped from the carriage onto the platform.

'I thought we could stop for a cup of tea before taking a stroll around the area. I would like to take you on to Gorey, with its busy harbour, but the train line doesn't extend that far. I believe there's talk about doing so at some point. We could take a carriage if you would like to go there.'

He looked around. 'This is very pretty. I'm happy to spend time here for now and come back for some refreshment a little later.'

Florence was happy to agree with him. They walked slowly, taking in the warm sea air, neither feeling the need to speak for several moments.

When they were a few feet onto the common, Mr Boot finally asked, 'Do you enjoy working at Rowe's? Or is there something else you would rather do?'

She wondered if he was referring to motherhood. Surely not. That would be far too forward a question for anyone to ask her, especially a man of Mr Boot's standing. To be safe she said, 'I'm happy at Father's shop. I love books and now we've branched out into art supplies, there's even more to enjoy and share with our regular customers.'

'You are very happy there then?'

Florence smiled. 'Yes, although I wish my father would allow me to arrange the shop a little differently. I'm sure I could make it work better than it does now.' Embarrassed to be thought of as complaining – or even worse: being disloyal to her father – she quickly added. 'Not that the shop doesn't do perfectly well.' She wondered if what she was saying could be construed as vulgar. 'Or that Father doesn't listen to me on occasion. Recently he agreed to let me order a couple of gold pen holders and holiday cards.'

'Holiday cards?'

'Yes, post cards.' She stumbled slightly and he caught her elbow, helping her right herself. 'Thank you. What I meant to say was that I merely wish for a little more freedom to try out a few new things.'

'I understand. My mother tended to see me as her child despite my advance in years and experience doing the work.'

She was relieved that he understood what she was trying to convey.

'Amy mentioned that you were a druggist,' she said, 'but you also have quite a few stores. Which work do you prefer?'

He thought for a moment and pausing picked a daisy from the high bank next to them, twirling it round between his right thumb and forefinger thoughtfully. 'I enjoy the creating of new medicines.'

Her face reddened, aware she had admitted some interest in him. 'Have you always wanted to do this work?'

He nodded. 'I have. I inherited this need from my father. He was concerned with helping improve living conditions in the lace market area. He realised that herbal remedies were cheap and over thirty years ago he opened an establishment at Goose Gate in a poor area of the town to provide herbal remedies to those who couldn't afford to pay for physicians. He learnt from his mother and he passed his knowledge down to me.'

She was fascinated by his story. 'So, it's very much a passion of yours then?'

'It is.'

What an incredible man this was.

He handed the daisy to Florence with a friendly smile. 'I am ambitious, but I find I am rewarded with much satisfaction by being able to help others.'

As her gloved hands took the daisy from his, the thin stem slipped through her fingers.

'Oh, I've dropped it,' she said, embarrassed by her clumsiness.

'No matter, there are many more.' He reached out to pick another one from the sloped bank, placing the flower in the palm of his other hand and waiting for her to take it.

'Thank you,' she said. 'I love daisies, don't you? So pretty, yet not at all . . . what's the word I'm trying to find.'

'Ostentatious?' Mr Boot suggested.

Florence mulled over his suggestion as she gazed at the plain white petals fanning around the egg-yellow middle. 'Yes, that's perfect.'

It was hotter than Florence had anticipated, and her corset was uncomfortable. One part of her longed to get back to her bedroom and remove the restrictive garment, but she was also enjoying herself much more than she had imagined.

'This common has the best view of any I've seen,' Mr Boot said, gazing at the view ahead of them. 'I presume events are held here at times?'

'Yes,' Florence said. 'There's horse racing occasionally, and the military come here to carry out training and exercises sometimes.'

'There's certainly the space for it.' They walked on a few

more yards. 'Your father has invited me to dine with your brother and his wife,' Mr Boot said. 'It really is very kind of your family to make me feel so welcome. I appreciate it.'

'We enjoy meeting new people. It gives us something different to discuss in the evenings.' She was joking, but only a little. 'Your life seems so different to ours and it fascinates us.'

His step faltered and he widened his eyes. 'Really? Why so?'

Florence hoped he would not think her forward or talking out of turn by saying such things. Her parents often scolded her for her forthright way of speaking to people they insisted she had no right addressing or giving her opinions to.

'You come from the mainland and the Midlands at that,' she said, hoping to show that she had paid attention to what he had been saying. 'You're a druggist; that is something unusual in itself. You also run factories and chemists. Not like the small chemist next to Rowe's at number twenty-nine. It's diverting for us to think about these things.'

He seemed pleased at her interest. 'I wanted to build up my business, because I believe that, the larger my business, the more I could buy in bulk and thereby afford to lower costs. I liked the idea of providing health for a shilling, because I believe the health of the poor man or woman is just as important as the health of someone with money.'

His sentiments matched hers completely. How incredible must it feel to be able to develop then produce and sell medicines, and know that products you had made could save your customers' lives. She struggled not to sound too in awe of him. 'Your work is very commendable.' She was painfully aware that she wasn't vocalising her thoughts as well as she had intended.

'You're very kind to say so. Thank you.'

'Do you produce all the medicines?'

'No. I was lucky enough last year to be able to open shops in Lincoln and Sheffield and take on my first qualified pharmacist. He is young man, not much older than you, and a marvel who creates and dispenses new medicines to my customers.'

'I envy him. To think he has the opportunity to work for a progressive man such as yourself.' Thinking she might have been too forward and spoken out of turn, Florence reddened. 'I didn't mean to offend by what I said.'

He patted her arm. 'No, my dear. I'm fully aware you did not. Nor have you. I am intrigued, and secretly delighted that I am considered interesting to others. It's not something I have ever presumed to be.'

Mr Boot might be older than her, Florence decided, but, for all his success, he didn't seem at all judgemental or priggish. She decided that if he asked her, she would agree to meet up with him again.

'I read that the train line from St Helier to La Corbière was opened earlier this month. Do you think you might consider accompanying me to see the lighthouse there?'

Florence wondered if he had been able to read her thoughts, then shrugged off the notion as nonsense. 'I would like that very much,' she admitted. 'In fact, it's been a few years since I went there myself.'

'Good,' he said, looking, she thought, rather pleased with himself for making the suggestion. 'Then we shall have to rectify that. What day do you next have time away from work?'

'Not until Thursday afternoon when we close half-day, I'm afraid.' She wished she didn't have to wait so long to spend more time with this interesting man who treated her as an equal despite her younger age and being a woman. 'However, maybe my father might make an exception as you are on holiday, and let me have time off before then.'

'I can ask him, if you think he will be more likely to agree?'

She thought that was a splendid idea and said so, trying not to show how excited she was at the prospect, as they continued their stroll to the seafront.

Florence was used to speaking her mind up to an acceptable limit, but for some reason she felt as if she was with a kindred spirit with this man. On the face of it they had very little in common – their ages were not similar, nor were their backgrounds – but there was something about him . . . something she liked very much.

Chapter 4

Later, as she lay back against her pillows in a quiet moment of solitude before being called for supper, Florence went over her day spent with Mr Boot. She had enjoyed herself in his company. She sighed happily, thinking of their next outing together. This time they would see the west of the island. For some reason she wanted him to love her homeland as much as she. She wasn't sure exactly why this need was so great in her, but she felt almost panic to show him as much as possible before the time came for him to return to the mainland.

She had never expected to meet a man with whom she felt this much at ease, or who intrigued her so much. She thought about the little he had told her about his work as a druggist. It all sounded fascinating. Florence loved her job and knowing that she made the Rowes' customers lives that much happier through the books and art supplies that they sold to them was an added bonus.

Maybe that was what connected them: their work. Hers catered for the customers' spirits, their creative side, either by helping them escape in a novel, or providing them with books on how to make something, while Mr Boot's business took care of their physical health. They were two sides of a coin that served the people living near them. The thought made her very happy.

Amy knocked on her door and opened it before waiting to be given permission. 'Father has asked that you come downstairs.'

Florence glanced at her small mantel clock. It was one her grandmother had left to her and Amy, which her sister hadn't wanted. 'It's earlier than usual tonight,' she said, wishing she could be left a little while longer with her thoughts.

'I have a feeling he and Mother wish to speak to you about something.'

Her stomach contracted slightly. On her return she had asked that she be allowed tomorrow off from work to accompany Mr Boot to La Corbière, but having already taken today away from the shop, she couldn't imagine her father would agree. She hoped he would though. Mr Boot only had one week left on the island and she wasn't looking forward to returning to find entertainment without his refreshing banter.

She checked her hair in the mirror and smoothed down her skirt. 'I'll be along directly,' she said, wanting a moment to collect herself.

Florence entered the small living room and was taken aback to see Mr Boot standing between her parents.

'Oh, I . . .'

'I hope you don't mind me calling on you so very soon after bidding you farewell this afternoon.' He gave her a polite nod. 'I was hoping to persuade Mr Rowe to allow you time away from the shop again tomorrow.' He looked at her father, apologetically.

Her father didn't look as cross about the prospect as Florence would have assumed. In fact, she thought, he seemed to be rather pleased.

'No, not at all,' she said, unable to hide her smile.

'Mr Boot has advised me that he's received a letter from home and must make plans to return to Nottingham a couple of days earlier than he had planned.'

Her mood plummeting, Florence had to concentrate on not showing her disappointment. 'Nothing is wrong with Jane, I hope, Mr Boot?'

He shook her head. 'No, Jane is well, I'm relieved to say. However, there is a business matter that needs my attention. My return has therefore had to be brought forward. Rather inconvenient, I'm afraid. It cannot, however, be helped.'

'That is a shame,' she said, not allowing herself to show her disappointment at hearing this news.

He cleared his throat. 'I have come today in the hope that we might take another outing tomorrow. If, of course, it's not too soon after our busy day out today?'

'No, of course not,' she said, without stopping to at least look as if she was considering his invitation. She gave her father an appealing smile. 'Father? Would you mind me taking the day off from work?'

Her father moved next to Florence and rested his right hand on her shoulder. 'I have given Mr Boot permission to go out with you tomorrow.'

She couldn't hide her surprise. Her father must like Mr

Boot very much to allow her another day off immediately after the one she took today. 'Thank you, Father,' she said, trying not to show her delight.

'I have a fancy to see the new lighthouse at La Corbière.'

Florence only vaguely heard him. She was too stunned by her father's permission for another day off to truly take in what Mr Boot had said.

He cleared his throat nervously when she didn't answer straight away. 'Only if you wish to accompany me, Miss Rowe. Please feel free to say if you'd rather not.' He passed his leather gloves from one hand to the other.

Horrified to have given him the wrong idea, Florence shook her head. 'Not at all, Mr Boot,' she said, trying her best not to sound too enthusiastic. 'I would very much like to accompany you to the lighthouse tomorrow. Thank you for asking me.' Her mother had a particular abhorrence of women having an unladylike enthusiasm for anything, and found it extremely distasteful.

She waited in the living room as her father showed Mr Boot to the door.

Her mother didn't appear happy at Florence agreeing to go on another outing with Mr Boot. She wasn't sure why, so felt compelled to ask her.

'Do you mind me accompanying Mr Boot on outings, Mother?'

Florence followed her mother as she walked into the kitchen, pulling the straps of her apron carefully over her head and tying it around her waist. She clattered about in the kitchen, not needing words to convey her feelings.

'Mother, is something the matter?'

'Nothing is the matter,' her father said, joining them. 'Your mother probably would like some help with the supper, or a little peace to continue with its preparation.'

'Peace would be my preferred choice,' her mother snapped without turning to address them.

Her father waved for her to follow him back to the living room. Florence shared her concerns.

'Your mother has nothing against Mr Boot,' he assured her as they sat opposite each other on the comfortable armchairs in front of the unlit fire. 'How could anyone have an issue with such a pleasant man?'

Florence couldn't say. 'Why then does she appear upset that I am to see him again? Is it something I've done?' If it was, she had no idea what it could be.

He leant forward and lowered his voice. 'She likes Albert. I suspect your mother is anxious that your affections will gravitate from him to Mr Boot. After all, Mr Boot is quite a bit older than you and you must have noticed his occasional pain when he moved.'

She had but couldn't understand what that had to do with anything. He was kind, entertaining and very good company. Surely that was what she needed from a man, not worrying about his age or the fact that once in a while he suffered pain in his legs.

'Albert and I are merely friends, Father,' she explained. 'I only let Mother think that we might end up courting, because it stops her fretting that I'll end up being a lonely spinster. Although, I can't imagine ever being lonely, and I have no issue with remaining a spinster, whatever Mother says.' As soon as the words left her lips, she wished she could recall them. She hated being rude to her parents and loved her mother, never intending to speak badly about her. 'That is to say . . .'

Her father rested his hand on her shoulder. 'Don't concern yourself. I don't like to think of your mother being misled. However, for the time being or until you've had a chance to change your mind about Albert's prospects as a husband, maybe allowing her to believe that you have a fondness for him is the best option. .'

'You prefer Albert over Mr Boot, Father?'

He considered her question for a moment. 'I don't believe it's a case of liking one man more than the other. I am only concerned that you, as with your siblings, choose to be with someone who makes you happy, be it Albert or Mr Boot.'

Florence was relieved to hear him say as much. Although she barely knew Mr Boot, she could not deny to herself that there was something appealing about him as well as his business ethics. Her disappointment at hearing about his earlier than anticipated return to Nottingham had given her quite a jolt. It made her realise that she was enjoying his company even more than she had ever supposed she might.

Chapter 5

Florence had spent the morning and previous evening planning how to make the best of her outing with Mr Boot. She was looking forward to spending time with him.

She walked down Mulcaster Street towards the Pomme d'Or Hotel, wishing she had thought to pack less in the picnic hamper she had brought with her. Maybe this wasn't the best idea of hers, she mused, moving the handle from her right to her left hand. It was far heavier than she had expected when she'd packed it up earlier. She didn't even know what foods Mr Boot liked, or if he would be happy with the idea of a picnic.

'I'm so stupid,' she murmured to herself. If only she wasn't using her mother's hamper, then she could maybe leave it with someone and ask if she could collect it later.

She wished she had a free hand to fan herself and hoped she wasn't too hot by the time she met him. The last thing she wanted to do was arrive in a flustered state. That really wouldn't do at all. She passed the entrance of the hotel and spotted him waiting for her outside the terminus building. He was looking up at the blue sky, and she followed his gaze, noting that there wasn't a cloud to be seen.

Seeing her, he waved and began walking to her. As he neared, he called out to her. 'Good day, Miss Rowe.' He noticed the hamper and reached out to take it from her. 'That looks rather heavy.'

Relieved he had taken the weight from her hand, she checked her hair was in place and her hat straight. 'Thank you. I hadn't thought about carrying it here when I was packing up our lunch.'

'I wished you had told me,' he said as they began walking; 'I would have collected you in a carriage. This really is far too heavy for a lady to carry.'

'Not at all,' she fibbed, not wishing him to think of her as weak. 'I'm used to lifting boxes of books, don't forget.'

He smiled at her. 'That's as maybe, but there wasn't a need for you to bring this hamper all this way, especially in this heat.'

Florence laughed. 'I have to admit, I was thinking the same thing when I was halfway here.'

They reached the terminus entrance. 'I've already purchased our tickets,' he explained, patting his chest pocket. 'The train is waiting for us to board.'

Once seated on the train, the hamper on the floor next to Mr Boot's feet, Florence relaxed slightly.

'Thank you for bringing a picnic,' he said quietly. 'I don't know the last time I've been lucky enough to enjoy one.'

This news made her happy. It had been worthwhile trudging down across town, after all. 'I hope you like the food I've packed for us.'

'I'm certain I will.'

As the train took Florence and Mr Boot from West Park to First Tower she gazed out towards the sea, silvery from the brightness of the sun, relieved she had not suggested they get tickets to travel by charabanc. Florence had noticed Mr Boot wince as he took his seat and at least the motion of the train was gentle and level, compared to the bumps in the road that the charabanc would no doubt find as the wheels hit them.

He cleared his throat. 'I haven't been to the west of the island yet. I'm told by Jane that it is more rugged than the east, with a long beach and Napoleonic forts dotted along the coastline.'

'She remembers our outing in a charabanc,' Florence laughed, recalling the fun day out they had with her friends. 'There were about twenty of us altogether. We travelled in two charabancs and we enjoyed a picnic on the sand dunes.'

Florence was glad that Jane had enjoyed her day enough to tell her brother all about it. They both obviously had fond memories of the day that had started out with the threat of rain. It had been so bad that there was a moment they weren't certain they would be able to go. But the clouds had parted, and everything had turned out perfectly.

'Is that the harbour where my boat docked?' Mr Boot asked, peering towards the granite pier walls to the left of the bay past Elizabeth Castle.

'Yes, that's correct,' she said, fanning herself with the pretty fan her sister Adelaide had bought her for her last birthday. She wondered if maybe she should suggest an outing to the castle on another day, unsure whether it would be easy enough for him to manage when the tide was low and the causeway there was exposed. Deciding not to say anything for now, she added. 'The sea seems so still today, doesn't it?'

'It does.' Removing his hat, he took his handkerchief from his pocket and wiped his forehead.

They fell into a companionable silence. Florence stole several glances at Mr Boot as he gazed out of the window at the seascape to the left of them. Fine lines ran from the sides of his eyes to the top of his cheeks. He seemed more relaxed even from the previous day and she was certain his visit to the island was having the desired effect on him.

He must have sensed her looking at him and turned, smiling as he caught her eye.

Shocked slightly to be caught out, her cheeks reddened.

'Sorry, did you ask me something?' he asked.

She shook her head, relieved he had thought she had speaking to him. 'Err, no. That is, yes. I was wondering if you find the island to your liking so far, Mr Boot?'

'I do,' he said, sitting back in his seat to face her better. 'Very much. I don't know if it's the sea air or spending more time than I usually would outside in the sunshine, but I am certainly benefitting from being here.'

'I'm glad.' Not wishing to seem forward, she added, 'I wouldn't want a visitor to the island going home without feeling that he, or she, had taken with them a true sense of well-being.'

'You can be satisfied then to know that I am feeling better than I have done for many, many months.'

She was glad to hear it. More than she expected to be. She smiled at him and they both gazed out of the window at the shimmering blue and silver view that the sea offered to them.

They passed The Tin Hut at West Park, along to the stop at First Tower where several passengers alighted, and others replaced them. Then they slowed to pass another rail car at Millbrook Station.

'It's a little warm today, don't you think?'

She nodded, wishing she wasn't wearing layers of fabric with her petticoats and cotton summer dress. 'Maybe there'll be more of a breeze when we reach La Corbière?'

He raised his eyebrows. 'Would it be so different? I didn't think it was too far away from here?'

Florence realised that most people would find it strange that on an island five miles by nine in size that there would be different temperatures. 'It's not much of a distance. The lighthouse is on a small peninsula adjoining two bays. The one to its right is a tiny bay, but that leads on to a larger expanse of beach. St Ouen's Bay faces west and there usually is more of a sea breeze in that part of the island. Odd, I know. My parents have friends who run a farm out that way and they never like coming into town on hot days, preferring to remain out there instead.'

'I'm looking forward to going there,' he said, a smile on his slightly pink face. 'The lighthouse is only a few years old, isn't it?'

She nodded. 'Yes, and it's the first concrete lighthouse in the British Isles. We're very proud of it here in Jersey. Apparently, on a clear night, the light can be visible up to eighteen miles away.'

The reached St Aubin, and Florence told him a little about the area, with its small harbour and busy waterfront.

'This is a new terminus building,' she said. 'It only opened at the beginning of this month.'

He gazed over to where the old shabby building stood.

The train took a sharp bend to the west and entered the tunnel.

'Not too long now,' she said, looking forward to reaching the next sea view. Florence didn't like tunnels, and this bit always made her slightly uncomfortable. Then, once again, they were back in the daylight and she relaxed.

They passed farmland and Florence pointed out a large herd of Jersey cows. 'They have to be the prettiest cows, don't you think?'

'I imagine you are right. Their faces are very pretty.'

'We're almost there,' she said, excited to reach their destination. 'I hope the journey wasn't a disappointment.'

'Not at all,' he said, smiling at her. 'I've enjoyed myself immensely so far. Thank you, Florence. It is very kind of you to accompany me here today.'

The train slowed, stopping at the station. Mr Boot lifted the hamper and disembarked, turning and proffering his hand, waiting for her to take it as she stepped down.

They walked away from the station and crossed over to the beach side of the road stopping at the top of the rocks and looking across the causeway to the splendid lighthouse standing proudly on the rocks at the end of the peninsular.

'What do you think of our lighthouse, Mr Boot?'

'Impressive, and well worth a visit.'

'Would you like to take a walk now?'

'Or we could find somewhere to sit and eat,' he said, 'and then take a stroll later when we've finished.'

'And then the hamper won't be as heavy.' She laughed.

'Then it's agreed. We'll eat first.'

Having scanned the area for a few moments, Florence pointed to a space at the top of the rocks where no one was yet sitting.

'We could sit over there,' she said, hoping they'd reach the area before any other visitors to the area would. She walked slowly so as not to rush Mr Boot, aware that he would be embarrassed if she made her slowness obvious.

They arrived at the spot she had chosen. He placed the hamper down next to two low boulders. 'These would make good seats, don't you think?'

She agreed, thinking that maybe he would find it easier to stand once more if he wasn't seated on the grass, but on something a little higher. 'It looks perfect.'

She lay the hamper on its side. Florence then unbuckled the soft leather straps holding the hamper closed, hoping to find the food in the same state it had been in when she had packed it. Raising the lid, she lifted the red and white picnic cloth and smiled.

'It looks as if everything has survived the journey here.'

'That's a relief,' he said, taking the cloth from her and opening it, lowering it until it was on the grass. Then, carefully lifting the open hamper he placed it on one side of the cloth.

Florence thanked him and knelt down next to the food to inspect it. She unclipped the two plates and took out her mother's second-best condiment set, placing it down.

'Would you like me to put some of the food on a plate for you?'

'That would be very kind.' He undid his jacket.

She was aware that he was watching her. 'I've made the food, so please don't expect it to be too delicate,' she explained, not wishing his expectations to be high, and then for him to be disappointed when he saw what she had brought for their lunch.

'I'm certain it will be delicious,' he said smiling at her. 'What have you brought for our lunch, if I may ask?'

She sat back and studied the tins of food. 'I've made us beef sandwiches, with a touch of horseradish. There are some cucumber ones also, in case you don't like the meat.'

'That sounds wonderful.'

Boosted by his enthusiasm, she added, 'I've also baked some scones this morning. Mother let me bring a small jar of her best strawberry jam and I bought some Jersey cream to go with it. We also have crackers with a small wheel of Brie.'

'You have thought of everything,' he said, breathing in deeply. 'This air is intoxicating.'

Florence thought so too. She was pleased that he was happy with her basic picnic. She took the two glasses from the hamper and placed them on to the lid, in case the grass was too soft, and they tipped.

'I made us lemonade,' she said, unsure of her choice. 'I tried some at home before leaving and I'm worried it's a little too tart.'

'Then it will be perfect for this weather.'

She handed him a glass, and, pulling the cork out of the

top of the lemonade bottle, poured a little into the glass for him to try.

Mr Boot took a sip and blinked a few times, despite keeping a smile on his face.

Florence couldn't help being amused by his reaction. 'I told you it probably wasn't very good.'

'It's delicious,' he fibbed, taking another mouthful. 'Truly.'

Unable to help herself, she laughed loudly at his attempt at saving her feelings.

'I don't believe you but thank you for being kind. I'm no cook, baker, or whatever you call a lemonade maker, but hopefully the food will be more palatable than the drink.'

Chapter 6

A week later, Florence thanked the postman as he handed her the mail in the shop. She exchanged pleasantries with one of their customers and opened the door for them as they left.

'Any interesting mail?' Amy asked, as she finished dusting the shelves and walked over to join Florence by the counter.

'Why?' Florence teased. 'Are you expecting something in particular?'

Amy scowled, peering at the letters in Florence's hand. 'No, but by the look of the top letter, you've received something?'

Florence turned her attention to the envelopes. Her sister was right; the top one was addressed to her. She didn't recognise the writing and inspected the other side, but there was no return address on the back.

'Who's it from?' Amy asked.

'I've no idea.'

Amy took the rest of the mail from Florence and sorted it out, putting it into small piles for her father, which included his personal and shop mail and one for her mother. She nudged Florence. 'Are you going to stare at it all day, or will you be reading it?'

Florence wasn't sure, but she hoped the letter was from Mr Boot. He had asked if he could write to her, but she knew his business took up most of his time and had not expected him to do so this quickly. If her intuition was correct, then he had enjoyed their outing to the west of the island as much as she had. Even her hopeless attempt at preparing a tasty picnic hadn't ruined their time together.

However, she wasn't sure that she wanted to be in company when she opened this letter, just in case it was from him. She pushed the letter into her skirt pocket just as the shop door jangled and announced the arrival of another customer.

The rest of the day passed achingly slowly. Finally, Florence finished her work for the day. She covered her mouth with the back of her hand to stifle a yawn, then tidied the last of the books and locked the shop door.

Amy chatted with their father as Florence stared out of the window at the street where people hurried to shops before they closed for the day. She turned the sign to 'closed', so that no more customers would think to try and enter Rowe's. She was desperate to read the letter that seemed to weigh down her pocket.

Unable to wait any longer, she said, 'Do you mind if I go and freshen up for supper now?'

Her father frowned at her question. She could understand his reaction, as she never usually asked to leave as soon as they had closed for the day.

'You are quite well?'

'Yes,' she said. 'Perfectly.'

'Of course, you may go.'

She began walking to the back of the shop, catching an amused smile from her sister as she passed her. She didn't have time for Amy's teasing, not right now.

She reached her bedroom, closed the door and unlaced her Boot, kicking them off as she sat on the cushioned chair next to a small table by her bedroom window. Pulling the letter from her pocket she opened it and withdrew the single piece of good quality paper.

It was from Mr Boot, she noted with relief. She stared at the writing for a moment thinking how distinctive it was in a slightly untidy way. Florence was nervous, yet excited to read what he had to say.

16–20 Goose Gate
Nottingham
1 September 1885

Miss F Rowe
27 Queen Street
St Helier
Jersey

My dear Miss Rowe,

Thank you for permitting me to continue our friendship through correspondence now that I have returned home to Nottingham.

I was sorry to cut short my trip and miss further outings with you to experience more diverse parishes in Jersey. I am still taken aback by the beauty and the difference in settings on such a small island. From the pretty cobbled back streets in your town to the expanse of sand and sea from the bays of Grouville and St Ouen. I can understand more fully now the reasons why my sister Jane enjoyed her visit so very much.

I was sorry to have to say goodbye to you and your parents. You and your family were very gracious in welcoming me and ensuring that my stay on the island was such a memorable and life-affirming one.

The business that I returned to Nottingham to deal with is now well underway. We have been developing our manufacturing facilities on Island Street and have come up against a few issues. It is a little more serious than I had presumed, but that is nothing unusual. Business always has its ups and downs, and very often unexpected events happen when you least foresee, or wish, them to.

I fully intend to travel back to Jersey as soon as I am able to take time away from my business. I hope that I may enjoy the pleasure of your company when I do. I have so much yet to experience of the island, and maybe we could attend a concert or a dance, or, if you would prefer, I could ask your father's permission to take you out to dinner.

Yours sincerely and very best wishes,
From your good friend,
Mr Boot

It had only been two days since Mr Boot had left on the ferry but already she missed his company. She had only known him a short time and hadn't expected him to make such an impact on her life. She needed to write a reply to him but hadn't managed to finish a letter that she was happy enough to post.

Florence had turned down a couple of invitations from Albert since Mr Boot's departure but was beginning to feel unkind to cancel their latest pre-arranged engagement to visit the Theatre Royal to attend one of the shows.

Albert was a kind man and a good friend. She didn't want to let him down again, so when he had popped in from the tea merchants earlier that day to deliver some tea for her mother, she had agreed to go with him and several other friends to a poetry reading.

Florence went up to the living room and offered her mother some assistance making supper.

'No, thank you,' her mother said. 'That won't be necessary. We're only having pork chops and boiled potatoes. It won't take a moment to prepare and will be ready shortly.'

Her mother came out of the kitchen, drying her hands and taking off her apron. 'Amy mentioned that you received a letter in today's post.' She didn't look very happy and Florence knew that her mother assumed it could be from Mr Boot.

'Yes, that's right,' she said. 'I'll quickly go to my room and freshen up.'

Not wishing to wait a moment longer, she ran upstairs. She wasn't sure what to write in reply but did not want to delay her letter to him in case he thought her uninterested in their correspondence. If she hurried and wrote back to him, he would probably receive it in the next day or so. She sat at her desk. Taking a piece of her favourite cream writing paper, she picked up her pen and began to write.

Deborah Carr

27 Queen Street
St Helier
Jersey
Channel Islands
4 September 1885

Mr J Boot
16–20 Goose Gate
Nottingham

Dear Mr Boot,

Thank you very much for your letter. I, too, enjoyed our outings and wish that you did not have to cut short your holiday on the island and go home to the mainland at such short notice.

I am happy to hear that you plan to visit us again. I will endeavour to make a list of the places you might like to see and the best places to enjoy a pleasant meal, or a dance. But there is still so much of the island that I have yet to show you.

You also haven't been to the north of the island, which is a little more dramatic than the south, with cliff faces that are breathtaking to look at. We could probably take a horse-drawn taxi out to the splendid breakwater at St Catherine's.

Please send my best regards to Jane; I hope that she is well.

With best wishes,
Yours sincerely,
Your friend, Miss Florence Rowe

She heard her sister leave her bedroom next door and walk down the creaky attic stairs to the main landing for supper. Then her mother's voice called for her to join them. She was unsure if her sister would come into her room for a quick chat before they went out for the evening. Florence quickly folded her letter and slipped it into an envelope, and wrote Mr Boot's name and address on the front.

She met up with Albert and her friends for their evening out. It was pleasant enough, although her mind kept wandering to Mr Boot and his letter. She had posted her letter on the way out and could barely wait for his reply to reach her.

Several days later, after surreptitiously checking the post each day, Florence was delighted to spot a letter on the mantelpiece. Her father would have opened his own mail by lunchtime and her mother rarely received mail from anyone. Excitement bubbled in Florence's stomach. This letter had to be either for either herself or Amy. She walked over to the mantelpiece and picked up the envelope. It was indeed addressed to her.

She couldn't help feeling surprised that his letters to her had come to mean so much and so quickly.

Florence didn't want her mother to see that he had written again. She didn't like to keep things from her family but didn't see the point in causing her mother any consternation if it wasn't necessary. She and Mr Boot were merely friends after all, weren't they? she thought.

Finally, it was her half an hour lunch break, and Florence made an excuse and raced up to her room to read her correspondence.

16–20 Goose Gate
Nottingham
7 September 1885

Miss Florence Rowe
27 Queen Street
St Helier
Jersey

My dear Miss Rowe,

How splendid of you to reply to my letter so quickly and with so much information about your beautiful jewel of an island.

I hope you won't be offended if I ask you to consider if I may perhaps address you by your first name in future? Please do not hesitate to dismiss this request if it bothers you at all; I would fully understand. If, though, it sits comfortably with you, then please may I ask that you call me Jesse and maybe I may refer to you as Florence?

I am trying to find a time in my calendar where I might have a week or so away from the office to visit Jersey once again. As soon as I do have anything planned, I shall let you know and then maybe we can make further plans about how to spend those carefree days.

My very best wishes, to you Miss Rowe.

Yours very sincerely,

Mr Boot (Jesse)

Florence checked her old mantel clock. She didn't have time

to write her reply, so put aside his letter for consideration later. She had no qualms about them using their first names to address each other. Weren't they good friends by now? A niggling thought crept into her mind. How would her parents take to this knowledge, especially her mother? She, Florence was sure, would not be as keen to think of her daughter being on first-name terms with a man she had not known for very long. After all, it wasn't as if they were courting.

Going back to the shop, she approached her father with an idea that she had been brooding over for the past few days.

'I was wondering if you would let me rearrange the back of shop display table. I thought I could move it further forward and change the way we arrange the display slightly.'

He looked askance at her. 'Whatever for? It's always been in the same place.'

She didn't like to offend him by arguing but was determined to try out her plan. 'I can't help thinking that if we moved it further forward and pushed the one in front slightly to the right, that it would make it easier to see from the window. It would also be easier to walk around and look at the books from each side of the table.'

She braced herself for his annoyance, surprised when it didn't come. 'Why not? Those books have always been the one to sell the least, even when they are the more appealing to the customers. Amy can help you move the table after closing and you can then redo the display in whatever way you choose.'

Stunned, she nodded her agreement. 'Yes, thank you,' she said quickly, before he had a chance to change his mind.

She took a deep breath to quell her rising excitement. She was determined to prove to him how well her ideas would work.

He took hold of both his jacket lapels and stared at her. 'You have a good head for business, Florence, especially for a woman.'

His comment jarred on her. She knew he didn't mean to be unkind but was aware he would never say such a thing to her brother Willie. However, she mused, she couldn't help being pleased with his compliment, no matter how back-handed it might be.

'I will allow you to leave it that way for a week and if it doesn't make any difference to the sales then you'll need to move it back to where it was.'

After rearranging the table and redoing the display, Florence was too tired to reply to Jesse. So, it wasn't until the end of the following day that she was able to do so. She didn't mind because this time she had something exciting to tell him. It would be interesting to see what he thought of her idea in the shop and the results after only one day. Would he be impressed with her acumen? She hoped so. He seemed to treat her almost like an equal already in other matters, and for him to see her as something other than a lightheaded woman would please her very much.

27 Queen Street
St Helier
Jersey
10 September 1885

Mr J Boot
16–20 Goose Gate
Nottingham

Dear Jesse,

Thank you for your most recent letter and, yes, I am happy for you to address me by my first name and I shall, as you see from the beginning of this letter, address you in the same way.

I am very much looking forward to your second holiday here. I was wondering if you would be interested in visiting some of the local shops? We have two large stores, A De Gruchy and Voisin and Company. They are probably the closest to the large stores in your area and I thought that you might find them of interest. Please do not think I shall be offended if you would rather not go to them. I understand that you will be taking time off work and probably will not be wishing to think of such things during your holiday.

There is an interesting adaptation by Mr D'Oyly Carte's Opera Company of Patience at the Theatre Royal in Gloucester Street. I went to see the show with my sister Amy and a few friends last night. I shall look at the theatre's programme when I know the dates of your visit and if there is something in it that I believe might interest you, I shall let you know.

The shop has been very busy over the past few days. Father has allowed me to move one of the display tables that was at the back of the shop forward to the front. He only agreed because I kept asking and assuring him that we would sell more books if I made the changes to the shop. To be honest I wasn't entirely certain that it would work, but I thought it worth a try, and, lo and behold, it did work, and we doubled the sales for those books today. I have to admit that I was very happy that my idea was successful. So was my father, although he didn't say as much.

I look forward to hearing from you again.
Very best wishes,
Yours sincerely, your good friend,
Florence Rowe

Chapter 7

The following days passed slowly. Florence was at a loss to how different she felt about her days. Until meeting Mr Boot, or Jesse, as she still was trying to get used to calling him, she had been carefree and excited to attend concerts, go on outings and generally spend her free time with her friends. Since her days out with him and then his subsequent departure, she seemed only to work and wait for the postman to bring the mail, and then, if his delivery did not include a letter from Jesse, her day was marred and grey.

She glanced up at the wall clock above the counter in the shop for the twentieth time that morning, willing the time to pass until the postman's arrival.

'What is so urgent that you keep staring at that clock all the time?' her father asked, his right index finger placed on his account book where to hold his place in his additions. 'Is there somewhere you wish to be?'

Embarrassed to have been caught out, she shook her head. 'Do you think the post is a little late today?'

He was about to answer when the door opened, and the brass bell announced a customer's arrival. Forgetting his conversation with Florence, he focused his attention on serving the lady and her daughter who were looking for a birthday present for an acquaintance. Florence couldn't help noticing that the lady appeared almost tearful and waited to see if she needed to provide the lady with a glass of water.

'I've brought Mother here to distract her,' the younger woman announced. 'My brother and his wife left the island yesterday to emigrate to New Zealand.' The older woman sniffed before dabbing her eyes with a corner of her handkerchief.

'I'm sorry to hear your son has chosen to leave Jersey,' her father said, 'but I've known of quite a few people over the past few years to take advantage of the offer of free passage for a chance to own their own land and start a new life there. I feel sure his prospects are good.'

'I'll miss him terribly though, Mr Rowe.'

'Yes,' her father said sympathetically. 'That is understandable.'

'This is a second family member to travel to the other side of the world,' she said, blowing her nose. 'My uncle and his family left for Australia about thirty years ago when I was a girl. That was due to the gold rush, but we've lost contact with them over time.'

'I'm certain you won't lose contact with your son. He is a fine man. Many times he came here to find small gifts for you, as well as sourcing his own stationery items.'

Florence wondered if she could ever move from Jersey. It wasn't something she had thought about much before, but having discovered more about Nottingham recently, it was occurring to her more and more that if she truly wanted to, she could embark on a new life away from the island. The thought excited her. She might think of herself as a modern woman, but was she brave enough to move away from here and start up a business elsewhere? She wasn't certain, but it was something she was determined to consider.

'He loved visiting this shop, Mr Rowe,' the woman explained.

Florence was relieved that the lady's attention had been diverted and immediately reverted to tidying the displays, relieved for the interruption. This letter was even more important than the others, she mused. She knew it probably shouldn't matter, but she felt the need for his approval of her changes to her father's shop that she had described to him in her most recent correspondence. For some reason, his reaction meant more to her than she had at first presumed.

A few minutes later the bell jangled once more and looking up, Florence saw Albert greet her father as he quickly made his way over to her.

'I shan't be long,' he said, glancing over his shoulder at her father. 'A few of us are buying tickets to attend a musical concert at the Royal Yacht Hotel. I thought you and Amy might like to join us. I think it will be a popular evening and we will need to purchase the tickets before they sell out.' He glanced at her father once again. 'It will be good to see you again, Florence. We've missed your company lately.'

Florence couldn't help feeling guilty. She had declined several outings with her friends and even cancelled going to a recital the previous week. She hadn't liked to let them down, but since Jesse's departure, she hadn't felt much like socialising. 'Yes, I'd very much like to join you. Thank you, Albert.'

'Will you ask Amy for me if she would also like to come along?'

'Yes, I will, but I'm certain she will want to join us, so do please buy her a ticket when you purchase mine.'

She liked that he didn't ask her why she had been absent recently. She needed to keep herself busy and decided that the days would pass until Jesse's return far more quickly if she kept up her usual social activities.

Jesse Boot. How had this pleasant, hard-working man made such an impact on her life? He had only ever been friendly to her. Never made any promises, or gestures to her that gave her any hope for anything between them in the future. Hadn't she always determined to remain unmarried and shared the intention with Amy many times? However, for all that she missed him and his conversation far more than she expected.

'Jesse Boot,' she whispered. 'What have you done to make me think of you so constantly?'

She was on her way upstairs to her bedroom to freshen up before lunch when her mother stepped out in front of her from the living room into the hallway.

'I'd like a word with you, Florence,' she said quietly, standing back so that Florence had no option but to do as her mother requested. She walked into the room, a little disconcerted when her mother closed the door behind her.

'Is something the matter?' she asked, hoping her mother wasn't going to ask about Jesse. She had seen her mother's expression when Florence had answered a few of her father's questions about Jesse one evening. She had hoped her mother hadn't heard when she had accidentally referred to Jesse by his Christian name in the conversation, instead of calling him Mr Boot.

'It is,' her mother replied, folding her arms across her chest. 'I have noticed letters arriving from Mr Boot every few days. I can only presume that as you are corresponding with each other that you are becoming closer.'

'I suppose we are.' What could her mother possibly be concerned about? She and her father knew the man well. They were both aware that he was a perfectly pleasant man and someone of a trustworthy nature.

'I've also learned that you were supposed to accompany Albert to a concert the other evening but cancelled at the last minute.' She frowned disapprovingly. 'I don't expect rude behaviour from you, Florence.'

Aware that Albert's mother and her own must have been speaking about the event, she tried not to show her annoyance. 'Albert and I were attending the concert with a group of friends. My cancellation would not have bothered him at all. In fact, he came to the shop this morning and asked me to join him and some friends at another event. He didn't appear at all upset by my earlier lack of attendance.'

Her mother appeared slightly appeased at this news. 'And are you going?'

'Yes.'

'Good. Albert is a good man and one who will, I feel certain, make a good husband to the right woman.'

Florence wished her mother give up on her hopes for Albert as a son-in-law. Yes, he knew how to run a shop, he was also a good family friend, but even if she had not met Jesse and become fascinated by him, Florence knew that she would never see Albert as a husband –whatever hopes her mother and his held for them both.

Her mother sighed heavily. This matter was obviously weighing on her mind, Florence realised. She also knew that the issue with Albert wasn't all that was behind this enforced conversation, but her correspondence with Jesse.

'And the letters to and from Mr Boot?' her mother asked, proving Florence's suspicions correct. 'Am I to understand that there is a closeness forming between you and that gentleman?'

Florence was aware that her answer to the question would have to be considered carefully. She didn't relish the prospect of having to deal with her mother's disapproval on a daily basis.

'He is a very pleasant man, as you and Father know, and I have enjoyed his company immensely.' She tried to resist, but was unable to help adding, 'You seem to hold issue with him for some reason. May I ask why that is?'

Her mother seeming to tire, and sat on the nearest chair. Florence thought it might be to give herself a little time to temper her words before she spoke them.

'Mr Boot is, indeed, a pleasant man. Your father thinks very highly of him and I am aware that you are also becoming fond of him. However, Florence, it can't have escaped your notice that not only is he older than you by at least a dozen years—' she paused for effect '—but also that the man is infirm.'

Florence's heart pounded faster as she battled to keep her temper. She loved and respected her mother, but she was twenty-three and a woman who had always held her own opinions. She could not bear to hear criticism against Jesse.

'I believe his age is what makes him more interesting in conversation. He has coped with many difficulties, and, yes, some of those are health related. However, it hasn't stopped him from working hard each day and building up a successful business with his mother, has it?'

'Maybe not, but I wish you would take care not to become too involved.'

'Whatever do you mean?' Florence had to work hard to hide her rising anger.

Her mother narrowed her eyes at her. 'You are not a silly girl, Florence. I believe you know perfectly well that I am referring to your future hopes for Mr Boot. And, if you are not, then I am unsure why you are writing to him with such regularity.'

Florence knew that her mother was only surmising at the speed at which she replied to Jesse's letters. It wasn't unreasonable for her to assume that in all probability he would only be writing in reply to a letter she had sent.

'I write to him because he is my friend and I enjoy hearing from him. I believe he feels the same. He was entranced by Jersey and was unhappy that his visit had been cut short.'

She watched her mother consider her words and eventually her tense expression eased slightly. 'Then I believe you need to take care not to encourage the man, Florence. Men can at times see interest in a woman where there may be none.'

'Mother,' Florence replied, wishing to be left with her own thoughts, 'Mr Boot has given me no reason to suspect he has any interest in me.'

Her mother didn't look convinced. 'I heard you refer to him as Jesse. He must have invited you to address him as such.'

'He did,' she admitted. 'He is only interested in my friendship; I can assure you of that.'

She was being honest and barely let herself wish that there was more between them. Maybe it was because he was so different to her and any other man she had ever met that her interest in him was so great. Maybe it was something else, but that wasn't something she wished to discuss with her mother.

They heard the bell in the shop and the distant voice of their current postman.

'You will want to go and check the mail, I shouldn't wonder,' her mother said sarcastically.

Florence bit back a retort. She wasn't used to being rude to either of her parents and didn't wish to start now. 'If you don't mind,' she said, determined to ignore her mother's comment. 'I'm also awaiting a delivery for some new art books that I thought might be suitable for the shop.'

'I'll let you go then,' her mother said, seemingly mollified by Florence's answer.

Forgetting her lunch break, Florence hurried downstairs to the shop. Her father was wrapping a parcel for a customer, so she made the most of the opportunity and sorted through the few packets and letters that had just been delivered.

Unable to help herself, Florence smiled at the sight of the familiar writing on one of the envelopes. Hopefully now she would be able to find out what Jesse thought of her improvements to her father's shop.

She picked up the envelope and pushed it deep into her skirt pocket. She didn't need her father to begin asking questions; it had been bad enough having to answer her mother's.

The customer left and her father turned his attention to the post. 'Anything of interest this morning?'

'Nothing very much, no,' she said lifting one of the small trunks. 'I'll take these through to the back and unpack them.'

She had to resist the temptation to run into the storeroom and walked sedately as her father followed behind her. She did not wish to give him reason to suspect anything; it was unlike her to be secretive but Florence felt she had little choice.

Chapter 8

16–20 Goose Gate
Nottingham
14 September 1885

Miss Florence Rowe
27 Queen Street
St Helier
Jersey

My dear Florence,

It was wonderful to receive your most recent letter and to be able to now address you by your first name.

I was delighted for you that your father agreed to try out your plans for the shop display and am not surprised that they were a success. You have a natural instinct for retail, it seems, and I am glad that you are able to express your ideas at Rowe's Stationers.

It is not often that I have come into contact with a friend who holds the same interest as I when it comes to my work, and although our businesses cater for the different *needs of the populous, we do, it seems, share the same wish to satisfy their needs.*

I am brought to mind of a customer from some years ago. She was a young mother with a sickly child. She had already lost three of her infants to various ailments and was panic-stricken that she would also lose this child. Like a lot of people in the poorer areas of the town, she did not have the funds to pay for a doctor, but came to my Goose Gate store, desperate for help. I was lucky to have the means to help and took her to the back of the shop to my mother who gave the woman the herbs needed to assist the child.

We still took payment, because we were too concerned about setting a precedent not to, but only took what she could afford. Not having any children, I could only imagine how terrified she must have felt having to find a way to keep her child alive. I can still sometimes hear her panicked voice and can recall the fear on her face. I decided there and then to find a way to provide health to my customers for the cost of a shilling.

Enough talk of business. This is a letter to a friend and, as mentioned in my previous letter, I am planning once again to visit your beautiful island. I believe that should matters go according to plan, that I will be able to travel to Jersey at the end of September. I would therefore be grateful if you could possibly agree to accompany me on outings, so that I may explore further the bays and interests that I was unable to enjoy during my previous holiday.

Work is, as always, busy, but satisfying. Last year I took on my first pharmacist, a Mr Edwin Waring. I had the idea to do this after a change in the law at the start of this decade that allowed limited companies to sell poisons and dispense prescription medicines. Mr Waring is a young man of 27 years and his hard work and vision has helped me make the move into the dispensing business for my company. With him at Goose Gate, we have halved the cost of prescription drugs and updated the packaging.

As a retailer I am sure you can see that this has not made me very popular, but it has made medicines more affordable to the public and that, to me, is a vital necessity. My father believed that everyone deserves the best health-care possible and it is something that I have continued to work towards since his, and now my mother's, death. Customers should not receive preferential treatment simply because they have the means to pay more than others. My aim is that medical aid is available to all, no matter where they stand in society, or where they live in the country.

My apologies. Again, I am discussing my work. Jane is always telling me that I need to step away on occasion and to at least try to focus on a life for myself. Talking of Jane, she came to my office to see me the other day and asked that I forward her best wishes to you and your family.

Until next time,
My very best wishes,
Your friend,
Jesse Boot

Florence sighed and pressed the letter to her chest. He had been pleased for her, as she had known he would. How many other men did she know who would express any interest in her working day, let alone care that she had come up with an idea and be impressed that it had succeeded. How many people cared as much as he did about those he didn't know? Jesse Boot was different, and very much someone with whom she wanted to keep contact.

She heard footsteps and quickly folded Jesse's letter and stuffed it with the envelope into her skirt pocket. She had enough time to open the trunk containing a delivery of coloured inks and stationery, and was lifting out a red leather writing folder when her father entered the storeroom.

'What is taking you so long?' He glanced at the paper in her hand. 'Are these from the new firm we ordered from last week?'

She nodded. 'I think so.'

'Good, hand that to me and get a move on unpacking the rest. I need to step out for a while after this customer has left.' He went to walk away then changing his mind, turned to face her. 'Amy is still out on deliveries, so I will need you to cover the shop.'

'Yes, Father. I won't be long now.'

Ten minutes later Florence watched her father put on his hat and walk out of the shop. It was a relief to have a moment to herself in between visits from customers to have time to absorb Jesse's most recent letter.

She was about to retrieve it from her pocket when she heard a commotion outside. A man's voice yelling for someone named Lily to 'come back here' resonated along Queen Street. Aware that her father would like her to remain inside the shop, but unable to resist from looking, Florence walked around the counter to the shop door and opened it.

She had barely peeked outside when she spotted a skinny young girl of about fourteen running as fast as her tatty shoes would allow her along the street from the direction of Snow Hill. Seeing Florence, she swerved and ducked inside the shop, stopping briefly to look around her before running breathlessly to the back of the shop and disappearing into the storeroom.

Florence was stunned for a moment. She saw the terrified girl staring back at her from around the storeroom doorway, a silent plea from her large brown eyes unmistakeable. Florence put a finger up to her lips to indicate that the girl remain silent and closed the door quickly.

'Lily! Where is that damn girl?' she heard a man's voice ask someone nearby.

She stared out of the window and saw an elderly woman pointing in the direction of her shop. 'Nasty woman,' Florence mumbled, hearing a whimper from the storeroom. She didn't want to alert the man who was now glowering in her direction. Carefully and without making it obvious, she didn't look at the girl but barely moved her lips and whispered, 'Shh, stay still.'

He marched up to the door, his fists clenched. Florence's heart pounded, although she felt sure it wasn't pounding nearly as heavily as the young girl in her back room.

He opened the door, glared at Florence and bellowed, 'Lily, damn you, where are you?'

Florence stood in front of him. She was tall and her father

had often said that when she took a mind to it, she could scare those less brave than herself with one look.

'How dare you enter my shop in such a fashion?'

'It isn't your shop, miss,' he snarled, saliva shooting out between the gap in his front teeth. He seemed only slightly unnerved by her stance, she realised. He stepped to the side to look past her, but Florence moved in front of him once more.

'It is my shop while my father is not here.'

'I want my daughter back. Now.'

She could see his fists clench and hoped it was simply to frighten her. The smell of drink hung around him, mingling with the unmistakeable stink of someone who had not washed for a long period of time.

'Sir, I do not know your daughter, although I have to admit that I pity the poor girl. She is not here and if you do not vacate these premises immediately, I will call for the centenier.' She knew that there would be a police constable or maybe one of the Honorary Police nearby who would soon assist her.

'Is that right?'

Albert slipped in behind the man and went to stand next to Florence. 'Yes, and if he doesn't come, I shall evict you from this shop myself.'

Florence wasn't sure how her skinny friend would manage such a thing against a drunken man twice his size.

The girl's father glanced from one to the other before opening his mouth to speak and being overcome by a coughing fit. They waited as he collected himself, wiping his mouth on the back of his mucky sleeve.

'If she comes this way, you tell her to get 'erself 'ome. She's got chores to be gettin' on with.'

'We will tell her, if we see her.' Florence moved to stand next to the door, waiting next to it for him to leave. After another glance around the room, no doubt to satisfy himself that his unfortunate daughter wasn't there, he grumbled something Florence couldn't make out and left.

Florence quickly closed the door behind him.

The sound of the bell alerted the hiding girl to chance a peek out from behind the storeroom door. 'Has . . . has he gone?'

Florence peered out to the street, relieved to see the man ambling away back in the direction of the public house. 'He has, for now. Stay there for a few more minutes in case he decides to come back and check for himself.'

She turned to Albert. 'Thank you for coming to help me.'

He shook his head, his face pink from temper. 'People like him infuriate me. He's nothing more than a drunken bully.'

Florence pulled a face at him to remind him that the man's daughter was still with them. He might be a lout, but she was his daughter and it wouldn't help her to hear them say things about the man that she would, no doubt, have to face at some point that day, or the next.

Florence pretended to busy herself, checking every so often that the man wasn't coming back.

'I'd better return next door,' Albert said. 'Customers won't be very happy with me if they can't buy their favourite mix of tea.'

'Of course. Thank you again.'

'Thank you,' said a timid voice from the back of the room. 'My name is Lily.'

Albert went to shake her hand. 'I think we gathered as much,' he said gently. 'Will you be all right to go home?'

She didn't look very sure for a moment. 'I'll wait until I know he's probably asleep. That's what I usually do. He'll have forgotten about this by tomorrow afternoon when he wakes.'

It occurred to Florence how very lucky she was to have a sober father and never to have to be concerned about being bullied by either of her parents. Her mother might have her own ideas about how she saw Florence's future, but she only had her best interests at heart. She smiled at the skinny, frightened girl and wondered how long it had been since she had eaten.

'Would you like something to eat or drink?'

The door opened and the girl gasped before disappearing back into her hiding place.

Amy strode in, looking from Albert to Florence. 'I can tell I've missed something, but what?'

'Albert was just leaving,' Florence said. 'Thank you, again.'

He gave her a brief nod. 'Amy, I'm sure your sister will tell you everything as soon as I've left.'

The door closed behind him and Amy took off her hat, hanging it on the coat stand near the front of the shop. She patted her hair to check it was in place and opened her mouth to speak, stopping when she noticed movement in the storeroom.

'Is someone in there?' she asked, concerned.

'It's all right, Lily,' Florence said quietly. 'This is my sister Amy. You can come out now.'

The girl did as she asked, her hands clasped together in front of her unkempt skirts.

Amy forced a friendly smile, as Florence knew she would.

'I'm sure Amy won't mind looking after the shop while I run upstairs and fetch you something to eat and drink.' She doubted the girl would have the confidence to follow her up to the flat and also wasn't certain her mother would take kindly to her bringing in a stranger without warning.

Lily looked nervously from one to the other of them. 'Yes, please.'

Amy walked over to the chair next to the counter and carried it to the back of the shop. 'You can sit here and wait if you like while Florence goes upstairs. Then while I'm sorting through these books, you can tell me about what has happened to bring you here.'

She glanced at Florence, her thin, pale face questioning whether or not to do as Amy asked.

'You don't have to say anything you don't want to,' Florence said, smiling at her, trying to put her at her ease. 'If you'd rather, you can look at some books, or our stationery. Don't feel you have to stay seated. It's up to you. Now, I won't be long.'

Upstairs, Florence explained to her mother what had happened. 'I don't know the last time she ate,' Florence said, concerned for her. 'The poor girl looks terribly thin and frightened. I hate seeing someone in such a state.'

'Do you think she will come upstairs to eat?' her mother asked, drying her hands on a towel. 'It would be more comfortable for her and she would be less likely to be seen by one of the customers or passers-by who could alert her father to her whereabouts. We don't want any further trouble when your father isn't here to help us. The father could reappear with his friends, if he thinks we're harbouring his daughter.'

Florence hadn't considered such a thing, but it troubled her. 'I'll go downstairs and invite her up here then.'

Florence hurried back downstairs and explained her mother's thoughts. 'My mother believes you would be safer and more comfortable upstairs in our living room. Then you can eat in peace. What do you think?'

Florence could see that what she had said about the girl's father coming back had unnerved her. 'Yes, I think I would rather be upstairs, for now. Me Dad is probably lookin' for me in The Exeter,' she said, referring to the public house across the street. 'I ran in there once before, but they'll soon chuck him out again. He's been banned from there for a long time.'

'Good,' Florence said, leading the way. 'Follow me.'

Florence settled Lily with her mother and hurried back to the shop to Amy. She wasn't certain that her father would take kindly to her bringing in trouble to his shop and didn't want to upset him.

She explained to Amy what had happened, knowing that her sister would have done the same in helping Lily to escape her father's drunken abuse. But Florence was aware that many simply turned their heads, not wishing to sour their day with unpleasantries. However, when she watched Lily, what she saw was a girl living on her wits. Whereas she and her sister's worst problem was what to wear, or in her case, whether her father had given her the same opportunity he would if she had been a boy, Lily had to contend with the humiliation of others knowing that her father was a drunken lout.

The contrast in their lives was vast and the thought of it almost brought Florence to tears. It occurred to her that it was only a matter of luck that she had been born into the Rowe family, where pleasing unpleasant customers was something she dealt with several times a week; in comparison Lily was alert to avoiding beatings from her father

'I'm not certain how we're to smuggle her out of here without her father or indeed one of his cronies spotting her?' She straightened a couple of books thoughtfully. 'She seems to think that if she can get away from him and wait for him to go home and sleep off his drink, then he'll have forgotten he was angry with her by tomorrow.'

Amy tutted. 'I've just noticed two men talking together across the road after stopping to stare at our shop. Maybe they're friends of Lily's father?'

'Possibly,' Florence said, concerned by what Amy had just told her. 'I only met him briefly, but I did pick up that he doesn't seem the sort of man to let someone get the better of him. Even though I insisted she hadn't come into the shop, that probably hasn't fooled him.'

Florence walked up to the window to see if the men were still lurking nearby. She spotted two men, now talking to a third and hoped they weren't the ones that Amy had been referring to. 'We need to find a way for her to leave the shop without them noticing her. We could try out the back.'

Amy looked at her doubtfully. 'If they're that intent on

catching her when she leaves, they'll probably have someone keeping watch out the back of the shop, too.'

'Yes, more than likely,' Florence said, disheartened and wondering if maybe her helping Lily had made things much worse for the girl.

Poor Lily, having to live in such a way. 'It makes you think how lucky we are to have a father who has never drunk alcohol; how very different our lived are to hers,' Florence said. 'And being a Wesleyan, Jesse will also not drink, like Father.' She heard her sister giggle and realised she had spoken her thoughts about Jesse aloud.

'Jesse, is it now? When did you progress from calling Mr Boot by his first name?' Her sister's eyes glistened with amusement.

Florence was annoyed at her slip, but knew Amy was only teasing. 'We've been corresponding since his return to the mainland.'

'I had noticed.'

She was about to explain their friendship, then decided that if she wanted to continue with her friendship with Jesse then she would and without any apologies for how it progressed to her family, or anyone else.

'More importantly, what are we going to do to help young Lily now?' Florence asked, concerned for the girl. She had witnessed other men bullying and on occasion slapping their female companions. It had always horrified her to see such things. She might not be able to help all the woman living nearby who survived difficult circumstances, but she was going to help Lily if she possibly could.

Maybe one day, she mused, she might even be in a position to help women on a large scale. The thought warmed her. She was unsure how, but it was something to which she intended giving thought. If Jesse's father had that ambition years before and Jesse was still working hard to assist those with less than himself now, then there was no reason for her not to find a way to do her bit to make a different to those less fortunate than she.

Amy took a deep breath. 'I'm not sure.'

The bell jangled and they both gasped as they turned to see who it was. Florence stared at the man standing in the doorway, smiling at her. Relieved it wasn't one of Lily's dad's cronies come to cause them trouble, it took her a few seconds to register that Jesse was standing there, waiting for her to acknowledge his arrival.

'Jesse?' she said, stunned. 'You're here?'

Amy laughed and walked up to him, welcoming him inside. 'I think that's plainly obvious, Florence. Good day, Mr Boot. How wonderful to see you again on our island.'

He touched the rim of his hat and gave her a brief nod. 'I am very pleased to be able to revisit you all sooner than I had anticipated.'

His smile faltered and he asked, 'Is there something the matter, may I ask? I did look into the shop briefly before entering and you both seemed involved in a very serious conversation.'

It dawned on Florence that Jesse's unexpected arrival was exciting in more ways than the obvious. She indicated the chair and asked him to take a seat. 'We have a problem that you might be able to help us find a solution for.'

He looked intrigued and took a seat. 'If there is anything that I might do to help you two ladies, then it will be my pleasure to do so. Please, tell me how I may be of assistance to you.'

Florence quietly and quickly told him all about Lily and what had happened to her earlier. 'So, you see, she needs to be helped to leave the shop, but we can't fathom out how.'

'And she is upstairs with Mrs Rowe now?'

The women nodded.

He stood up. Florence noticed him wince, but he covered it up almost as soon as he did it. 'I have the perfect solution,' he said, making her heart soar in more ways than one. 'I have a carriage waiting for me a little down the street. I shall go now and ask him to draw up next to the shop, while you go and fetch Lily. I can then take her to wherever it is that she feels she'll be safest while she waits for her father to sober up. At least then she will be away from him and his friends until that happens. I doubt that they will dare interfere with a horse and carriage with a driver and male passenger. These men are usually cowards.'

It was a brilliant idea and Florence was delighted that Jesse had come to their rescue.

'I'll go and speak to Lily and bring her down,' Amy said. 'You keep a look out here, Florence, while Mr Boot arranges for the carriage to pull up outside.'

She watched him leave. How perfect that Jesse was going to help resolve their problem of how to help Lily get away. He was such a kind man, so thoughtful and resourceful. Hearing voices coming down the stairs from the flat, Florence went to join Amy and Lily in the hallway.

'Amy has explained everything to you?'

Lily nodded.

'And you've had something to eat and drink?'

'Yes, thank you,' Lily said in a quiet voice.

Amy went to the window to check on the carriage, before turning back to Lily. 'Now, remember, if your friend isn't at home, you can always come back here. Be careful to ensure that your father's friends aren't about first, though, because you don't want them to know that you have our shop as a place to come and wait.'

'I'll remember.'

'Good girl.'

The carriage drew up alongside the front door and Jesse stepped down, immediately coming to join them in the shop.

'Are you Lily?'

'Yes, sir,' she said, her voice more timid than ever.

'This gentleman is Mr Boot,' Florence explained. 'He's the man accompanying you to your friend's home. You can trust him.'

Florence and Jesse exchanged glances. She could see the kindness emanating from his eyes and knew without doubt that she and others could trust this man with their lives, should the need arise.

'I'll send you a message later, when I'm settled,' he said quietly to Florence, before turning his attention to Lily. 'Come along then, young lady. I believe it's time we took you away from here.' He walked out to the pavement and checking the street quickly before waving for her to follow him. She glanced at Florence for a second before running to join him.

Taking her hand, he helped her up into the carriage, wincing as he stepped up to join her. Florence noticed how badly the poor girl trembled. She gave her a friendly wave as Jesse instructed the driver to leave.

As the carriage moved away, Jesse touched the rim of his hat and gave Florence a nod, and then they were gone towards King Street and the other end of the town.

Amy and Florence barely had time to register what had happened when their father arrived back at the shop. He took off his hat and hung it on the coat stand before walking to stand behind the counter.

'Sorry I was longer than expected.' He opened the till, as he always did when he had been out. 'Has it been busy here today? Anything of interest I should know about?'

Florence glanced at Amy, unsure what exactly she should tell him.

She saw him staring at her and realised he had noticed their exchange.

'Florence? Have I missed something?'

Chapter 9

Florence's father was intrigued, as she had known he would be. 'I'm very proud of you two girls,' he said, hugging them both. 'And of your mother for her part in the girl's rescue.'

'Thank you,' Florence and Amy said in unison. It was wonderful to receive praise from him, Florence thought, aware that she would have not done anything differently even if her father was opposed to their becoming involved in the event.

'That poor mite,' he said, after they had finished explaining what had happened. 'And me absent and unable to help you. We shall have to pray for her at chapel on Sunday.' He opened his till book and wrote something down. 'At least Mr Boot arrived when he did,' he said after he had finished. 'That really was fortunate.'

'It was,' Florence said, ignoring her sister's amused grin as she looked at her from the rear stationery display.

'I hadn't realised he was coming to the island again so soon.'

Amy grinned. 'I don't think any of us had. Had we, Florence?'

'Sorry?' Florence suddenly realised her sister had been speaking to her. 'No, I hadn't expected him here so soon.'

Two customers came into the shop, and, after checking that they didn't need any assistance, her father walked over to where Florence and Amy were sorting through new books.

'Is he staying at the Pomme d'Or again?' her father asked.

'I'm not sure,' she replied. 'I assume so. He said he'll send me a message later.'

Her father thoughtfully straightened several pen holders either side of a wooden tiered display of gold fountain pens. 'I suppose you will be hoping for more time away from the shop, no doubt?'

She hadn't dared hope he would give her more time, not yet. She had only just allowed herself to think about spending more time in Jesse's company, but not when, or where, she might see him.

'If you don't mind.'

He raised his hand to touch her right cheek, smiling at her fondly. 'My independent, funny, middle daughter,' he said almost to himself. 'I never expected you to find any man interesting enough to spend time solely with him. You always seemed to prefer the company of groups of friends.'

'I know,' she said, half to herself. 'The surprise is as big to me as it probably is to you all.'

He lowered his hand. 'And I am happy to allow you to take the time to accompany our friend around the island. It will do you good to go out and see places you probably haven't thought to go to for several years. I'm also remiss at doing the same.'

'Me, too,' Amy said, smiling to the customers as they left without buying anything. 'I think we often don't put ourselves out to do things because we know we can do them any time.'

Florence couldn't help agreeing. 'And then we don't bother to do them at all. It's a shame really, when you think about it that way.'

Another customer entered the shop and her father clapped his hands to hurry her and Amy to start doing some work. They heard the gentleman ask about scrap books for his wife as they both rushed off to find something to keep themselves busy.

Florence went to the storeroom to carry out a small check of the recently delivered portable leather goods for their female and male customers that her father had begun stocking against the order she had made. She couldn't help being distracted by her thoughts of Jesse's unexpected arrival. The thought of him wanting to see her again made her stomach flip. The prospect was exciting.

Thankfully Florence didn't have to wait very long until a delivery boy from the Pomme d'Or arrived with a folded piece of paper for her. She retrieved her small change purse from her pocket and tipped him, but he told her that he was to wait for a reply and take it immediately back to Mr Boot at the hotel.

Florence would rather have read the note in private but didn't like to keep the boy waiting any longer than was necessary. Smiling at the familiar writing, she hurriedly read Jesse's script.

Dear Florence,

*I wish to report that your young friend was safely deliv-
ered at her friend's home in Hue Street. She asked that I
pass on her thanks to you and your family for their concern
and assistance.*

*I am, once again, ensconced at the Pomme d'Or Hotel.
I would very much like to ask you to join me for Afternoon
Tea in the splendid gardens at the back of the hotel, this
afternoon. I understand, however, if this it too short notice.*

The messenger will wait for your reply.

My best wishes,

Jesse

'One moment, please,' she said, waiting until her father
finished wrapping two books for a lady's maid at the counter.

When the girl had left the shop, Florence quietly asked
him if she could have time off that afternoon.

'I have no problem giving you permission,' he said, 'but
you will have to let your mother know before you leave for
the hotel.'

'Can I not simply say that you are happy for me to go, if
she asks me?' she pleaded, nervous to ask her mother in case
she refused to let her go.

Her father took her lightly by the shoulders. 'I know you
are old enough to know your own mind, but your mother
worries about you no less than she did when you were younger.
You may tell her that I am happy for you to go, but also that
you would like her permission before accepting the invitation.
It would show her that you do consider her feelings still.'

As much as she would have liked to argue with her father, she knew better than to attempt doing so. She also couldn't ignore that what he said made sense.

'I shall go upstairs and ask her now,' she said, not wishing to keep the boy waiting.

She found her mother in the living room dusting the mantelpiece.

'Mother,' she said quietly, not wishing to give her a fright so that she dropped the precious porcelain dog she was holding in her left hand as she wiped underneath it, 'would you mind very much if I accept an offer of afternoon tea at the Pomme d'Or gardens this afternoon with Mr Boot? Father is happy for me to go, but I wanted to be certain you did not mind.'

Her mother slowly replaced the ornament, staring at it for a second before moving it slightly. She turned to Florence, a knowing expression on her face, and shook her head.

For a horrible moment Florence thought her mother was going to withhold her permission. Then her mother shrugged. 'I have my reservations about Mr Boot, as well you know, but I cannot in all honesty refuse you permission to take tea with him. Not if your father is happy for you to do so.'

Florence had to resist the temptation to hug her mother. It wasn't because her mother rarely showed emotion, but because she knew that if she did, her mother would realise quite how important being allowed to spend time with him was to Florence. It was not something she had even come to terms with yet and it wasn't something she was ready to share with anyone.

'Thank you, Mother,' she said calmly before leaving the room, delighted to be able to give the boy the answer she had hoped for.

As soon as the boy had left, her father said, 'As your sister will be covering for you this afternoon, I think you should redo the leather goods display she was going to be working on this morning.'

Florence agreed. She couldn't wait to go and see Jesse again and the thought of keeping busy and helping the time to pass was an appealing one. 'I'll start immediately.'

As she worked, she planned what she could wear. Earning her own money, albeit not a high wage due to her job being with her family's business, it still gave her the freedom to keep up with most fashions when it came to dresses and hats.

She had recently treated herself to a new summer dress and, although she had worn her new hat on her outings with Jesse, her dress hadn't quite been ready. Yes, she thought satisfied, I'll wear my new white dress with the blue trimmings.

Despite being busy, the next two hours still seemed to take an age to pass. The shop was busy, and Amy didn't look too impressed that she was, once again, being given time off from the shop. Florence knew that she would have to offer to cover for Amy to have some time away from work once Jesse had gone back to the mainland again. It was only fair.

Although her mother had shown her concern at Florence's growing closeness to Jesse, the calm way her father had accommodated Jesse's request to see her that very day with little notice, made her believe that he didn't have such qualms. It was a relief. Her mother was a strong person and stood up for what she considered right, but Florence's father always seemed to have the final word, and on this occasion that was a welcome relief to her.

'Florence,' her father called, when the shop was empty, 'you may go and change for your outing, if you wish.'

She took twenty minutes to freshen up and change into her new summer dress and hat. She studied her reflection in the mirror, and, satisfied, took a deep breath to gather herself, picked up her bag and went downstairs to say goodbye to her father and sister.

She was very much looking forward to meeting Jesse again this afternoon. She had just reached the doorway at the side of the shop when her father motioned for her to wait.

'Ask Mr Boot if he would like to accompany us to chapel on Sunday. He might wish to go on his own elsewhere, of course, but I think we should invite him to join us.'

'Yes, Father,' she said, happy to have another reason to spend time with the man she realised she was becoming fonder of with every encounter.

Florence decided to walk to the hotel to meet Jesse. It was a beautiful day and thankfully not too hot. It would give her time to prepare what she would say to him once she was in his company. The streets were busy, but that was to be expected in mid-September when the weather was still warm and the holidaymakers enjoying the afternoon air.

She arrived at the hotel in good time. Walking through the arched entrance from the front, Florence entered the beautifully manicured gardens at the rear. It took a moment for her to spot Jesse, but there he was, looking suave in a pale-brown suit. He was seated at a table shaded by one of the trees and looked relaxed as he studied the people around him, his right hand resting on the top of a dark-coloured wooden cane.

The gardens were busy with waiters scurrying back and forth, carrying trays of silverware, or cake stands displaying finger sandwiches, scones, cream, jam and delicate fancies.

The maître d' saw her and hurried over. 'May I help you, miss?'

'I'm here to meet Mr Boot,' she said. 'He's a guest at your hotel.'

'Boot?' He checked his list of bookings. 'Ah, yes, of course. Please, follow me.'

She did as he asked, both of them having to step to the side of the path a couple of times to avoid the busy waiters. She wondered if it was always this busy on a summer's afternoon. She assumed so; it was protected with the building walls high on three sides of the garden, sheltering the outside space from the worst of any winds that might blow in off the sea.

Jesse looked up as they neared and, smiling widely, stood to greet her. 'Miss Rowe,' he said formally, for the maître d's benefit, 'how wonderful to see you again.'

The man pulled a chair out for Florence, pushing it closer to the table as she sat. Once the two of them were settled, he said, 'Afternoon tea for each of you?'

'Yes, please,' Jesse said. He smiled at Florence. 'I'm told it is the best on the island.'

Happy with this compliment, the man left them to go and deal with their order.

'Is it?' Florence asked, intrigued. She wouldn't be at all

surprised, going by the amount of people seated in the gardens.

'I don't really know,' Jesse admitted. 'However, looking at the food as it's been placed on the nearby tables, and the cheerfulness of the people here, I presume it must be one of the top venues to enjoy such a treat.'

Florence giggled. It occurred to her that she sounded like a silly young girl and blushed slightly. She pretended to be absorbed by the tables nearby until her face cooled a bit.

'It is wonderful to be able to see you again, Florence,' he said, smiling at her and looking, she thought, very handsome.

'I was very happy to see you so unexpectedly at the shop earlier today,' she said. 'Thank you, too, for helping with poor Lily. I have to admit I still feel a little shaken by the whole incident. I hate to think of her having to deal with such things at all, let alone at such a young age.'

'Unfortunately, there are too many families spoiled by the vice of drink,' he said thoughtfully. 'I know of too many to focus on just one or two. As I've mentioned before, I've worked with my chapel for many years trying help improve the living conditions of the residents, the education of their children and their working conditions in the factories in my area as much as possible.

Recalling his Wesleyan practices, she asked, 'Father said to ask you if you'd like to accompany our family to chapel on Sunday. Unless you already have a preference for an alternative chapel that you would like to attend.'

He shook his head. 'No, I haven't. I was going to ask at the hotel tomorrow for some suggestions. I would very much like to join your family.'

She couldn't help smiling. 'Father will be pleased,' she said, unsure whether he knew that it was she who would be the most delighted for him to accompany them.

'Where do you worship?'

'Grove Street,' she said. 'It's on the same street where my family lived when I was born. We've always attended the same church. It's beautiful inside and I always love going there.'

He opened his mouth to reply, when two waiters arrived at their table and set down the silverware, food and accompaniments, pouring the first cup of tea for each of them.

'This looks splendid,' Jesse said, waiting for Florence to indicate the sandwiches she fancied and then doing the same. 'I've been looking forward to this since I was last here.'

'You have?'

'Yes.' He smiled. 'I have to admit that I was intending asking you to join me for afternoon tea during my previous visit here, but when it was cut short, I had to wait. I had already seen others enjoying this and have dreamt of sharing an afternoon such as this with you.'

Her eyes widened in surprise to hear him vocalise his thoughts in such a way. For a moment she could not think of a thing to say, despite being happy to hear him profess such a thing. 'Well, this all looks delicious. Thank you very much for inviting me.'

They both ate a cucumber sandwich and Florence couldn't help thinking how lucky she was to have met this attractive and caring man. Her life that she had thought so enriched before meeting him seemed dull and far less interesting now that she had spent time in Jesse's company.

She noticed a couple who were friends of her parents sitting at a table in a far corner. The wife, usually such a timid woman, was craning her neck to see who Florence was with, oblivious that Florence was watching her, too. The woman then spoke behind her hand to her husband. Silly woman, thought Florence; it wasn't as if she could hear what they were saying from so far away. Maybe that was the woman's point, she realised. She wanted Florence to know she was gossiping about her.

She smiled, satisfied when the woman blushed and turned away.

'Do you know them?' Jesse asked, amused.

'Yes, a little.' She thought she had better explain their behaviour. 'This is a small island and they know you're not local. They are probably trying to work out who you are and why I'm here with you this afternoon.'

He narrowed his eyes, staring at them for a few seconds. 'I'm happy to go and introduce myself, if you think I should,' he suggested.

'No. They'll only make up what they want to anyway.'

'Fine. Then I suggest we ignore them.'

Florence smiled. She liked his way of thinking. 'Good idea,' she agreed. 'There are probably others here who will recognise me, either from chapel or the shop. They might also be wondering what I'm doing spending time taking tea with a stranger.'

He took a drink from his cup before replacing it onto the saucer. 'But I'm not a stranger, am I?'

'No,' she said, relieved that this was the case. 'You are not.'

They ate the rest of their sandwiches, passing the time in light conversation. The waiters came and removed their plates, replacing them with fresh crockery and holding a cake stand for them to choose what they would like to eat next. Cakes chosen; Jesse waited for them to leave.

'Do you think your father will allow you time away from the shop to come out with me somewhere tomorrow?'

Florence, delighted to have already had the conversation with her father, smiled. 'Yes, I believe he would. Where would you like us to go?'

Chapter 10

'I was thinking of seeing another part of the island. Maybe somewhere on the north coast? Jane often recalled how she had enjoyed her train journeys there.'

'I'm afraid the trains only go east or west,' Florence said, concerned that she needed to ensure the journey wasn't too arduous for him. 'We could go by charabanc though. That wouldn't be as comfortable as the train, but they are fairly quick and only slightly less comfortable.'

A shadow passed across his face. It was brief but unmistakeable. For a moment Florence thought she had upset him, and it worried her. He was a proud man and she imagined that the thought of her trying to rearrange their day to accommodate any health issues he might be dealing with was not something he would accept kindly. He had never mentioned anything about his condition, but she had noticed him covering a grimace when the pain took him unexpectedly.

As quickly as the shadow had appeared, it vanished like a mist she was certain she had seen, but couldn't otherwise prove. He smiled at her, although it didn't reach his hazel eyes and she saw a sadness there that she had never noticed before.

'Florence,' he said lowering his voice, 'I am older than you and I have my—' he hesitated, staring at her thoughtfully '—crosses to bear, but I hope that you would never change anything about yourself, or your plans, because of me.'

Unsure of his meaning, she hesitated. Keeping her voice low so the next table could not hear, she said, 'You are a strong man, Jesse. You have a dream to make the lives of others better in all ways, like your father did before you. You are working hard to achieve that and so much more. I feel certain that you will do all that you set out to do. But—' she hesitated, uncertain whether to continue. She was either going to become a closer friend to him by what she was about to say or ruin any closeness they had. But if she acted the part of a timid lady now, then that would set the scene for their future, whatever that might end up being.

No, she had to be true to herself. Jesse had liked her character enough so far to want to take time out of his busy schedule running his businesses to see her, and she owed him the honesty to show her true self.

She felt the intensity of his gaze on her and forced herself to continue. 'You are not infallible and need to know your limitations. We all do. I, as a woman, am reminded of mine constantly, by my parents, my friends and societies parameters. You don't have the same barriers to overcome because you are a man. Your—' she struggled to find the right word.

'Continue, please,' he said, his eyes softening.

She took his gentle tone not as one of suppressed anger that someone trying to trick her into saying her piece might use, only for them to then use it to end a friendship, but of someone wanting to honestly know her thoughts.

Buoyed by this, she added. 'Well, your own restrictions. We each have them, just in different ways and some are more obstructive than others.'

He considered her words silently, their tea and cakes forgotten in the heaviness of their conversation. After a moment's thought, he smiled. 'My dear Florence, you are correct in what you say. I like to hide my – what was the word you used? – limitations, even from myself. I am never used to hearing about them from anyone else.' He smiled. 'In fact, you are the only person who has had the courage to mention them to my face.'

'I don't mean to offend you, just be open with you.'

'I see that, and I am touched that you care enough about me to be honest with me.'

Florence sighed heavily. 'Do you really not mind me saying such things?' She thought he was being honest, but really, how well did she know this man? she wondered.

'Yes.' He shrugged and took a drink from his cup. 'It is not something I wish to discuss on a daily, or even monthly, basis.' He gave her a smile that this time did reach his eyes and softened his words further. 'I feel that in you I have met a very decent soul. You are a strong, kind woman, Florence. An independent thinker who doesn't let other people's reservations stand in your way. I don't believe you are aware of how refreshing you are to others. To me.'

It took a few seconds for her to process what he was saying to her. She had never been given such high praise before.

Mostly her life had consisted of her parents doing their best to ensure that she kept her opinions to herself. They worried that she was too assertive and ready to follow her own independent thoughts. Their constant reminders to ensure she be seen and not heard had resounded through Florence's life. It had made her very aware that she was expected to repress her opinions – not that she succeeded in doing so very often.

Jesse Boot, however, was sitting opposite her and telling her that she was refreshing. She couldn't help but smile. He had not taken what she tried very clumsily to say to him in the wrong way. In fact, she realised, he was complimenting her on her character and all the things that her parents had tried to suppress in her. This man really was someone she could see being in her future. They suited each other very well; she felt certain of it.

He cleared his throat quietly. 'Through you I have discovered that although working hard to achieve the dreams my parents and I have been aiming for is a good thing, there is also far more to life than work and ambition alone.'

Hearing him saying these things made her happier than she had ever felt before. He was a man who had achieved so much and someone she admired greatly. For him to think of her in such a way was remarkable. Florence took a steadying, calming breath, determined not to make a fool of herself by over-reacting. She listened, awestruck, as he continued.

'You have shown me that taking time to experience life is also vital to one's health and well-being; to enjoy the pleasures that travel, sunshine, friendship and quiet moments of reflection by the sea offer. There is a value to knowing that these things are as important as spending hours inside an office, or factory walls, nursing an ambition.'

She was unable to hide her happiness from him any longer, nor did she want to. Wasn't it this joie de vivre that he liked so much? Florence wiped away a stray tear with the back of her lace-covered hand.

'Thank you, Jesse. I have to admit that it makes me happy to think that I have added so much to your life,' she said, feeling more satisfied with her existence than ever before. 'You, too, have brought much joy to mine.' She took a moment to assemble her thoughts.

'Becoming friends with you and our time spent together has taught me much about myself. I am ambitious,' she said, keeping her voice low, so as not to sound vulgar to anyone nearby, 'which for a woman is not often something that is encouraged, or indeed praised. You, however, don't see my dreams for my future as a bad thing, nor do you have issue with my independent ways, as my mother likes to refer to them. That is refreshing to me. A precious commodity,' she added as it occurred to her how much she valued his approval and encouragement of her.

Buoyed by his smile, she continued, 'My earliest recollections are in shops. Mostly I remember toddling round the counters at my father's side and watching him at work. He always told me, and still does, that all labour is dignified and that to be courteous and obliging is a great asset in the business world.'

'I agree with him,' Jesse said, nodding.

'As do I. He also believes that working in a shop ought to

be a high calling and thought of in that way by others.' She smiled. 'I'm proud to do the work that I do.'

'Good. It is a job that provides much to others in many ways.'

Satisfied with their continued agreement about how they saw their business lives, Florence realised her mouth was becoming dry after so much talking. She picked up her teacup and finished the cooling liquid. She placed the fine bone china cup back onto its saucer.

Jesse looked thoughtful and didn't speak for a moment.

'I don't wish to offend your father by keeping you out too late,' he said, standing and walking around to behind her chair and pulling it back as she rose. 'I'll see you home and speak to your father properly about tomorrow.'

She was disappointed that their afternoon was coming to an end. Their time together had flown by and she could have happily stayed there with him for several more hours. However, like Jesse, she had no wish to annoy her father by arriving home late. She stood up and walked with him slowly, making their way through the town to Queen Street. Florence couldn't help thinking how natural it felt to be in Jesse's company. She could not deny he was more mature than her friends, both in age and behaviour, but whereas she had enjoyed their company, she couldn't help feeling that she was meant to be with someone like Jesse. They even shared similar ambitions and he didn't seem as if he would feel threatened by her independent ways, not like she expected most men would be.

He might be older than her, but he was refreshing in so many different ways. He had proved his kindness too, by going out of his way to help her and Amy rescue Lily, forgetting his own plans. He didn't know Lily at all. In fact, despite the girl being nothing to him, he had still helped her without a second's thought.

'Penny for them,' he said, interrupting her thoughts.

Florence laughed. 'I'm not sure I want to share them.'

'Then shall I share mine with you?'

She resisted from replying instantly, not wanting to sound too forward. 'If you wish to,' she said, giving him a smile. 'I suppose, as we're walking together, I won't have much choice but to hear them anyway.'

'I suspect you are teasing me, Miss Rowe,' he said, laughing. 'And so I shall share them with you.'

'Good.'

'I was thinking that maybe I should ask your parents if they wish to come out tomorrow. I assume Amy will be needed to run the shop, if you and your father are absent. What do you think?'

Think? She was confused and not a little disappointed. Hadn't he asked her to accompany him out tomorrow? She hadn't thought that he had also been meaning to invite her parents. She battled with her emotions momentarily before being able to speak without exposing her true feelings.

'I'm sure they would be happy to accept,' she was finally able to say.

They walked on in silence for a few minutes. Acquaintances of her parents stopped to wish her a good day. She could tell that they were really interested in being introduced to Jesse because when she mentioned his name, neither the husband or wife reacted, apart from the husband shaking his hand and asking how his businesses were doing in Nottingham.

They walked on and Jesse said, 'I presume they already knew who I was when they stopped to say hello to you?'

'It would seem so,' she said, glad of the change of subject. 'This is a small island and in this town most of the people know each other's business. Us having tea together this afternoon will be the talk at quite a few dining room tables tonight, I think.'

As they walked up King Street, Jesse slowed his walking even further. 'You don't mind me asking your parents to join us tomorrow, do you?'

Shocked that he should ask her opinion, she couldn't think what to reply. Then she remembered that this was Jesse, the man who enjoyed hearing her opinion. She was about to answer him honestly and tell him that she would rather that they didn't have company for their next time out together, then realised how forward that would be. And not very ladylike.

She took a moment to process her thoughts. She wished she could admit to Jesse that she wanted him all to herself. They had so little time to spend together before he must return to his life in Nottingham, and she would rather not have to share his presence with her parents.

Aware that she could not possibly act in such a blatant way, she simply said, 'I'm certain my father will be delighted to receive your invitation, as will my mother.'

* * *

'Please, take a seat,' her father said, having greeted Jesse and welcomed him into the flat. Her mother said hello and then went to continue with whatever she had been doing in her room.

Florence remained standing and waited for Jesse to speak to her father about the following day's proposed outing. The room was filled with the scent of lilies that her mother had probably bought at the Central Market earlier in the day. She loved to have flowers to brighten up their sunny living room and each week there was a new display in one of her crystal vases.

Florence gripped the top of her mother's empty armchair and waited while her father mulled over the invitation.

'Mrs Rowe and I would have liked to join you, very much,' her father said sombrely. 'However, we are both already committed to appointments that we will be unable to break.'

'I understand,' Jesse said apologetically. 'I should not have asked. I'm aware it is very late notice to offer an invitation to you both.'

'Not at all,' her father said, shaking his head. 'We appreciate you doing so.' He thought for a moment. 'You are joining us at church on Sunday, aren't you?' Jesse nodded. 'Then, why not come for lunch here with us. We would love to have you here?'

'That would be delightful,' Jesse said, glancing briefly at Florence.

She would rather go out somewhere, but to know he would be coming to their home to take part in their family meal was something to look forward to and she would just have to wait until then to see him.

'I have no issue with you going out with Florence again tomorrow though,' he said, his voice quieter.

Florence suspected it was because he didn't want her mother to know about the outing until a little later. She presumed that he would then spend time persuading her mother that it was fine for him to have given his permission.

'Thank you, Mr Rowe. Florence has been very kind taking the time from her work to show me your beautiful island. I appreciate you giving her the time off.'

'As do I, Father,' Florence said, slightly stunned to have more time off. Her father must really like Jesse, she decided, relieved. It helped to know he wasn't against them becoming friends, especially when her mother had reservations about them spending time together.

Her father offered Jesse a cup of tea, but he refused politely. 'I really ought to leave you good people in peace. I feel I've taken up a lot of your time lately and should be on my way.'

'Not at all,' her father argued. 'It has been enjoyable meeting and getting to know you, Mr Boot.'

'Please, I believe we are friends and I would be delighted if you would agree to call me Jesse.'

Her father beamed. 'It would be my pleasure,' he said. 'And you must address us as William and Margaret.'

Florence couldn't help smiling at her father's pleasure in Jesse's request. She was thrilled that they were becoming good friends and hoped too that her mother would begin to soften in her attitude towards the man that she was becoming more fond of each day.

He stood up to leave. 'Goodbye, Miss Rowe. What is your preferred time for me to collect you here tomorrow?'

'Ten-thirty?' she said, unsure, but presuming that would be early enough for them to have time to visit the north coast if that was what he still hoped to do.

'Perfect,' he said, picking up his stick and following her father out of the room.

She waited until she heard the front door closing before going into the kitchen to see her mother.

Chapter 11

'Don't think I missed your father giving you permission to go on yet another outing with Mr Boot tomorrow,' her mother said in a low voice without diverting her attention from peeling a bowl of potatoes. 'I don't understand how I am the only one to see the danger in this—' she hesitated as if struggling to find an acceptable word '—relationship.'

'Mother, I . . .'

Her mother spun round to face Florence, her eyes narrowed in barely controlled temper. 'I hope that I'm proved wrong,' she said, oblivious to the potato in her hand dripping onto her prized linoleum flooring, 'but I can't help worrying that you are becoming embroiled with a person with whom you have very little in common. Despite what you may think.'

Upset to think that her mother saw so little potential in her friendship with Jesse, Florence opened her mouth to argue.

Her mother noticed the puddle at her feet. 'Now look what you made me do,' she scowled, facing the sink once more and dropping the potato back into the bowl. 'Fetch the mop and clean that mess up immediately.'

She did as she was told, determined to have her say. When

the floor was once again dry, she put away the mop and went to stand by her mother. 'Would you like me to take over the peeling?'

'No,' her mother said. 'It's keeping me busy while I try to calm down.'

She wasn't used to her mother being so open with her feelings and the thought depressed Florence. If her mother had taken such a dislike against Jesse, maybe there was something wrong in her allowing their friendship to deepen. She clasped her hands together, trying to work through what she could have missed in his character for that to be true. No, she was certain her mother was mistaken.

'If you knew him better, Mother,' she said quietly, 'you'd see he really is a thoroughly decent man.'

Her mother didn't speak as she continued peeling the potatoes, dropping the final one into the pan of water on the table next to her. She tipped the scraps into a bucket to the side of her and placed a lid on the top of it.

'That will be full soon so you can send for Mr Colesby to collect the scraps for his pigs.'

'Yes, Mother,' she said, wondering if now was her chance to put her side of the argument to her mother. She stumbled over her words, trying to find the right way to broach the subject of Jesse and her friendship, as her mother dried her hands on a towel.

'Whatever is it, my girl?' her mother eventually said, sighing heavily. 'I know you aren't happy with my thoughts about Mr Boot and are desperate to speak to me about it. So, go on, tell me why I'm wrong to think of him as I do.'

Stunned by her mother's words, Florence stepped back. She was never allowed to argue with her. She and her siblings had always been expected to accept what their parents said as law and, for the most part, had done so. This matter was too important to her to be able to simply accept what her mother had said, but getting her point across was another matter entirely.

'Come along, Florence,' her mother snapped. 'You're never usually lost for words.'

'I . . . well, I'm trying to think of the best way to say what I think,' she replied honestly. 'I'm not usually asked for my opinion when you've made up your mind so firmly about something.' Florence straightened the cuffs on her sleeves as she thought about what she wanted to say.

'Stop fiddling with your clothing and say whatever it is you need to,' her mother said, her voice weary. They rarely disagreed and Florence could see that she was finding this difference of opinion as upsetting as she was.

Florence took a deep breath. 'I feel certain that if you maybe knew Mr Boot better than you do now, then you might see him in a more favourable light. That's all.'

'You do?'

'Yes, Mother. I do. He's a good, kind man. He cares about those who work for him and his family.' She finally decided to say what was bothering her most. 'I simply don't understand why you don't like him.'

She heard the catch of emotion in her own voice and found that she was on the verge of tears. It wasn't like her at all. Then again, feeling this deeply about a man wasn't at all like her either.

Her mother reached out and placed a hand on Florence's right forearm. 'Dearest Florence. You are a loyal and hard-working daughter. My feelings are nothing to do with Mr Boot's character, or against him personally. Although, it is true that I don't know him very well. But can't you see that he already has health issues? These will only increase, and I would hate for a daughter of mine to spend her married life caring for an invalid.'

'Mother, he isn't that.'

'I want a strong, fine, husband for you: someone who will look after you – not a man who needs you to care for him. Don't you see that?'

She stared into her mother's eyes, unable to miss the fear emanating from them. She tried to see Jesse from her mother's point of view. 'I suppose I can see what you're trying to say,' she admitted, 'but there are more ways that someone can be strong. It doesn't have to be in the physical body alone, surely?'

'Florence!'

Her face reddened. 'I only meant that Mr Boot has so much more about him than the fact that he sometimes struggles physically. He is entertaining and we think along the same lines in business, too.'

'Business,' her mother sneered. 'Honestly, my girl, you have always been too ambitious for a woman, but that really is too much.'

'He doesn't think so,' she said, knowing as soon as the words were out of her mouth that it was the wrong thing to say.

'Oh, doesn't he?' Her mother glared at her. 'That's enough now. You go to your room and freshen up for supper before we both say something we regret.' She stared at Florence silently for a moment as if she was trying to find the person she knew behind the woman Florence had become. 'I want no more argument about this man, otherwise I'll insist your father revoke his permission for you to go out with him again tomorrow.' She rubbed her temples and closed her eyes. 'This situation worries me greatly, Florence. It's upsetting and I do not wish to discuss it a moment longer.'

Florence, aware that they had broached territory neither had touched on before, turned and left the room.

'You're a changed woman since that man came to this house,' her mother called after her.

Florence didn't reply. She wasn't able to. The exchange with her mother had upset her deeply. She wasn't sure if it was the cross words or discovering how deeply her mother worried about her becoming close to Jesse that made her the most distraught. She stopped in the hallway, placing her hand on her chest, trying ineffectually to calm herself.

Did her mother have a point though? she wondered. Jesse's health was only going to worsen as he grew older. Did she have it in her to be someone's nurse, especially if that someone was her husband? It wasn't something she had ever considered before now. She could hear her mother grumbling to herself in the kitchen. Florence realised that she probably shouldn't feel too surprised by her mother's reaction. Hadn't she always told her mother that she would never marry? That she was determined to retain her independence?

Florence rested a hand on her bedroom doorknob. Could she in all honesty become the wife that Jesse would not only want, but also need? She didn't know why not. If she loved him then surely she would be able to forget all her previous notions about her future.

Florence heard her father's footsteps coming up the stairs, stepped into her bedroom and closed the door behind her. She sat down on the edge of her bed and replayed the exchange with her mother. Why couldn't she give Jesse a chance? Why was her mother so determined not to trust her strengths to be able to adapt?

Muffled voices emanated from the kitchen moments later. Her father and mother's harsh tones were unmistakable. Florence tried her best to hear what they were saying, but only heard her father mention Jesse several times.

She tried to remain calm. Her parents rarely argued. In fact, she could only recall hearing them doing so on two occasions, and that had been when she was very much younger. She hated to think that she was the cause behind their annoyance with each other. Her parents, though very different, had a happy marriage. She would have to go and say something, she decided, trying to think what exactly.

Someone knocked on her door, giving her a shock. Before she had time to ask who it was, or answer it, Amy opened the door and stepped inside, closing it immediately behind her.

'What have you done?' she asked gently. 'I heard Father mentioning your name and Mother snapping back at him. It was something about Mr Boot. I didn't wait to hear more. I don't want to become embroiled in whatever it is that's going on.' She sat on Florence's bed next to her. 'Are you all right? Nothing untoward has happened, has it?'

Florence shook her head. 'Jesse asked Father if I could go out again with him tomorrow.'

'Again?' Amy shook her head. 'But you were only with him this afternoon, weren't you?'

Florence nodded. 'I was. But he's only here for such a short time,' she said, trying to explain why she should see him so frequently. 'And he needs a friend to show him the sights on the island.'

Amy raised an eyebrow. 'And that has to be you each time, does it?'

'Why?' she asked, irritated. 'Would you rather be the one to accompany him?'

Amy thought for a moment. Florence watched her, willing her not to give the wrong answer and wishing she hadn't asked such a leading question.

'He is a very nice man,' Amy said thoughtfully. 'I wouldn't mind at all.' She smiled suddenly. 'I'm only teasing. I know it's you he favours and—' she studied Florence's face for a moment '—if I'm not very much mistaken, you rather like him, too. Don't you?'

Florence didn't reply. She wasn't going to commit to anything without knowing exactly how much Jesse liked her, or what, if any, his intentions were towards her.

Amy sighed. 'I know I'm right.' She glanced at the bedroom door as the voices outside rose slightly in volume. 'Are they quarrelling about you seeing Mr Boot too much, or is it that

Mother frets about you becoming too close to him? Is that the trouble?'

Florence stared at the floor. She felt utterly miserable. 'I hate to hear them angry with each other. They never have cross words.'

'No,' Amy said, grinning and nudging her gently, 'Mother gives her opinion and Father overrides it.'

'Not always,' Florence said, feeling slightly better that at least her sister wasn't angry enough with her not to want to try and cheer her up a little. 'And I thought that he usually did what Mother wanted. He simply likes us to believe it was his idea.' Was she right, or Amy? she wondered.

Amy lay back against the wall. 'Like you I have no idea, though I do wish they wouldn't argue.'

Supper was a silent affair. The food was mostly cold because her mother had called their father back into the kitchen for more angry words. Eventually, after an awkward, troubled evening, Florence and Amy washed the dishes and went to their respective bedrooms.

Florence lay awake for several hours hoping that her mother wouldn't persuade her father to change his mind and stop her from going out with Jesse.

She thought of her older sister, Adelaide who had surprised them all by marrying a shipwright called Francis a few years earlier. It occurred to Florence that maybe her mother's shock at her oldest daughter marrying a man thirty years older than her hadn't helped her own cause when she wanted to spend time with Jesse. She pushed the notion aside. Her sister seemed happy enough with Frances, so surely her mother should not worry on that account. Maybe it was the issue of wanting grandchildren, Florence mused, or the concern of ending up with a second son-in-law who was a similar age to her.

Florence had no idea, neither did she know how long Jesse would be able to remain on the island. He was a busy man and a conscientious one and staying away from his business was not something he was able to do for any stretch of time. She knew that she had been lucky that he had chosen to return so soon after his first visit, but it seemed that their luck was running out.

Chapter 12

The following morning when Florence woke, it took her a moment to recall that she was once again going out with Jesse. Unless, that was, her mother had managed to persuade her father otherwise.

She decided to be positive, so washed and dressed herself as if she had every intention of going on an outing. Florence wanted to do something a little different with Jesse and decided that, if he was willing, they would join a group of other people and go on a horse-drawn charabanc ride to the north coast. She wasn't sure if the roads would be too treacherous to Bouley Bay, but would enquire at Weighbridge and see what was available.

She made her bed and opened her curtains. Walking to the living room she was greeted by her parents, sitting with Amy, having their breakfast of poached egg and rashers of bacon.

'I've left yours in the kitchen,' her mother said without her usual smile. 'I only made it a few moments ago when I heard you moving about in your bedroom, so it will still be warm.'

'Thank you,' she said, going to the kitchen to collect her food. She was feeling a little out of sorts after the previous evening's events, but if her mother was choosing to act as if little had happened then she had no wish to upset her further by referring to it in any way.

She sat down and ate, grateful when Amy began speaking about one of the customers from the previous day who had bought ten books.

'She said she simply couldn't choose which ones to leave behind.' Amy laughed. 'It was so funny. Although the poor maid who was with her wasn't all that amused.'

'Did you not think to offer to deliver the books?' their father asked, horrified by Amy's story.

'Yes, naturally. I think she was being a little mean to the poor girl. I had the feeling that there had been some argument between them and the lady was seeking her revenge by insisting she took all ten books immediately.'

'That's mean,' their mother said.

'It is,' Florence agreed, picturing the maid trying to carry so many books for any distance. 'Poor girl and I should imagine there would have been purchases from other shops for her to carry, too.'

'I wouldn't be at all surprised. I thought the same as both of you,' Amy said, before putting a mouthful of egg and bacon in her mouth.

They continued their breakfast with little conversation. Florence was determined not to say anything that might give her mother cause to continue their disagreement from the previous evening. She wasn't hungry and would rather have asked to leave the table but knew that would only antagonise her parents. Her mother had taken the time to cook her breakfast and she would be polite enough to eat it, however difficult it was to swallow.

Finally, her mother placed her knife and fork down on her plate. As always, she was the last one to finish and Florence wondered sometimes if it was something her mother made a point of doing. She wasn't sure, but either way all she was hoping for was that her parents let her go out with Jesse today and not tell her that her father had changed his mind. She would not have put it past him to be persuaded by her mother to do such a thing. He was perfectly capable of sending a messenger to let Jesse know that their plans had changed, and Florence was needed in the shop after all.

She dabbed her mouth with her napkin before refolding it and rolling it up to push it through the napkin ring with her initials on it.

'Once you've washed your hands, I would like you to go down to the shop with Amy for an hour to help set up for today's customers,' her father said, just as her mother stood and began taking plates to the kitchen.

Amy glanced at her, took hers and Florence's plates and followed their mother.

Was this the point that her father would tell her he had changed his mind? She hoped not.

'Yes, Father,' she said, remaining calm as best she could. 'I'll go down with you now, if you wish.'

Moments later she was checking orders and placing them together so that Amy wouldn't have to during the day. Her sister would need to be very organised if she was to be working alone for some of the day while their parents were out, she mused, feeling guilty for taking more time away from the shop and leaving her sister to cover for her.

'I'll look for a trinket to buy her today,' she mumbled to herself as she worked.

'What was that?' her father asked, making her jump.

'I was feeling badly towards Amy,' she admitted. 'I've taken so much time away from the shop recently.' She knew she was tempting fate and that her honesty might cause him to change his mind about her going out, if he hadn't already done so.

He smiled at her. 'You're a good and hard-working girl, Florence,' he said. 'Amy will have her time.'

She wasn't sure if he meant that she would have time off work or if she would have her own turn at going out with a gentleman.

Unable to bear not knowing any longer, Florence put down the two books in her hand and looked at her father. 'I'm sorry to have caused so much trouble.'

He shrugged. 'Don't fret. Although I do understand your mother's concerns, I personally believe that Mr Boot is a decent fellow and I am happy for you to make his acquaintance.' He took a moment to think something through, before adding, 'You have not wished to spend time with anyone as much as you have this man. I trust your judgement and I am happy for you to see him while he is on the island.'

It was a relief to hear him speak in this way. Florence smiled and gave him a hug. 'Thank you, Father,' she said, relieved to know that her plans with Jesse had not changed. 'He is a good man and I know that Mother only has my best interests at heart.' She didn't want to add that she disagreed with her mother's concerns about Jesse's health, fearing that to do so would only antagonise her father and be disrespectful to her mother. But after a moment's hesitation, she heard herself say, 'I understand that Mother is being protective of me and doesn't want his health issues to impact on my future life. Surely, though, this should be my decision. I'm twenty-three and haven't I proved that I have strength of character and know my own mind?'

'You have both those attributes, Florence,' he said. 'However, you have never been married and don't have the experience in life to oppose your mother about this.'

'That's true, Father,' she said, wishing it wasn't the case, 'but Jesse isn't only about his health. He has a brilliant business mind and surely being a part of that side of his life would make up for any other issues that being with him might bring, don't you think?'

'I think you need to be aware of the reality of a life with him,' her father said, his voice solemn. 'And I'm not certain you are as equipped as you might think you are.'

He walked away, leaving her to mull over his words while he served a customer.

After working for a while, Amy joined her. They worked hard to prepare for Amy's day alone.

'I'm sorry to be leaving you here again,' Florence whispered when their father was serving a customer. 'I know it's unfair the amount of time I've had away from Rowe's.'

'It's perfectly fine,' Amy said. 'If Father allows you this time, then he'll let me have time off to make up for it at some point. He's a fair man and always tries to keep things even between us.'

It was true, and Amy's words made her feel better about her day out. She glanced up at the shop clock and saw that it was a quarter to ten. Excitement rose inside her and she indicated the time to Amy.

'Father's still busy and I don't want to disturb him. Do you mind if I run upstairs to freshen up and collect my hat and bag?'

'No, silly. You go. I'll explain if he asks where you are.'

She smiled at her thoughtful sister and hurried upstairs, hoping not to be confronted by her mother again. She knew that, despite accepting their father's decision, her mother would not be pleased to have been overruled on something that she clearly had a strong opinion about.

Florence freshened up, checked her hair was still immaculate after pinning on her hat, and grabbed her small bag. She loved that her bag hung from her wrist. She didn't have to keep putting it down when she sat and remembering to pick it up again whenever she stood.

She left her room, closing the door to find her mother standing at the living room door, arms folded across her chest.

'You're going then, I see,' her mother said, pursing her lips.

'Yes,' Florence answered, hating the discord between them. 'I do wish you wouldn't mind so much, Mother.'

'As do I, Florence. However, I am your mother and I see things differently to your father, that much is obvious. A mother has different instincts towards her children. I sometimes wonder if fathers have any at all.'

'I'm sure they do,' Florence said, stepping forward to give her mother a kiss on the cheek. 'I won't be late.'

'Good,' her mother said, her voice slightly softened, Florence was pleased to note.

Florence ran downstairs feeling much happier now that her mother was less angry with her.

Amy was waiting for her by the back door to the shop at the bottom of their stairs. 'Mr Boot has arrived,' she whispered. 'He has a carriage waiting for you both and is speaking to Father.'

Florence's heart raced. She took a deep breath and strode into the shop with as much confidence as she could muster.

Jesse stopped speaking to her father and both men looked over at her. Jesse smiled.

'Good morning, Miss Rowe. It looks like we have another fine day for our outing. I feel very spoilt by all this sunshine.'

'Good morning, Mr Boot.' She glanced out of the storefront window, already aware that the weather was perfect for them again today. 'It does look splendid, doesn't it?'

'I have a carriage waiting for us outside,' he said. 'I know you wished to book tickets to go on a charabanc to the north coast, but when the concierge of the hotel tried to find some available seats, he found that several large parties had already booked them.'

'We don't have to go to the north coast, if you'd rather go elsewhere.'

'He did suggest us taking a carriage instead, if you didn't mind. We can still follow the charabancs and join in any fun.'

She didn't mind at all. If they were the only ones in their open-topped carriage, then their conversation would not be interrupted.

'You'll probably have more comfortable seats, if I'm not

mistaken,' her father said. 'Let me see you out before the next customer comes by.'

Her father held her hand as she alighted the carriage and waited for Jesse to climb in and make himself comfortable on the seat beside her.

'Have a splendid day,' he said, smiling at an inquisitive customer who'd stopped to watch them at the shop door. 'I look forward to hearing all about it later. Mrs Du Val, please, let me open the door for you.' Her father gave them a brief wave before following his customer inside Rowe's.

'Drive on,' Jesse said. 'We are to go north and then to Rozel.'

'Yes, sir.' The driver picked up his reins and made a clicking noise.

Florence spotted Lily in a shop doorway and gave her a smile. She couldn't help noticing that the young girl appeared to be a little better than the last time she had seen her. Could it be because her usually pale face had been slightly bronzed by the sun, or was her home situation any better? If Lily's tatty dress was anything to go by, nothing much had changed in her personal situation. She wished she could visit her at home to check up on her but, recalling the drunken behaviour of the girl's loutish father, knew that to do so would possibly only make matters worse. Florence didn't want Lily to be punished for bringing an outsider to her family's door.

She turned back to Jesse. 'This is a lovely idea,' she said, hoping to have a chance to speak to Lily soon. She would like to enquire how the girl really was and if there was something Florence could to do help make her life easier in some way.

The carriage reached Don Road and the horse broke into a trot. She was relieved that their journey was underway, aware that part of that relief had something to do with her concern that her mother might put a stop to their outing at the last minute.

'I have been looking forward to our outing today,' he said.

'So have I,' Florence agreed, relaxing for the first time since she had seen him.

The rhythmic sound of the horse's hooves as it trotted along La Grande Route de St Jean was soothing. Florence felt like she, too, was on holiday. The breeze was cooler the further they went from the town. It was a relief. Despite wearing her best summer dress with its cooler thinner fabrics, it was still a little warm for St Helier.

She pointed out the imposing Methodist chapel at Sion. 'I believe this is almost the centre of the island.'

'Have you ever been inside?' Jesse asked, as the driver slowed to let them study the vast gothic building.

'No, not that one.'

'Would you like to now?'

She shook her head. 'I'd rather continue to the north coast. I can't wait to show you how beautiful it is.'

He told the driver to drive on and after a little while they reached the north coast and turned right.

'The view along here is very different to the one on the south coast,' Jesse said a few moments later. 'More dramatic, but no less majestic.'

Florence agreed. It was a while since she had come this way and again, like her other outings with Jesse, it was a joy to see, from someone else's eyes, the sights of the channel and these almost vertical cliffs down to the navy sea.

'It's much cooler too,' she said, thinking how hot he must have been today in the heat. Here in Trinity and being in the open countryside was far more comfortable.

Florence spotted two charabancs ahead. 'We must be going faster than they are to have caught up with them already,' she said, slightly disappointed to now have company.

'They look as if they're having a lot of fun.' Jesse smiled as they neared and the sound of the laughter coming from the two groups increased. 'It makes me happy to see people enjoying themselves. There are so many complications in all our lives that to have days when you are taken away from them must be good for the soul.'

Florence couldn't help agreeing with him. She wished Lily could have a day out like this too, but doubted very much that even if her family did have the spare money to pay for an outing that she wouldn't be allowed to go on one. The thought occurred to her that if she ever had any spare funds, she would find a way to arrange days out for people who usually spent their days working long hours.

'I think days such as these remind us that there is more to this world than our small lives and the problems that we focus on each day.'

He turned to her. For the first time she saw what she suspected was love in his eyes. She hoped, very much, that it was. It dawned on her that her feelings for Jesse had evolved into a deep love for him, too.

Chapter 13

Florence waved back at the children as the charabancs and carriages reached the first cottages just before Rozel harbour. Their tanned, rosy-cheeked faces beamed up at them, and she wished she had thought to bring some sweets to hand to them.

'Seeing these children makes me wish that all youngsters and older people might have the luck to live in such a pretty place where the sea air fills their lungs and where they are surrounded by beauty,' Jesse said wistfully.

'There must be pretty fishing villages on the coasts in England?' Florence asked, trying to picture them.

'There are, but it's the people living in the cities where the pollution is high that I'm mostly thinking of.'

She felt a little silly, having misunderstood his comment. 'Yes, of course. Wouldn't it be wonderful to be able to arrange outings for many people to be able to enjoy a peaceful, healthy place such as this?'

'It would, Florence. It really would.'

The people in the charabancs ahead of them climbed down off their carriages as soon as the driver stopped at the end of a narrow road leading to the harbour. Their driver halted his horse behind them.

'I presume this is the end of the line?'

'This is Rozel Bay,' Florence told him as he stepped down and held out his hand for her to take. She placed one foot on the metal step and then another onto the road. She breathed in deeply. 'I do love being by the sea.'

He smiled at her, his blue eyes twinkling in amusement.

'What?' she said, as they began walking towards down the road.

'Sorry,' he replied, unable to help laughing slightly. 'It's just that you live on a small island that's surrounded by the sea. Don't you always feel that you are breathing in the sea air?'

She thought about his question for a moment. Did she? 'Actually no, I don't,' she said, as they passed tiny granite cottages. 'I suppose that does sound a little strange. When I'm in the countryside I forget how close to the sea we are and when I'm in town, I presume it feels like being in any town. I don't think that I'm only a ten- to fifteen-minute stroll to the seaside.'

'Good morning,' a man coming out of one of the houses said to them. 'If you wish for refreshments, there's the Rozel Bay Hotel, but it's going back the way you came, turn left and at the corner at the end of the road it's on the right. You'll be well cared for in there.' He indicated the opposite direction that they were going.

Jesse thanked him. 'I'm sure we will take time to do as you suggest,' he said. 'Once we've had a walk along the harbour.'

They walked on. 'Do you think he might work there and

is looking for business?' Florence asked quietly when she was sure they were out of ear shot.

'Very possibly. Mind you, I will be happy to sit in the cool and have a bite to eat and something to drink,' Jesse said. 'I suppose we are close to lunchtime, or will be after our walk.'

They reached the sea wall and stopped. 'Look at the way the sunshine glistens on the gently rolling waves,' Jesse said, indicating the small bay with the small curved harbour wall to their left, with the rising hills either side. 'This must be a very sheltered place for the fishermen to moor their boats.'

'I believe so,' Florence said. 'This is one of my favourite places.' She noticed amusement in his face again. 'What have I said now?' she asked, giggling.

'You have a few favourite places.' He held up his hand. 'I'm not trying to be insulting in any way,' he said anxiously. 'You have every right to love this beautiful island. It's peaceful and has such an individual way about it. I know most of the locals speak English, but it has a very French way about it. I've noticed the French road names and have heard many French accents in St Helier when walking through the streets. There's another language I keep hearing, but I can't work out what it is.'

'It's probably Jèrriais,' she said. 'The local patois. Some people refer to it as Jersey French, or Jersey Norman French.'

'Your parents speak it, do they?'

She shook her head. 'My mother was born in Cumberland and doesn't speak it. I speak French, as do my sisters, because we were sent to school in a convent in Normandy. My mother wasn't happy that we were sent there, but my father thought it important that we were fluent with our French neighbours.'

'I wish I spoke a second language,' Jesse said thoughtfully. 'Though I haven't really had call to do so living in Nottingham.'

Shrieks and laughter came from below them on the sand by the water's edge where some of the other visitors were paddling.

'I like to see people enjoying themselves,' he said. 'Life is far too short not to take time to do something different if you possibly can.'

'Is that something new you've discovered?' she teased, feeling comfortable enough with him to believe that he wouldn't take any offence.

He nodded. 'It is. In fact, it's another thing that I've learnt during my time spent with you, Miss Florence Rowe.'

She loved the way he said her name. It sent shivers down her spine. Florence didn't like to dare hope too much, but she couldn't help thinking that he might be building up to wanting to ask her father for her hand. Was that too fantastic to imagine? She was surprised to realise that she hoped it wasn't.

When had she changed from the girl determined to remain a spinster and forge an independent life for herself, to this woman who wanted to spend the rest of her life by a man's side? Was the change in her plans due to Jesse treating her so much like an equal, rather than as a gentlewoman who should be seen and very much not heard giving an opinion? Or, could it be because he enjoyed conversations with her about business and encouraged her to share thoughts and dreams for the ambitions she might have in her future? He certainly was unlike any other man she had met before. Maybe that was the reason for her complete change of heart. Jesse was special and unique and she suspected that a life with him would be filled with excitement, adventure and many challenges.

She noticed that he was waiting for her to say something.

'Sorry, I was miles away,' she fibbed. 'It's so pretty here, I can't help wishing I had a little cottage somewhere, over-looking the bay, so I could sit and watch the sea on days like these when it's a rich navy and in stormy weather when it's a vibrant jade.'

'I like the sound of that,' he said, his voice soft. 'That would indeed be something to aspire to. A house by the sea. Perfect.'

She noticed a shot of pain pass his features. She didn't want to remark on it but had an idea. 'Shall we take a breather on that low wall over there?' she suggested. 'It's in the shade of that house and would be the perfect place to sit and take in all this beauty.'

'If you wish,' he said, walking with her to take a seat. He sighed contentedly. 'You are right; this is a good place to enjoy the scenery around us.' He paused. 'Florence, there is some-thing I feel I need to address.'

She didn't like the way he spoke and could tell by his tone that it was something she probably wasn't going to like.

'I'm older than you.'

He took a breath to add something further, but not wishing to hear anything negative, Florence quickly said, 'Yes, I know that and it's fine.'

He turned to face her fully. 'Florence, if it was just that I wouldn't mind either. However, I have rheumatoid arthritis.' He held his hand up to stop her when she went to interrupt. 'No, we need to have this conversation. I'm in pain some of the time and as I age it will only increase and my ability will lessen. I need you to understand this.'

'I do,' she said, wishing he would stop this conversation. She loved him and surely all that mattered was that she was with him.

'Really, understand though. I don't want you to be with me because you feel sorry for me.'

She couldn't imagine ever feeling such a way towards this strong, determined man, and said so.

'Or, that you are with me for any reason other than you wish to spend your life with me.'

She realised that she needed to reassure him rather than argue with his comments. 'Jesse,' she said quietly, 'I have never met anyone like you before. You intrigue me, you think like me and I love being with you. I don't care about your age and, as far as your arthritis is concerned, we will find a way to help you. There are always improvements in medicines, you know that better than most people. Who knows what the next year or two will bring in that area? You might be worried for no reason.'

He stared at her briefly before smiling, his eyes shining suspiciously. 'You are a marvel, Miss Florence Rowe; do you know that?'

'I hope I am,' she said, 'then maybe I will be able to keep up with you.'

'I'm glad we've had this talk,' he said, taking her hand and giving it a gentle squeeze.

'So am I.'

They sat in silence for a while, each lost in their own

thoughts. It was a comfortable silence and Florence sensed that their relationship had taken a deeper direction. She was happier than she could recall being for a very long time.

They watched the other visitors from the large horse-led charabancs having fun on the beach. The women stood with their parasols shading them from the sun, while one or two of the younger men took off their shoes and paddled in the shallows.

Florence noticed them begin to gather and discuss something. Then the men who had removed their footwear put them back on.

'I have a suspicion that they are going to soon make their way to the Rozel Bay Hotel,' she said, standing. 'I think that if we would like a table for ourselves then we need to make our way there now, before they catch up with us.'

He laughed. 'You don't miss much at all, do you, Florence?'

She shook her head. 'Not when I want to ensure that my companion is able to enjoy a good luncheon.'

He stood and they began walking in the direction of the hotel. 'I should have thought to ask that man who spoke to us earlier if he would ask the hotel to reserve a table for us in their dining room.'

It was a good idea, Florence thought, deciding to remember it for next time – if she was lucky enough to be invited to join him here again.

They were given a table by the window. It gave them light, but no sea view. The food was tasty, and Florence was relieved to be out of the heat for a while in the cool stone-floored restaurant.

'I'm sorry your parents were unable to accompany us today,' Jesse said. 'I would have liked to treat them to a day away from the town. Not that I think St Helier is unpleasant in any way, you understand,' he added hurriedly.

'I'd never think that,' she said, wanting to put him at his ease. She was glad he had mentioned her parents and hoped he would continue to do so.

He glanced around them and, lowering his voice, said, 'Your parents have been very gracious towards me, Florence.' She smiled, waiting for the 'but' in the conversation. 'However—' he thought for a moment '—I don't wish to say this in a derogatory way, but I sense that Mrs Rowe isn't as, shall we say, comfortable as Mr Rowe might be with you spending time with me. Would I be correct in saying as much?'

She considered her reply carefully.

'Please don't feel you must answer my question. I'm aware it probably isn't the best one to make over luncheon.'

Florence didn't want him to mistake her thoughtfulness for upset, so shook her head and smiled. 'I don't mind you asking at all.' She didn't want to reference Jesse's frailty so simply said, 'She is a little unnerved by our age difference, maybe?'

He seemed satisfied with her answer and nodded. 'I can understand her thinking in this way.' He took time to cut his roast beef before placing a forkful into his mouth and chewing.

'Mother is very protective of us girls,' she added, wanting to reassure him that her mother's reaction would have been the same for either one of her daughters.

'Naturally. I can imagine I would be the same with my

own children, especially daughters, if I was lucky enough to have them.'

She continued eating her meal, her enjoyment of the perfectly cooked beef, carrots and roast potatoes lessened by her mother's attitude to Jesse and the fact that this kind man had picked up on it enough to remark about it. Why couldn't her mother simply trust in her daughter's instincts, Florence mused miserably. She hoped that her attitude to him wouldn't ruin the rest of his visit to the island. They were becoming close and she would hate for anything to destroy that friendship.

'I shan't ask your father to let you have any further time away from Rowe's Stationers until after I've spent time with your family at chapel on Sunday. Hopefully at lunch afterwards your mother might get to know me better. I will try my best to make her soften her concerns about me. I would like her to discover that despite my being over a decade older than you, and my health issues, I have the support system in place to ensure that you would still have a happy and fulfilled future with me.'

She hoped so too. She was sad to think that had to wait another two days to spend any more time with Jesse. Tomorrow was Saturday though, and, as their busiest day at the shop, she knew she would have felt too guilty to ask for time away from her job.

They finished their lunch and, after a brief walk while their food digested, they made their way to where Jesse had pre-arranged to meet their carriage. After settling themselves down in their seats, the driver clicked the horse to walk on.

'This has been a wonderful day out,' Florence said. 'Have you enjoyed today as much as I have?'

He smiled at her. 'I believe so, Florence.' He hesitated briefly and glanced at the driver before speaking. 'I was hoping to speak to your father.'

'Really?' Florence said, unsure if he meant to speak to her father about her, or if he was still referring to her mother's reticence towards their friendship.'

'Yes.' He cleared his throat and took her left hand in his. 'Coming to Jersey has been an incredible experience for me.'

'I'm pleased you think so,' she said, delighted to hear him repeat his enjoyment of the island.

'Not only because I've discovered this gem of a place, but because of my meeting you, Florence.'

'Oh, is that so?' she asked, unsure how to react or what exactly she was reacting to.

'Yes. You might, or might not, have guessed that I have developed feelings towards you. Feelings of love, rather than mere friendship.' His face reddened slightly.

Florence's heart constricted with love for him. He looked as if he wanted to say more, so, rather than interrupt his thoughts, she waited for him to continue.

Jesse took a deep breath. 'I know I'm older than you, but at this moment I feel like a schoolboy unable to form an intelligent sentence. Florence Rowe, I know that my trip here has to end soon, but I find that I am unable to imagine my future without you in it.'

'Future?' she couldn't help asking, her voice wobbly. Her

heart pounded. Was he broaching the subject of marriage? Was Jesse about to propose to her? She hoped so with all her heart.

'Yes, dearest Florence.' He took her other hand in his and gave her a gentle squeeze. 'Would you mind very much if I speak with your father this evening on our return to your home? I am aware of your mother's feelings, but maybe if she knows that my intentions towards you are to give you not only a good home and family of your own, but a rewarding life that will satisfy your needs, she might soften her resistance to us being together. I am aware of what my future entails—' he indicated his walking stick '—I don't want you to think that you will be wholly responsible for any care that I might need. I have always been an independent, proud man and I aim to continue in that way.'

'Do you mean you wish to speak to him about . . .?' She couldn't finish her sentence. What if she had taken the wrong meaning from what he said.

Jesse sighed, his eyes exuding all the love she had never dared hope to be the recipient for.

'Yes, Florence. I'm sorry. I'm acting like a bumbling fool. I wish to ask your father for his permission to marry you. If you are happy for me to do so.' He frowned, seeming momentarily concerned.

Her feelings for him threatened to overwhelm her and she didn't know whether to cry out or laugh. Instead she took a deep breath to regain some control and said, 'I . . . well, I would be delighted if you spoke to my father, Jesse.'

'Truly?'

She couldn't help laughing. Then, aware that her cheeks were wet, realised that she was crying too. 'I'm sorry. I don't mean to be so . . . I don't even know what I'm saying. Sorry.'

He took a white handkerchief from his top pocket, and, shaking it slightly to unfold it, gently dabbed at her eyes before drying her cheeks and handing it to her.

'Please, dearest one, don't apologise. I am only too relieved that my feelings towards you are reciprocated.' He leant forward and, placing the tips of his fingers underneath her chin, gently lifted it and kissed her. 'I believe we could have a magical future together.'

Florence was taken aback by his actions and for a moment couldn't think how to respond to the delightful sensation of his lips on hers. 'As do I, dear Jesse,' she said, wiping her eyes once more, willing her mother not to come between their plans to marry.

She stared into his eyes. Why did this happy time have to be blighted by her mother's concerns towards Jesse? Could she possibly ever walk away from this man and his proposal to appease her mother? Florence wondered miserably. She doubted it very much. She wanted her future to be with him, to share all the excitement and dreams that he had confided in her. She gave a shuddering breath. The thought of having to make a choice between the man she loved, and her mother hurt made her throat constrict with unshed tears. One of them was going to suffer heartbreak at her hands; it was unavoidable. She loved them both and to hurt one of them was going to devastate her.

An hour later, Florence was barely able to contain her

disappointment. 'Father's out?' she said to Amy, looking about the living room as if her father might be hiding behind a chair. 'Do you know when he'll be back?'

'I've no idea,' Amy said frowning. 'Why? What's so important you need to speak to him now?' She took Florence's hand in hers. 'Nothing's wrong, I hope?'

'No,' Florence assured her, trying to sound calmer. 'Mr Boot is outside in a carriage. He's waiting to hear if Father is available for him to speak to about something.'

'What?' Amy asked.

'I can't tell you now,' Florence said. 'I need to go and let him know that Father isn't here. Maybe he can speak to him after chapel on Sunday.' She couldn't help feeling let down that this most important of conversations would have to wait two days, but knew how busy her father would be the following day. She would simply have to do her best to wait with as little impatience as possible.

She ran down the stairs and up to the carriage. Jesse beamed at her and went to stand.

'Is he there?'

She shook her head, unable to hide her disappointment. 'I'm afraid not. He's out visiting friends with Mother. Tomorrow is always a busy day for him,' she said. 'He always does his paperwork after closing the shop on Saturdays and won't thank me for asking him to interrupt his routine. We'll have to wait until Sunday to speak to him. Do you mind?'

He leaned down to her. 'I've waited my whole life so far for that conversation and can wait another forty-eight hours.'

Soothed slightly by his calmness, Florence nodded. 'I shall

see you at chapel then. Will you want to meet us here and walk down with the family, or should we meet you there.'

'I'll take a carriage direct to the chapel. Unless you think your parents would like to ride down to Grove Place with me?'

She shook her head. 'No, there will be too many of us. We'll meet you there, just before eleven.'

'Perfect. Goodbye, Florence.' He sat upright in his carriage seat and gave her a nod. 'I'll see you all on Sunday then and look forward to it.'

She smiled and waved as his carriage moved on. 'As will I,' she whispered as the carriage took him along Queen Street. Florence would just have to be patient and hope that the family's get together with Jesse at chapel and later at lunch would go some way to dull her mother's fears about the future she would have, should she marry Jesse.

Chapter 14

Florence stood chatting nervously to Amy near to where their parents chatted friends with Adelaide and her husband. She hoped Jesse hadn't changed his mind about coming. Could he have changed his mind about speaking to her father? She tried not to give in to her panic and kept a smile plastered on her face to greet friends and acquaintances that she was used to seeing each Sunday.

'Here's his carriage,' Amy whispered, nudging her gently. She narrowed her eyes in amusement. 'You didn't think he would come, did you?'

'I did,' Florence argued, keeping her voice at a whisper so as not to alert anyone else. 'Don't tease. This is an important day for me.'

'I wish you'd tell me why,' Amy said. 'We always confide in each other. I don't know why you're keeping something from me now, especially when it's obviously worrying you deeply.'

'It isn't,' she fibbed. 'Anyway, I can't tell you. Not yet.'

'Why not?'

Florence didn't want to tempt fate, but then again, this was Amy and she was right; they did always confide in each other.

Amy stared at her silently. Unnerved by her sister's eyes boring into hers, Florence looked away. Her sister knew her well enough to pick up on the fact that something was troubling her, she felt certain of it. She didn't want Amy to know, at least not until Jesse had had a chance to speak to their father; but first they had today to get through.

Amy grabbed her arm and squeezed it tightly. Florence glared at her. 'Ouch, that hurts.' Then she realised that her sister was staring at her open-mouthed. Florence could tell that she had guessed her secret.

'Is he going to ask Father if he can marry you?' she whispered breathlessly. 'You have to tell me. I'm right, aren't I?'

Florence glanced around them, horrified in case anyone else heard. 'Shush.'

'I am. I knew it,' she said clapping her hands together, obviously excited by this news.

'Fine, you're right,' Florence whispered back at her anxiously.

'No!' Amy gasped, her exclamation alerting others around them who turned their heads to see what the excitement was about.

'Amy!' Florence hissed, horrified that her sister might blurt out her secret. 'Please. Stop it. You're making people look at us and I don't want Mother to know there's something I'm keeping from her. Not yet, at least.'

Amy grimaced. 'Sorry. I didn't mean to do that,' she whispered. 'You've finished the book already?' she asked loudly, hopefully putting them off the scent of their real conversation.

Florence was relieved when everyone soon lost interest and continued with their conversations again. They were no doubt bored at the thought of two women discussing books to want to waste time listening in on their conversation.

'Honestly, Amy,' she whispered. 'Please, don't do that to me.'

'Sorry. I wasn't thinking.'

A murmur arose around them as Jesse's carriage came to a halt at the bottom of the chapel steps. Their father, spotting him, called out to welcome him and went to greet him as he stepped down.

'Mr Boot, how splendid of you to join our congregation here today. We're very happy to see you.'

Florence watched as her father took Jesse to introduce him to everyone. She smiled back at him when he glanced over briefly at her, soothed to know that it wasn't long now until they could hopefully go public with their relationship.

Everyone took their usual places in the large church and Florence tried her best not to keep sneaking peaks over at Jesse, sitting next to her parents in the pew in front of where she sat with her sisters, brother and their families.

Eventually, after what seemed like a much longer sermon than usual, they all made their way outside.

Florence walked up to stand near her parents who were introducing Jesse to more of their acquaintances. Finally, a couple of them began speaking to each other and her parents about an event they had all been invited to in a couple of weeks, and she and Jesse were left by themselves.

'Hello,' he whispered, his gloved hand grazing hers, sending static through it despite their skin not actually touching.

'I'm glad you came today; I feel like I haven't seen you in days.'

'It has only been two,' he teased.

'It feels like many more to me.'

He sighed. 'Good, I'm glad to hear you say so. It felt like more to me, too.'

Two women came over and spoke to Florence, waiting obviously for her to introduce Jesse to them. After some small talk, she was relieved when they spotted another person they were wanting to catch up with.

She opened her mouth to speak, when Amy appeared next to her. 'Good morning, Mr Boot,' she said. 'You're still coming to lunch with us today?'

'Yes. I'm looking forward to it very much.' He gave Florence a quick glance before adding, 'Your parents were very kind to invite me to join you all today.'

'We're delighted you could be with us,' Amy said. 'Mother would have liked to cook a roast, but because of chapel we usually have cold meats and Jersey Royals with salad. I hope that is to your liking?'

'Very much so.'

Florence's parents came over to them. 'Are you ready to go back for some lunch now?' her father asked.

They strolled the ten-minute walk up Halkett Place. Florence stopped every so often to speak to friends as they and other families walked on their way from church either to their homes, or to visit relatives and friends. She much preferred to be out walking on a Sunday, when everything was more sedate, rather than any other day of the week when horses trotted along the cobbles and wooden wheels noisily rumbled past the shops, and employees rushed from their place of work to deliver at customers' homes.

They reached 27 Queen Street and her mother led the way upstairs to the living room.

'Please take a seat,' her father said to Jesse before offering him a refreshment.

Florence and Amy went to help their mother in the kitchen. Most of the preparations had been carried out before they left for chapel, but her mother was boiling the Jersey Royals so that they were hot when served.

Florence took two glasses of the cold lemonade into the living room for her father and Jesse.

Jesse thanked her and when he took the glass from her hand, she noticed his was trembling. She realised he was building up to speaking to her father. She barely had time to think of whether this was the right time, when Jesse stood up.

'Mr Rowe,' he said quietly. 'I was wondering if we could have a brief word in private once Miss Rowe leaves the room?'

Her father frowned. 'Is something the matter?'

Jesse swallowed and seemed to stand up taller before replying. 'Hopefully not,' he said. 'Are you happy for me to do this, Miss Rowe?'

'Yes,' she said, hearing the unmistakeable tremor in her voice. Jesse gave her a nod.

Her father turned to Florence. 'Is everything all right?' he asked her. It was typical of him to check that she was happy with what was about to happen.

'Yes, Father. I am aware why Mr Boot wishes to speak to you. I'll leave you both for the moment and go to see if Mother needs more help in the kitchen.'

She left the room. Her heart pounded rapidly as she closed the door, willing her father to agree to Jesse's proposal. Florence heard her mother's voice as she asked Amy to pass her the colander and her stomach fluttered anxiously. What if her father agreed to them marrying, but her mother put a stop to it? Her concern was certainly real, but she hoped that her mother would listen to reason and be persuaded that her marrying Jesse was her dream.

She strained her ears to hear what they were saying but was unable to pick out any particular words. She soothed herself with the thought that at least there were no harsh tones emanating from the room. That was something to be positive about, she decided.

Eventually, after what was probably only minutes but seemed to Florence to have taken hours, the living room door opened. She studied her father's face. He seemed happy. Although on second glance she saw an underlying nervousness about him. Was it because he had giving his permission with the knowledge that her mother would need to be persuaded that Florence marrying Jesse was the right thing to allow them to do?

'Florence, please come in, will you?' He let her pass him into the room and stepped out of the doorway, calling for her mother to join them.

Her mother took a moment, no doubt to dry her hands and remove her apron, Florence mused.

'Yes, William,' she said, her voice light, until she stepped into the room and caught Florence's eye. Her eyes hardened and she looked from Florence to Jesse and then to her husband. 'William?'

She said his name in a question, but didn't hide the underlying threat in her voice, Florence noticed.

'My dear, I have been speaking to Mr Boot alone. He has asked for Florence's hand in marriage and I have—'

Before he could finish his sentence and make Florence the happiest woman alive, her mother shook her head. 'I will speak to you alone for a moment, please, William.'

'Stay here with Mr Boot, Florence,' he said. 'I'll ask Amy to come and join you both while I speak with your mother.'

She stayed in the room alone with Jesse, the door closed firmly behind her parents. Just then Amy walked in.

'What's going on?' she asked, frowning. 'Mother looked very stern when Father told me to come in here.' She stared at Jesse. 'Is something wrong?'

He shook his head. 'I asked your Father to give me his blessing so that I might ask Florence to marry me.'

'Jesse, tell me what Father said,' Florence asked, taking Jesse's hands in her own and hearing her parents' whispers becoming more urgent and angry in the next room. 'Quickly, before they return. I have a horrible feeling that today isn't going to end how we would have wished it to.'

Jesse frowned. 'Why not?'

Florence glanced at Amy, who had sat on the chair across the small room and was watching them apprehensively.

'I suspect that Mother has her reservations about us

marrying and she does not want Father to give us his blessing.' She sighed. 'Therefore, before they come back to the room, please, tell me what Father said, so that I can enjoy it for at least a moment.'

Jesse gave her hands a slight squeeze and gazed into her eyes. 'He gave his permission for us to marry,' he said, his voice gentle and filled with a love that mirrored her own. 'We are going to be married, Florence. Isn't that wonderful?'

They hadn't heard the door opening.

'I am afraid that if you do marry my daughter, Mr Boot, that it won't be in the near future.' Her mother stared at Florence's hands in Jesse's as they both stood up. Florence saw that her mother was unable to meet Jesse's distraught gaze.

'Mrs Rowe, Mr Rowe? I don't understand,' Jesse said, letting go of Florence's hands, his face ashen.

'We all need to remain calm,' her father said. 'My dear, please, take a seat.' He looked at Jesse. 'Mr Boot? If you wouldn't mind doing the same. And you, Florence.'

They did as he asked.

'William,' her mother said, her voice hard as she clasped her hands together on her lap.

Her father remained standing and cleared his throat. He studied first Jesse and then Florence. 'Your mother believes, as do I, now I think of it, that it wouldn't be seemly for the two of you to marry too soon. She suggested that you postpone any engagement until next year.'

'Next year?' Florence was horrified.

'You have known each other such a short time,' her mother said, concern sharpening her tone.

'I understand what you are saying,' Jesse said, his voice calm. 'However, how are Florence and I going to be able to become better acquainted when I have to return to my work in Nottingham and she is living here?'

'You may correspond by letter,' her mother said after a brief hesitation.

'Yes, both take the time to be certain that you are right for each other,' her father continued, clearing his throat.

Florence knew that her mother had forced her father's hand in this decision. He wasn't worried about her marrying Jesse; otherwise he would have put a stop to the conversation when Jesse broached the subject. No, this was all her mother's doing. She had managed to enforce her anxiety about Jesse's age and health onto her father, Florence mused, angrily. She was unsurprised but hurt that her mother didn't trust her to know what was best for herself.

She looked at Jesse, unable to miss the hurt in his gentle face. He wasn't a stupid man and she could tell that he knew that her mother would not choose him as her daughter's partner. Was that why he wasn't saying anything? She scowled in her mother's direction, catching her eye and wondered how she could be so mean as to insist on this proviso to their marriage.

'I explained that you have asked for Florence's hand in marriage and that I had agreed. However, I'm sure you will understand that under the present circumstances this situation will have to change.'

'But, why?' Florence cried, frustrated with how things had turned out. 'It doesn't make sense. This is about Jesse's age, isn't it? And the fact that he has rheumatoid arthritis.'

Her mother's face reddened. Florence knew how she hated confrontation and believed that people should not discuss certain things with others. Things just like these.

'Fine, if you insist. Then yes, I am concerned about Mr Boot's age and, well, his health.'

'But how is a year apart going to solve those issues? It doesn't make any sense.'

'There's no need to give me that look.' Her mother scowled. 'You are my daughter. I love you and want the best for you.' She seemed to realise what she had just inferred and addressed Jesse. 'Mr Boot, I'm sorry; I don't mean to insult you.'

'Please, do not concern yourself,' Jesse said quietly.

'Father, please.' Florence was unable to resist pleading to him, although she knew it was probably a waste of time.

'Florence, that is enough,' her mother said, glaring at her. 'William, continue please.'

'Yes, as I was saying, Mr Boot, Mrs Rowe and I have discussed this matter.' He cleared his throat and glanced at his wife before continuing. 'And we're in agreement when I say that I feel the need to rescind my permission.'

Florence gasped. She covered her mouth with her hands to stop from crying out. It wasn't fair. How could her parents do this, and after her father giving his permission already? She daren't look at Jesse, but could feel his humiliation from where she was sitting feet away from him.

'We have also agreed that it would probably be better if you go back to the mainland as soon as you are able. You are, as you say, a very busy man. If Florence is to spend her future with you then that is something she will need to become used to.'

She looked at Jesse to gauge his reaction. His face was ashen and his eyes wide as if he had been slapped. Despite this, he was sitting calmly, listening to what her father was saying. His controlled reaction made her love him even more. He might have physical frailties, but mentally this man was strong. Strong and determined, and he loved her. The thought reassured her a little.

'As I mentioned, we have no issue in you corresponding by letter. We also believe that if your feelings are as strong for each other next summer, say, July, as they are now, then I will give my permission and assure you I will not stand in your way if you still wish to be married.'

Florence watched him conclude his speech. Her mother mumbled something to herself, but Florence, aware that this resistance had come from her mother, was unable to look at her in case she saw how much she resented her at that moment.

She should be planning her wedding to Jesse right now. Celebrating their exciting news and writing to her friends to share their joy. Not sitting here, lost for words, trying to find a way to bear what seemed like a terrible unjust loss.

Jesse stood. 'I have no choice but to accept your terms, Mr and Mrs Rowe. Would you mind if I take a moment to speak with Florence alone, briefly?'

Florence waited for her mother to reject his request, but her father surprised her by agreeing.

'Come along, dear,' he said to her mother, leading her and Amy out of the living room. 'I will wait in the hallway for you, Florence.' He cleared his throat and reached out his right hand for Jesse to shake. 'Goodbye, Mr Rowe. Until we next meet.'

As soon as her father was out of the room, Florence turned to Jesse, and taking his hands in hers, whispered, 'I'm so sorry they've reacted in this way,' she said, her voice tight with emotion. 'I wish . . . I wish.' She struggled to find the words to explain how heartbroken she was that he would soon return to England and she would be left behind here in Jersey. The thought of not seeing him for several months devastated her.

'Hush, now,' he soothed. 'Your parents want to protect you. I have to respect that. As much as I am disappointed not to be returning to Nottingham with you as my bride, or at least as my betrothed, we don't have too long to wait until we can make our dreams a reality.'

'But a year!' she cried, unable to stop her tears from slipping down her cheeks.

'Not that long,' he argued, taking his handkerchief and handing it to her. 'You'd better wipe your face. Your father will forbid me from ever seeing you again if he walks in and finds me doing it for you.'

She took the handkerchief and dabbed her eyes and cheeks. She had never felt so much emotion as she had since meeting Jesse. Him coming into her life had stirred up feelings she had never experienced before and now she was to be without him again. It didn't seem fair.

'It is ten months, not even that,' Jesse reassured her. 'We can write in that time. I will be busy and I'm certain you will be, too. The time will pass quickly, you mark my words.'

Calming and collecting herself a little, Florence focused on the positive. 'We can plan our wedding in our letters, can't we? Discuss all the things that we would otherwise do if we were together.'

He smiled and whispering, added, 'We will plan our wedding so that when I do come back to Jersey, we won't have to wait too long to be married. What do you say to that?'

She sighed deeply. She had no choice but to accept the situation and make the best of it. She was strong. She would find a way to prove her mother's fears to be unfounded. Florence resolved to make the most of this time away from Jesse, to get to know him better through his letters. She might have to wait for Jesse, but she could do that. She was determined not to be deterred. She would marry him and then show her parents that they were a perfect match for each other, regardless of his health and her youth.

'Yes. We will put everything into place, so that all that needs to be done is have the banns read on your return to the island next year and set the date.'

He glanced at the door. He stepped forward quickly and kissed her damp cheek. 'All will be well, I promise you, dearest Florence.'

She believed him.

Chapter 15

She showed Jesse to the door and watched him walk away from her down Queen Street. It was the last time she was going to see him for ten months and she couldn't look away until the pavement curved, and he was out of sight.

A wave of emotion hit her. She had to hurry back inside and close the front door before anyone saw her make a spectacle of herself. She ran upstairs and into her bedroom, slumping down on her bed and giving into the sobs that had been threatening to come.

She had tried her best to be brave in front of him and her parents and sister, but she was unable to hold back her tears any longer. She had no idea how long she had been crying when there was a light tap at her bedroom door.

'May I come in please?' Amy asked.

Unable to speak without crying, Florence didn't answer. Amy knew her well though and after a brief wait let herself in coming to sit next to her on the bed.

Florence brushed away her tears with the back of her hands and sat up.

Amy rubbed her sister's back lightly. 'I'm so sorry that

this has happened,' she said. 'I wish Mother had left well alone. You seemed so happy earlier and I can't bear to see you this heartbroken.' She got up and going to one of Florence's drawers, pulled open the top one and took out a laundered handkerchief. 'Here, dry your eyes and blow your nose.'

'Thank you,' Florence sniffed. She took a moment to tidy herself up and pull herself together. She never let emotion take over and always kept control of herself. 'I don't know what has become of me, acting in such a hysterical fashion. I rarely cry but seem to be doing rather a lot of it lately.'

'You had expected to end the . . . I was going to say luncheon, but that never happened, did it.'

'No.'

'Anyway, as I was saying. You were expecting to be celebrating your betrothal to the man you obviously love.' She caught Florence's eye. 'You really do love him, very much. Don't you?'

'I do,' Florence said. 'I hadn't realised quite so much until today, if I'm honest.'

'I had no idea.'

They sat quietly for a few minutes, each lost in their own thoughts as their parents' voices hummed through the walls from the living room

'Mother really annoys me sometimes.' Amy frowned, her cheeks pink with suppressed temper.

'It's not her fault,' Florence said, feeling the need to defend their mother despite her actions ending the chance of her going to Nottingham a married woman this side of Christmas. 'She only did what she thought was right.'

'That's a matter of opinion,' Amy scowled.

'No, it's true. She's only doing what she thinks is best for me, however much I might dislike it.'

'You're not angry with her?'

'Yes, I am. Furious, in fact. But I know that she has acted this way because she loves me and believes she is protecting me. So, as much as I'm hurt and cross, I . . . oh, I don't know.'

Amy stood up and opened the bedroom window a little wider than it had already been. 'It's hot in here. Would you like me to fetch you something cool to drink?'

'Thank you,' Florence said, grateful for her sister's kind thought. Amy left the room and Florence stared at the blue sky above the opposite building to theirs. Ten months wasn't that long, she tried to persuade herself, walking over to the small table beneath her window and sitting down to write her first letter to Jesse.

Jesse might not have left yet, but she was going to ensure he arrived home to several letters from her. She wanted him to know that he was going to marry a woman of character and strength, one who wasn't floored by disappointment and others nastiness. They would have a future together. Just not as soon as they had hoped.

27 Queen Street
St Helier
Jersey
20 September 1885

169

Mr J Boot
16–20 Goose Gate
Nottingham

Dear Jesse, she wrote, feeling much better now that she had a plan.

I am sitting in my room trying to come to terms with what happened earlier this evening. I find I am unable to believe that matters took such an unexpected turn. To think that one moment my father had given you permission to ask for my hand in marriage, only for my mother to then deliver a blow so heartbreaking that I am almost at a loss for words.

You left our home minutes ago and have probably not yet arrived at your hotel, but already I feel your loss. I console myself with the knowledge that my father will stand by his word and my belief that your feelings towards me will not alter before next summer arrives.

I must trust that if I keep myself busy with my work and friends, then the time will pass speedily. At least we are not forbidden from communicating through letters; that is something I am relieved about.

Safe journey home to England. I hope the weather is kind to you and the sea is not rough.

I look forward to receiving a letter from you.
Your dearest,
Florence

Florence struggled to still her mind enough to fall asleep. Finally, after several hours, she fell into an exhausted slumber only to dream that she was standing in front of a congregation and everyone was staring at her in horror. For a moment she couldn't understand why, then, turning to face her groom, she realised she was alone. Where was Jesse? She stared from face to face, but he was nowhere to be seen.

Florence cried out and woke with a start. Sitting up immediately, it took a moment for her to realise that she was in her bed at home. Relief coursed through her as it slowly dawned on her that she had been having a nightmare and had not been humiliated publicly.

She took a moment to allow her heart to stop racing, then flung off her bedsheet and light summer blanket. She rubbed her face to help herself come around and swung her feet out of the bed.

Florence stared at the curtains. It was light outside. She walked over to them, and, holding back one side, she peaked out at the dawn. She usually liked waking early before the rest of the household stirred. But not this morning. She was going to be exhausted by the evening, having woken at such an early hour. She drank some water from the glass on her bedside table and opened the curtains, aware that she was too traumatised by her nightmare to sleep.

Slowly the events of the previous evening came back to her and she sank back onto her pillows trying to rationalise how to deal with the fact that her immediate dreams had been quashed. Well, she thought, trying not to dramatise her and

Jesse's situation, maybe not, but they had been delayed for almost a year.

She was unable to face her mother just yet. She was aware that they would be eating breakfast in the next two hours, so Florence washed and slowly dressed, sipping at her glass of water. An hour later, desperate to keep her mind from racing, she went downstairs to the shop. She wanted to be alone, but busy, and so quietly went in and began refilling spaces in shelves and dusting before her father and Amy joined her.

She rearranged a display of fountain pens that had arrived the previous week. What must Jesse think of her. She knew he loved her, but would he be put off by her family when he had time to consider the previous night's scenario?

She was deep in thought as she worked, so didn't hear Amy enter the shop.

'How are you feeling?' her sister asked, making Florence jump at the sound of her voice and drop one of the pens she was holding.

She bent to pick it up, checking it for damage. Relieved it wasn't damaged, Florence placed the pen back on the stand. 'Humiliated,' she said, honestly. 'Heartbroken.'

When Amy didn't say anything Florence stared at her, surprised to see her sister close to tears. 'What's the matter, Amy?'

Amy pulled her into a hug. 'I'm so sorry this happened,' she said, loosening her hold and stepping back. 'You were so happy last night before . . . well, before Mother said her piece to Father and persuaded him to change his mind.'

'I told you,' Florence said miserably. 'We mustn't blame her. She was only doing what she thought was right.'

Amy sighed heavily. She didn't look convinced. 'It's all so unnecessary,' she snapped. 'You're twenty-three. Surely you're old enough to make your own decisions by now?'

'It will be fine,' Florence reassured Amy, suspecting she was trying to do the same thing for herself.

'Poor Mr Boot. I could see he was mortified when Father rescinded his approval for you two to become engaged.'

He had, Florence thought miserably. She wondered if he had written to her yet and when he might arrive at his home in Nottingham.'

'What will you do?' Amy whispered, glancing at the closed back door of the shop that lead to the bottom of the stairs to their flat. Their father should arrive at any moment and Florence knew her sister wouldn't want him to overhear them discussing this incident.

'We are allowed to correspond by letter,' Florence said, relieved that this was the case and that her father hadn't forbidden any contact at all. 'I wrote to him last night and will continue to do so until I next see him.'

'Good. I'm certain he will be writing to you as much. I don't know why I hadn't noticed it before, but that man is very much in love with you.' Amy thought for a moment. 'I knew he liked you, but I thought it was because you were happy to show him the sights. It didn't occur to me that you two would fall in love.'

Florence hadn't expected it to happen either and said so, adding, 'Was it because he is older than me?'

'What, that I didn't think you two had become so close?'

Florence nodded. It felt good to speak openly about Jesse

to Amy. She wanted to hear her sister's thoughts about their relationship.

'Yes, and also because he didn't seem to be the type of man I ever expected you to fall in love with.'

'Because he sometimes uses a walking stick?'

'What? No,' Amy said, sounding offended at the accusation. 'I'm not that shallow.' She seemed offended. 'No, I had thought Albert was more the sort of man you'd end up with. Someone livelier, always wanting to socialise with people, go dancing, that sort of thing. Mr Boot seems to favour quieter outings, that's all.'

Florence could understand why her sister would think this way. She had done, too. 'You're right,' she admitted. 'I know Albert is nothing more than my friend, but before meeting Jesse—' she ignored her sister's surprise at the use of his first name but chose to ignore it and continued '—I would also have thought that if I ever met a man fascinating enough to make me want to give up my independence and get married, he would be a sociable person, one that likes to be entertained, travel, take adventures. Someone who liked music and being out at events.' She realised she didn't even know if Jesse had plans to travel or if he liked the theatre. 'However, with Jesse, I feel like I've met my soulmate. I feel utterly at ease with him.' She gazed out of the window, recalling Jesse collecting her by carriage outside the front door, and smiled at the memory of their outing to Rozel Bay. 'I am as happy talking to him about business, or the places we wish to visit, as I am to sit in his company in complete silence.'

She stared back at her sister and saw the wistful expression on her face.

Amy gave a shuddering sigh. 'How romantic. I hope to find that connection with a man of my own someday. If not, I'm going to remain unmarried. I'm not going to settle for a dull man who might boss me around from morning till night.'

'You will find someone special,' Florence said, certain that if she had then surely her younger sister would be lucky enough to as well. Amy was a kind, fun-loving girl who deserved to be happily married with her own home and family.

Amy opened her mouth to speak, when they heard the unmistakeable sound of their father's footsteps on the wooden staircase in the hallway. Both instinctively turned away from each other and busied themselves in their work.

He opened the door, surprised to see Florence there. 'You didn't come to breakfast,' he said, as if he was telling her something she didn't know.

'I wasn't hungry,' she said, unable to look him in the eye.

'Florence,' he said, walking up to her. 'Look at me.'

Feeling her face reddening, she did as he asked.

'I know you're upset about what happened last night. You probably blame your mother and me for our decision to ask Mr Boot to return to the mainland.'

'Yes, I have to admit that I am upset.' Before he could reply, she added. 'But I do understand why you did what you did.'

'You do?' He didn't look convinced.

'Yes. I can't say in all honestly that I'm happy about it, but I know that you only have my best interests at heart.'

'Then why are you missing breakfast and keeping to yourself?'

Did he really not know? 'Because I'm . . .'

'She's heartbroken,' Amy said in her defence.

'That's enough, young lady,' their father snapped. 'I think Florence is stronger than you imagine. Now, get back to your work. Florence is more than capable of speaking for herself.' He looked Florence in the eyes. 'Aren't you?'

She nodded. 'Yes.'

'I'm glad that you understand my decision,' he said, his voice gentle and, she noticed, with a hint of sadness about it.

Florence suspected that her mother was hoping that she or Jesse would tire of the other before he could return to Jersey, or any wedding banns could be read the following summer.

'I can't say I'm happy about it,' she said honestly, 'but I do understand.' She decided to be careful not to give her mother any further ammunition to use against her or Jesse over the coming months. She was determined to see their separation through and marry him next summer, whether her mother gave her blessing or not.

Chapter 16

'Good morning,' Albert said cheerily, when Florence walked into the grocers next door a few hours later. 'How are you this fine morning, Miss Florence Rowe?'

Despite her misery, Florence couldn't help smiling at his sunny disposition. 'I'm well.'

It was true; she was in fine health. She always was. Albert didn't need to know what had happened the evening before.

He narrowed his eyes and studied her face. 'You don't seem as happy as you're making out,' he said. 'I have a suspicion not all in your life is as cheerful as you're making out.'

She forced a brief smile, letting it slip when he crossed his arms in front of his chest and rubbed his chin. He had been her friend for so long that he was beyond fooling.

'Come, take a seat,' he said, indicating the prettily upholstered chairs near the back of the shop. 'You know I believe tea to be the answer to most ailments and troubles. I'll make us a pot and you can tell me everything.' Before she had a chance to make an excuse he disappeared into the tiny room at the back of the shop. 'A deliciously fragrant new blend was delivered yesterday and I'm yet to sample it.'

She sat, hoping he wouldn't take too long, and that her father would be too focused on customers to notice how long she was missing. 'Thank you,' she said, realising how thirsty she was at the thought of a cup of tea. 'That would be very welcome. Do you have any biscuits?'

Albert soon came back carrying a tiny porcelain pot and two cups and saucers. 'I am a connoisseur,' he said with mock indignation. 'I will not be offering any accompaniment with this fine sample.'

'I thought you said you hadn't tried it yet?' She couldn't help teasing him. Albert never failed to brighten up her day.

The realisation gave her an understanding why her mother had held hopes of them making a couple at some point. The thought of her mother's issues with her and Jesse being together brought a lump to her throat. If only she could see Jesse's good qualities and not worry so much about everything else. Surely if she wasn't worried about marrying Jesse and he was a good man, which she knew her mother was well aware that he was, then everything else shouldn't matter. Should it?

'Deep in thought?' Albert said, pouring the tea and sitting back, watching her. 'Now, before a customer comes in tell me what it is that's making you so miserable.'

'I'm not miserable,' she fibbed.

'Troubled, then.' He held up his hand when she went to argue. 'And please don't think that you can dissuade me from finding out what is wrong, because you won't. You're my dearest friend and it upsets me to see you unhappy. Now, take a drink of that delicious blend and tell me what you think of it.'

She did as he asked, raising the fine porcelain teacup to her lips and taking a tentative sip. The hint of orange and something else. 'It's delicate and I have to admit I do like it. What is it?'

'It's Earl Grey's Mixture. Black tea flavoured with the oil from the rind of bergamot orange.'

'Orange? That's different.'

'You haven't tried this tea before then?'

She shook her head. 'No, I don't think so. I'm sure I would recall if I had.'

They drank in silence for a few moments and then Albert, finishing his tea, placed his cup back on its saucer and sat back in his chair. 'Tell me.'

She took a little time to finish her drink and gather her thoughts. How much did she want to share with him? She wasn't exactly certain. She stared at his kindly face, aware that he was more than a little intrigued. 'I've been seeing something of Mr Boot.'

'Your father's friend who you accompanied on outings several times?'

She stiffened briefly at the mention of Jesse being her father's friend. It made him seem so much older and she wondered, briefly, if that's how her mother saw him too.

'Well, he was initially introduced to me by my father, yes. However, he is more of a family friend. He's become my friend over the weeks,' she admitted quietly.

Albert sat forward. 'Go on. I can sense there's more.'

'We've become close and he . . . well, he asked for father's blessing last night.'

Albert's eyes widened and for a second his mouth dropped open. 'He did? What did your father say?'

'Yes, and then after a conversation with my mother, changed his mind.' Her voice wavered with emotion.

'I don't understand. Does your mother not trust your judgement?'

He voiced her exact thoughts and she told him that had been the case. 'He is older than me, and she's worried that I will end up being married to an infirm old man as time goes on.'

Albert frowned. 'By then you'll probably be an inform old lady. It doesn't make any sense.'

It was a relief to hear him echo her thoughts. She needed to feel that she wasn't being ridiculous when she thought to marry Jesse.

'Thank you, Albert. You're a good friend.'

He smiled. 'There's no need to thank me. So, what has happened with Mr Boot now then?'

'He's travelling back to Nottingham on the first available boat. We're allowed to communicate by letter, which is something at least. Then, if we both still feel the same way about each other next summer, Father said he will give his blessing.'

'But you're already twenty-three. Why not let you make your own choices?'

She laughed. No wonder she and Albert got along so well, they both thought about things in the same way. 'They're not as modern as we are, though, Albert. They're from an older generation, and I suppose I have to abide by their decision.'

Someone walked up to the shop door and Albert stood up, but they peered in and then turned around and walked away.

Florence decided it was time she went back to work before her father became annoyed. She stood as Albert tidied up after them, straightening the chairs and walking her to the door.

'Try not to worry. You will probably find that this forced separation will give you both time to get to know one another. I find that writing letters can sometimes be a better way to find out more about the other person. I tend to forget my reservations and shyness in a letter.'

'You, shy?' Florence teased. 'I've never met anyone less so.'

He made a point of looking at the wall clock. 'Oh, is that the time?' He opened the door and stood back. 'Go and earn your living, Miss Rowe, and leave me to earn mine,' he said smiling. 'Come and see me tomorrow, if you can. We can make plans to go with our friends. They'll cheer you up. We could catch the train to Georgetown and go to the orchestral concert at the Casino de Jersey. Maybe have a meal there first. What do you think?'

She didn't want to ruin his idea, but said, 'Sorry, I really don't feel like doing anything much at the moment.'

'What, you'd rather stay in your room and read your books?'

Right now, she couldn't think of anything she would rather do. Apart from be with Jesse, of course. 'Yes. I'm not in the right frame of mind to go out with people. I'd only ruin the mood by being quiet all evening.'

'Then you must gather yourself, put a stop to this moroseness of yours and make yourself see your friends. It's the only way to take yourself out of this mood.'

'What if I don't want to?' she asked. She didn't have the

181

energy to dress up and try to be fun and entertaining, which is what her friends would expect her to be.

'Nonsense, Florence,' he replied. 'You're always the life of every party. You're the most outgoing, sociable person I know. If this is how your affection towards Mr Boot makes you react then I'm glad he's gone home to England.'

Florence gasped, horrified that Albert could be so unfeeling towards her and say such a mean-spirited thing. 'Why would you say such a horrible thing, Albert? Mr Boot is a fine man and I won't listen to you being nasty.'

He grimaced. 'That came out wrong. But I've only ever known you to be outgoing and good fun. You're never morose and quiet. And, I'm sorry to say this, Florence, but it simply does not suit you. There, I've said it.'

She was stunned by his response. 'Albert. Stop it, this instant. You're making me sound dreadful.'

He shook his head. 'No, I don't mean to. It's just that I don't recognise this side of you. I want you to be the Florence I know so well. You've never behaved this way before and it concerns me.'

She should have known he would be honest with her when she opened up to him. He had always been to the point but never this brutally. Then again, she mused, he had probably never seen her this down before. He was right, she thought, locking eyes with him and seeing the sadness within his. Just because she was miserable, that did not give her an excuse to behave in a way that brought those close to her down too. It was selfish of her and she hated to think of herself as being that way.

She took a deep breath. 'I refuse to quarrel with you. I have a lot on my mind at the moment and don't wish to go out anywhere tonight. However, I will consider doing something later this week, if you wish to arrange an evening out for our group of friends.'

His mouth drew back into a wide smile. It was how she was used to seeing him and it was a relief to see the concern on his face vanish. 'Truly?'

'I said so, didn't I?' She smiled. 'Now, I must hurry back to the shop before Father fires me.'

'Yes, you must,' he agreed. 'When I see you tomorrow, I'll tell you who'll be joining us. I'll try and make plans for all of us to go there one evening.'

'If you insist,' she said, intrigued.

He tapped the side of his nose. 'I do. You'll thank me for making you focus on something other than this fellow of yours. Truly you will.'

She wasn't sure he was right, but left feeling much better than when she had arrived. Opening the shop door quietly, she winced when the brass bell alerted her father to her arrival.

'Where have you been?' he whispered as she passed the counter. 'We've been busy and could have done with your assistance here.'

'Sorry, Father,' she said, spotting a customer holding up two leather bound notepads and comparing them.

'May I be of assistance?' Florence said, hurrying over to the woman.

* * *

183

'You're looking a little happier, I've noticed,' Amy quietly remarked later. 'You've been to see Albert, I suppose. He always amuses me too.'

'He is funny,' Florence said, telling her sister about the tea and how he'd insisted on her telling him what had happened to upset her. 'He's a good friend. He was bossier than usual today and gave me a stern talking to.'

'Good for him,' Amy giggled. 'I'm glad you listen to someone.'

Florence concentrated on serving as many customers as she could get to before her father. She was determined to keep herself busy and this was the best way to keep her mind from slipping back to thoughts of Jesse and how she was already missing him. How she was going to last their enforced separation, she really didn't know.

She must have been busy, because she missed their postal delivery and it was only later when she had gone back upstairs to the living room that she saw a letter for her propped up against her father's wooden mantel clock.

Florence picked it up and, quickly checking the kitchen for her mother, listened briefly to hope that no one else was in the flat with her. She opened the letter and read its contents.

16–20 Goose Gate
Nottingham
21 September 1885

Miss Florence Rowe
27 Queen Street
St Helier
Jersey

Mrs Boots

Dearest Florence,

I will be leaving Jersey Harbour mid-morning and have asked a messenger from the hotel to deliver this letter to you in order that it reaches you as soon as possible.

I feel certain that you will be as downcast as me to know that we are about to begin a long period of separation, but as I leave to take the ferry back to the mainland, I know that the time will pass quickly and that once it is over we will be married and then no one will ever have the right to part us again.

I have much planned for the coming months and hope that you, too, keep busy, not only working at Rowes but with your sisters and your friends, with whom I feel sure you will find distraction and support. Write to me often, so that we may share our daily lives. I will then be able to imagine you at work, reading, going for strolls along the beach, taking outings with your friends and attending chapel on Sundays.

I wish that I had been able to stay on the island long enough to buy you a keepsake of our time together here, but will send you something small enough to enclose in a letter on my return to Nottingham.

I am being called now and must sign off so that this reaches you today.

Remember, dearest, that this too will pass and in no time we will once again be together.

My love, until then,
Your most sincere,
Jesse

Florence hugged Jesse's letter to her heart. He had been thinking of her this morning while she was silently pining for him, as she knew he would. She re-read his words and then, hearing footsteps on the hall stairs, hurried to her bedroom to put the letter away in the drawer of her mahogany writing slope that her father had given her on her previous birthday. It was her favourite possession and he had seen her polishing it over the months in the shop. Opening the gift had been one of her most special days.

Now it would hold her precious private letters from Jesse. She couldn't think of a better place in which to store them.

She washed her face and hands and sat down to write back to him.

27 Queen Street
St Helier
Jersey
22 September 1885

Mr J Boot
16–20 Goose Gate
Nottingham

Dearest Jesse,
Your letter was a welcome treat for me to discover after I finished work today. Thank you. I have been trying to keep occupied all day, but, despite my good intentions, my mind keeps slipping back to you and the wonderful times we have shared.

I went to see Albert at the grocer shop next door earlier and he, as usual, cheered me up. He suggested we attend a concert at the Casino de Jersey later this week with friends. I tried to tell him that I was not in the mood to do so, but he insisted that it would be the best thing to cheer me up. I hope you don't have an issue with me going. I don't assume that you will, but want to be certain.

Apart from that, I have nothing much to report. I am a little concerned about Lily and thought I saw her through the shop window walking passed on the opposite side of the road, but when I went to the door intending on speaking to her, I realised it wasn't her at all. I can't help worrying about her and hope to see her soon, to ensure she is well.

By the time you receive this you will probably also have the letter I posted to you this morning. I hope your journey wasn't too tiring and look forward very much to hearing from you again.

With fondest love,
Florence

She finished her letter and placed it on the small table in her room ready for posting first thing in the morning. She supposed that if they did keep in constant contact it would help ease their separation. If Jesse had already written to her even before leaving the island, then surely she could trust him to write to her often enough to keep her mind busy, either mulling over what she had written to him, or her thinking of information she could include in her letters back to him.

She took another piece of paper and began listing all the

things she would be able to write to him about in the coming months. The rest of summer, fun with her friends, customers at work, even the soon-to-be-planned-for Harvest Festival at chapel. She thought of Christmas and her mood dipped to think that they would be apart on what should have been their first Christmas together. She could at least buy him a gift and would ensure that she posted it to him early so that he received it in good time to place it under his Christmas tree so that he would be reminded of her and know that she was thinking about him at all times.

Chapter 17

Florence was working on her list of things to write to Jesse about when her mother knocked on her bedroom door. 'Florence? May I come in?'

She quickly turned over the piece of paper, hoping the ink was dry enough not to smudge her table, and screwed the lid back onto her fountain pen. She placed the pen onto the table.

'Yes, Mother,' she said, standing up to go and open the door. What could her mother wish to discuss with her that had to be done in the privacy of her bedroom? she wondered. Florence wasn't in the mood to discuss Jesse again. She would not have minded speaking about him to Amy, or even Adelaide, or Albert, but knowing her mother didn't approve of them being a couple soured the subject.

She walked over to the door and opened it. 'Please, come in,' she said, standing back to let her mother enter her room.

Her mother stood at the end of her bed and scanned the room. Florence could see her taking in the tall sash window high above the busy street. Despite the streets being much quieter than earlier, the sound of chatter drift into the open window.

'I remember when we chose that for you,' her mother said,

indicating the floral wallpaper that she and Florence had picked out several years before when Adelaide had married her husband and moved out of the flat into her own home. Florence had been excited to finally have her own bedroom then. It was a new experience after sharing her private space with Amy since they had moved to the flat at Queen Street.

'You have everything laid out very well,' her mother said approvingly. 'I don't know why I'm surprised; you've always been excellent at creating impressive displays downstairs in the shop.'

Florence was secretly thrilled at her mother's compliment. She rarely gave them. She had told her children when younger that to over compliment a child would risk the chance of them becoming over-confident and that was something she would never tolerate. Hearing her being so open about her liking of this room and the way Florence arranged the displays made her slightly anxious. What was her mother leading up to?

'I so rarely come into this room,' her mother said wistfully. 'And you've changed it somewhat since the last time I did.' She walked over to the window and peered down at the people outside. 'It's noisier than most of the rooms, but sunnier too. I remember when we set it up for you after Adelaide left.'

'So do I,' Florence said, unsure where this conversation was leading.

'You were very excited.'

'I was. I still love it in here,' Florence said, although resisted adding that despite her love for this room she would give is up in a heartbeat to be with Jesse.

'Shall we sit?'

Florence nodded and sat on the edge of her bed letting her mother take the bedroom seat.

She watched her mother smooth down her skirts, her bony hands adorned with her thin gold wedding band that Florence noticed for the first time was worn after so many years of wear.

'I don't wish for us to become estranged over this business with you and Mr Boot,' her mother said eventually.

Florence wasn't surprised at her mother's usual blunt and to-the-point comment. She would have been more concerned if she had not got straight to the point.

'Neither do I,' Florence agreed. 'But I can't help feeling upset by the restrictions you've insisted Father put in place until next summer.'

Her mother gazed at her, studying her face until Florence became uncomfortable. What was she looking for so intently?

'I am your mother and, despite what you may think right now, your happiness is of the utmost importance to me.'

'Yes, I know that,' Florence admitted, wishing she could argue but knowing it would be disrespectful to do so.

'I'm aware that you yearn for your own home and your independence, but I worry that by marrying Mr Boot you will not end up with the independence that you so crave. Can you see how that could happen?'

Could she? Florence thought about it. Did she truly not see an issue as Jesse aged, or was it that she was simply ignoring any chance that their future together could be marred by his progressive arthritis? Was it that she was so focused on the excitement of a new future with him that she was blind to any hint of troubles that might work their way into their married lives, or was it that she simply loved him enough not to care about what may lay ahead for them?

'Mother, I love you dearly, you know that, but I also love Jesse and now that he has shown his intentions towards me are in a marriage, I love him even more. I am so excited for our future together and can't imagine that anything could mar them.'

Her mother's face darkened, as she stood. 'Then you are being a fool.'

Angry that her mother didn't allow her the freedom to make her own decisions about something as important as her future, Florence said, 'Maybe so, but didn't you decide to marry Father without knowing what was to lie ahead in your future? Doesn't every woman who accepts a man's hand in marriage do the same?'

'Your father was healthy,' she snapped, walking to the door. 'He still is remarkably strong for his age.'

Florence could feel her hackles rising. 'That's as maybe, but, in your case, surely the issue wasn't one of health, but one of finance.'

Her mother spun around. 'What on earth do you mean? You know nothing of our finances.'

Florence had heard arguments behind closed doors between her parents over the years. She was aware that there had been times her father struggled to keep the shop going and the roof over their heads. She had found her mother in tears several times during her childhood and later wondered if this had been due to money worries. Why, she wondered, did parents feel the need to hide so much from their children, especially when they were grown up, like Florence and her siblings were?

Chapter 18

It was three days before Florence received another letter from Jesse. She was beginning to worry that something had happened to him on his journey home when nothing arrived with the post the previous day. Now, though, she spotted his handwriting on an envelope at the top of a pile on the counter and slipped it into her pocket to read as soon as she had a moment to herself.

'I'm just taking a quick break,' she said to Amy after the lunch rush had dissipated. 'I'll only be twenty or so minutes. Do you mind?'

Amy shook her head. 'No. Don't be any longer though. Father will be wondering where you are otherwise.'

She ran up the stairs to the flat and quickly went into her bedroom to open it. Without waiting to take off her Boot, Florence sat on the edge of her bed and opened his letter.

16–20 Goose Gate
Nottingham
24 September 1885

Miss Florence Boot
27 Queen Street
St Helier
Jersey

My Dearest,

I have arrived home after a rather lengthy journey, with far too many delays along the way. I have to admit it was made all the less bearable by my sadness of our last meeting and having to leave you behind. I am aware that should your father have agreed to my proposal for your hand that I would not be arriving home alone now and kept trying to remind myself of that fact. Somehow it did little to alleviate my having to leave you behind.

I am aware that my previous letter to you was full of positive notions and intentions, and, maybe when I wake tomorrow refreshed after a good night's sleep, I might be in a better frame of mind. I probably should not be admitting my low spirits to you. Perhaps I should be less selfish and pretend to you that all is well. Today, though, I find that I am unable to.

I have now changed and had some hot, sweet tea. My soul feels salved by it somewhat and I had considered discarding this letter to you and starting afresh. Then I thought of you, dearest Florence, and I realised that you are a woman who is truthful and would want the same in return. So, I am continuing with the same letter and hope that I was right to do so and that you are not offended by me doing so.

I have spoken to my secretary and arranged for a full

diary to be kept for me for the next few weeks, or at least until I am in better spirits and more able to focus on looking forward to the joys that lie ahead for us when we are able to begin our lives together. I long for us to be the decision makers in our future and not to have to bear the choices of others, albeit they make these decisions with your best interests at heart. Of that I am certain, even though I do not enjoy having to abide by them.

I must sign off now. My carriage is waiting for me outside ready to take me to my first port of call at the factory where I have urgent matters that will no doubt keep me busy for the rest of the week.

I long to read your next letter and will have more to tell you when I reply to it.

With the fondest of wishes,

Yours very truly,

Jesse

Florence re-read his heartfelt words before resting his letter on her lap and staring out of her window at the darkening skies. Winter was coming and it seemed that Jesse was suffering as much as she over their enforced parting. She couldn't help feeling guilty that his sentiments made her feel slightly better. Was that selfish? Probably, but at least it reinforced her feelings towards him and confirmed to her, yet again, that he did love her as much as she loved him. The thought gave her a warm feeling. Today had been a far more satisfying day than she had dared hope it could be when she woke that morning.

She didn't want Jesse to feel sad though, so immediately took off her Boot and sat down to write back to him.

27 Queen Street
St Helier
Jersey
27 September 1885

Mr J Boot
16–20 Goose Gate
Nottingham

Dearest Jesse,

I'm sorry that your journey was not as I had hoped it would be for you. I am relieved, however, to hear that you are now back at home and have returned to work.

Please, do not ever hold back from speaking your truth to me. I wish to know all that you feel and if it is sad, then so be it. Mostly I hope that you are happy, and, despite your missing me, that you are keeping yourself busy with your businesses.

We must be honest with each other at all times. If we are to get to know the real people that we both are then facing our sad days is surely as important as facing and sharing our better, happier times.

The weather today in Jersey is miserable. It is misty and wet and all the customers coming into the shop today moaned about it in varying degrees. I had to walk to the post office for Father and as I walked I thought of poor

Lily and her worn Boot and how they would be wet through. It made me think of the destitute families you mentioned living in or near the Lace District in Nottingham. How difficult it must be for those poor people to cope at any time, but especially when the weather deteriorates.

When we are married, we must make a plan to help the people in the Nottingham area as much as we are able.

Until next time, as always,

Florence

Chapter 19

Florence kept as busy as possible over the next few weeks. It was now mid-October and she was slowly getting used to finding ways to keep her mind from dwelling on what could have been.

She wrote to Jesse and was even persuaded by Amy to accompany her during two evenings at poetry readings, but she knew that her best days were the ones where she received a letter from Jesse. She decided she would need to find a way to focus her attention to keep from becoming too dependent on the arrival of his letters. Her good intentions were forgotten though when the postman arrived and handed her a letter with one hand and a bundle for her father with the other, two days later.

'You bin waitin' for this, Miss Rowe?' the man asked cheekily.

Amy marched over from where she had been working on a display of picture postcards that her father had brought in from a contact in France. 'I'll thank you not to be cheeky to my sister,' Amy said, marching over and glaring at him.

'Sorry, miss,' he said, his face reddening as he marched out of the shop.

'Well, really,' Amy exclaimed, shaking her head at Florence and turning to go back to what she had been doing.

Florence was walking back to the counter when she heard a cry and the postman snap at someone. 'Get out of my way, they don't want the likes of you in this shop.'

Shocked to hear him speak to someone in such a way on their behalf, Florence spun round to look out of the door and see what was going on. She saw him push a young woman out of the way. It was Lily, who, she noted, was about to do as he instructed and walk away.

Florence hurried up to the door. She had waited a long time to catch up with the young girl and an insolent postman was not going to send Lily off on Florence's behalf.

'Lily, stop,' she pleaded. Lily waivered and for a second Florence thought that she would have to race after her down the street. Then Lily, glancing at the postman, did as Florence asked. 'Come inside a moment, will you?'

Florence could see Lily wasn't wearing a shawl over the threadbare dress. She would need to do something to rectify that, she decided. First, though, she needed to speak to the postman.

She waved the young girl in.

'Amy, could you come and look after Lily here for me please. I won't be long.'

Amy nodded. She smiled at the red-faced girl standing nervously in the shop staring at her worn shoes.

'Come with me,' Amy said, instantly taking over and allowing Florence the time to go after the rude postman.

Florence hurried after the man. 'Excuse me,' she called,

catching up with him outside the chemist next door to Rowes.

'Yes, Miss Rowe,' he said, shocked to see her behind him. 'Did you want me to take any mail for you?'

She was desperate to give him a piece of her mind but forced herself to remain calm. The last thing she wanted was for any of their neighbours to see her squabbling with this man in the street. She raised her chin, standing as tall as she could. She towered over him and as she did so, he seemed to reduce in statute and confidence. Maybe, she thought, he now has an inkling of how he made Lily feel.

She lowered her voice, but kept a smile on her face in case anyone should see them talking. 'I would be grateful if you did not presume to speak to our customers in the fashion to which you have just done.'

'Err, I, um.'

She could tell he was completely bemused by her reaction to what had happened. Florence had to wonder if he spoke to young girls like Lily so often with such disdain that he didn't even realise how rude and threatening his behaviour seemed.

'That young lady you pushed out of your way next door is a friend of my family's. I would be grateful if you refrained from speaking to her in such a fashion, or, indeed, any other of our customers in such a way.'

'I . . . um.'

'You probably frightened the girl,' she said, glowering down at him. 'And I'm sure you will agree that none of us like to be frightened, do we?'

'No, Miss Rowe,' he said, shamefaced.

'Then I will thank you not to do so again in the vicinity of Rowe's Stationers.'

'Sorry, Miss Rowe. I can assure you it won't happen again.' He moved from one foot to the other and Florence could see that he was desperate to get away from her and continue on his round. 'Thank you. Is that all, Miss Rowe?'

'Almost.'

His shoulders slumped. 'I would also ask that you do not take it upon yourself to decide who we do and do not wish to serve at Rowe's Stationers. I do not believe it to be your place to firstly make that decision and, secondly, inform the person involved. Do I make myself clear?'

'Perfectly, Miss Rowe.'

'Thank you,' she said, satisfied that her words had had the desired effect on him. 'Then I shall say no more about it. Good day.'

'Err, good day, Miss Rowe.'

She turned on her heels and, head held high, marched back into the shop. She noticed two women from across the street pretending not to be watching her. Florence was aware others saw her as a little overbearing at times but put it down to the fact that she was tall and didn't suffer fools.

She arrived back at the shop and opened the door. Seeing Lily speaking quietly at the back of the shop with Amy, Florence went to join them.

'Lily, I'm so terribly sorry about that man being so rude to you.'

Lily shrugged. 'I'm used to it, Miss. He's probably right in what he says; this beautiful place isn't somewhere I should come to.'

'Stuff and nonsense,' Amy snapped. 'The man is a buffoon, which I'm sure my sister has already told him.'

Florence saw Lily stiffen and didn't want to frighten her further. 'Not at all, Amy,' she said, keeping her voice soft. She didn't want Lily to be put off from visiting them again. 'I merely explained that it was not up to him to decide who our customers could be.'

'Now, Lily,' Florence said, smiling. 'It's wonderful to see you again. We've been thinking about you, haven't we, Amy?'

'We have been a little concerned not to see you,' Amy admitted. 'How are you keeping?'

Lily shrugged one skinny shoulder. 'I'm doin' fine,' she said, not sounding at all convincing to Florence's ears. 'My dad was—' she hesitated '—away for a few weeks, so it was quieter at home.'

Florence assumed that Lily had meant her father to have been locked up in Newgate Street jail but didn't like to ask.

'Is he back at home now?'

Lily shook her head. 'Tomorrow, we think.'

Florence could feel the girl's tension and wondered if this was why she had come back to visit her and Amy, hoping to be given some sort of comforting words.

'And are your mother and siblings all well?' Amy asked, glancing at Florence over Lily's bent head as she picked at her bitten fingernails while she decided how to answer the question.'

'They are.'

'May I ask if you still go to school?' Florence asked, unsure how old Lily actually was.

Lily frowned at her. 'I'm fifteen, Miss Rowe. I left school a long while back.'

Mortified, Florence winced. 'I'm sorry, I didn't mean to offend you. I thought you were younger.'

'I know I look younger than my age,' she said. 'I'm always being mistaken for one of my smaller sisters.'

'We're about to have some tea and biscuits,' Amy lied. 'Would you like me to bring a cup for you, too?'

Lily glanced at the door, then at Florence and Amy. 'If you really don't mind.'

Amy smiled. 'I wouldn't have offered if we did.'

Lily's face lit up. 'Then I'd like some very much.'

Florence showed her over to the back of the shop and indicated the two chairs. 'Please, let's sit for a while. It's quiet in here this afternoon, so we won't bother anyone if we do.'

She noticed Lily shiver. 'You're cold?'

Lily stared down at her hands again. 'I, um, lost my shawl,' she said. 'It was silly of me.'

Florence couldn't help doubting the girl's story. Her clothes were very worn, but Florence could see that they were clean, and that Lily took pride in the way she tried to make the best of her dress and shoes.

Wanting to take Lily's focus from her situation, Florence changed the subject. 'What dreams do you have for yourself, Lily?'

Lily's eyebrows knitted together in confusion. 'Dreams?'

'Yes,' Florence said, wondering if anyone had ever asked

her such a thing before. 'You must have dreams for your future. About the things you want for yourself. Where you'd like to live, get married, that sort of thing?'

Lily stared at Florence thoughtfully. 'I don't know.'

'You must have some, everyone does.' She wasn't certain of this. She believed that if Lily had the realisation that there was more to life than the squalor that she lived in with her bullying father, then maybe she had a chance to escape it at some point.

'Well,' Lily said, the hint of a smile appearing on her pretty, drawn face, 'I have always wanted to work in a shop. One like this, or maybe a dress shop.'

Florence's heart lifted at the young girl's words. She had ambition. It was all Florence wanted to hear. Ambition, hard work and someone giving her the chance to make something of herself was the most likely way Lily would find a way out of her current circumstance.

She decided she would speak to her father about maybe employing Lily on Saturday mornings. She doubted he could afford to employ her for more hours than that. Florence decided that she would offer her own wages to be reduced to cover Lily's, if her father approved of her idea. She kept her thoughts to herself, not wishing to get Lily's hopes up only to quash them should her father refuse to do as she asked.

'And there's no reason why you shouldn't work in a shop, as you wish to do.'

Lily gazed down miserably at her dress. 'They're not going to take me on wearing clothes like these, though, are they?'

Florence couldn't argue with that, Lily was right. She

wasn't presentable enough to work in a shop, not as she appeared now.

Amy arrived back into the shop carrying a tea tray and, Florence noticed, a plate of the nicer biscuits her mother kept for guests.

'This is just what we all need on such a miserable day,' she said, pouring a cup for Lily and handing it to her.

For a couple of seconds, Lily seemed terrified of the cup and saucer and Florence noticed her hands shaking slightly. 'Put it down on that small table next to you, and take one of these.' She took the plate from the tray and held it out to Lily. 'Take a couple; they're delicious. Mother baked them yesterday.'

Lily placed the cup and saucer down on the table, the porcelain cup clattering against the saucer noisily and then did as Florence suggested. Her eyes widened as she stared at the plate of biscuits.

'They have chocolate in them,' Amy said. 'Our father has a sweet tooth and Mother makes them for him occasionally.'

At the mention of their father, Lily's hands pulled back from the plate. 'Won't he be angry if we eat them?'

'No,' Amy argued. 'There are plenty more for him still in the tin. Now, take a couple before I eat them all.'

Florence smiled. Amy would never eat more than one, or two in a day. She wasn't a big eater and preferred savoury treats to sugary ones. Now, Florence, mused, if this was a plate of cheese, they would probably not be able to eat more than a scrap each.

They watched as Lily took a bite from the biscuit in her

right hand, closing her eyes as the sensation of the chocolate melted into her mouth.

'They're good, aren't they?' Florence said, satisfied that Lily was enjoying herself.

'We told you they would be,' Amy giggled.

Lily nodded. She shivered slightly. 'That was the most delicious thing I've ever tasted.'

Florence glanced out of the window. It had stopped raining, but was still gloomy and the wind had increased by the looks of people's clothes. She couldn't let Lily walk home without a shawl. Aware her father wouldn't like it if Lily came home with a good shawl, she recalled that she had an older one that her mother had knitted for her several years before.

'I'm just popping upstairs briefly,' Florence said. She couldn't let the girl go out in the rain without at least giving her something to put over her head.

Florence went to her room and rummaged through the oak drawers where she kept her clothes. Finding what she was looking for, she held the pale-green knitted shawl open. It appeared a little worn, but she knew that to give Lily anything new would probably only result in her father selling it.

Going back to join her sister and Lily, she handed the shawl to the girl.

'I'd like to give this to you,' she said. 'It's an old one of mine that I don't use any more and I thought it might do to replace the one you lost.'

Lily stared at it momentarily. 'Are you certain you won't need it again?'

Florence nodded. 'I have a couple of others. To be honest

this one is a little small for me now. I hope your parents won't be offended by me passing this on to you.'

'No, they won't,' Lily assured them. 'I'll tell them that it's a hand-me-down from my cousin Brigit. She'll cover for me.'

'Put it on,' Amy said, as Lily shivered again. 'Let's see how it looks on you.'

Lily glanced from one to the other of them before standing and doing as Amy suggested. She wrapped the soft wool around her shoulders and crossing it in front of her, tied the ends together behind her back.

'It's ever so warm,' she said beaming at them. 'Thank you very much.'

'It's my pleasure,' Florence said, wishing she could also find a pair of Boot for Lily, but knowing firstly that to do so would probably insult her, and also that no one in their family probably had feet as small as Lily's. 'Now, drink your tea before it gets too cold.'

Lily sat back down and finished her tea. After another cup, she placed the cup and saucer onto the table and stood to leave.

'I'd better be going home now, or my ma will be wondering where I am. Thank you very much, though,' she said her cheeks reddening slightly. 'You're both very kind.'

'Not at all,' Amy smiled at her.

'We don't want you being a stranger to us, Lily,' Florence said, walking with her to the front door. 'Please come back and see us here again soon, won't you?'

'Yes,' Lily said, smiling up at her. 'I will.'

Florence watched her go, waving when Lily turned to smile

at her as she walked down Queen Street looking much warmer than when she had arrived. She hoped that the next time Lily came to the shop that she might be able to offer her some work. First, though, she needed to speak to her father and ask him for permission to do so.

She restocked some of the shelves and wondered what Jesse would think of her idea on how best to help Lily. She would write to him as soon as the shop was closed. Yes, she thought, he'll know what to do.

27 Queen Street

St Helier

Jersey

11 October 1885

Mr J Boot

16–20 Goose Gate

Nottingham

Dearest Jesse,

I hope you're keeping well and that you're not working too hard. Please ensure you take time to rest and eat properly.

You'll never guess who came to visit Amy and me at the shop this afternoon? Yes, Lily Buttons. Do you remember the poor girl with the bullish father? You were so kind to her that day, stepping in instantly to remove her from what appeared as if it could become a dangerous incident, for her, at least.

She is probably thinner than the last time we saw her. She said her father has been away and I believe that he may be in Newgate Street prison, which could account for her thinness. He might not be the most pleasant of men, but I gather that he does earn a living from time to time and without his income they must have had to get by on less food than usual.

She came to the shop today after an unfortunate incident with someone who tried to turn her away. I'm sure you can imagine mine and Amy's fury at someone presuming to do such a thing, firstly, to a young girl who was doing nothing wrong at all, and secondly, at Rowe's where the man had no authority to take it upon himself to evict anyone from our property. We invited her inside because she was cold. I gave her one of my shawls. Oh, Jesse, it was pitiful how grateful she was. The dear girl. I only wish I could have helped her more. Do you have any ideas as to how I could help Lily further, without her taking offence and thinking of it as accepting charity?

I did have one idea and have decided to ask Father if he might consider employing Lily for several days each week. Maybe this is my best way to help her? I've just read this letter back and it seems that I've answered my own question, but if you do think of anything else, please do write and tell me. I would be most grateful for any advice from you, dearest Jesse.

I do believe that if Lily is given the opportunity of coming to work at the shop and learning how things are done, then she will agree to do so. She's a determined girl and seems to want to help her family and make up for her father's occasional lack of support for them.

It will be busier in the shop in the weeks leading up to Christmas. Lily needs an income and, I believe, to know that there are people on her side who are looking out for her. Father has always believed that we, as a family, are enough to run Rowe's and I don't know if he will agree to my suggestion. I need to find a way to persuade him but am unsure what to say.

Thank you, dearest Jesse. I know that you have helped many of the poorer people in Nottingham in various ways, one of which being to give them work and the skills to earn their own living. I can't imagine anyone being in a better position than you to help me with this.

I look forward to receiving your thoughts and long to hear your own news.

As always,

Florence

She folded her letter and washed her face and hands. She put on her house shoes and went to join her family for supper. Lily had made her think more deeply about others in a similar situation to hers. How did families like Lily's manage during the winter months? she wondered.

She didn't have long to wait for Jesse's reply. It was a relief because her father had caught her gazing out of the window on several occasions over the next few days trying to spot the girl. She couldn't help worrying about Lily and how helpless she had seemed with so many obstacles against her.

16–20 Goose Gate
Nottingham
15 October 1885

Miss Florence Rowe
27 Queen Street
St Helier
Jersey

Dearest Florence,

I am well and taking good care of myself. Not that I have to do much, except return home to a warm house with fires lit by my servants and food prepared by my cook. I am not working too hard, so please, do not fret about me. Thank you though for caring so much.

Now, about your thoughts with regard to Miss Lily Buttons. I think it a marvellous idea. The best way to assist anyone and help them find their way out of poverty is to give them a hand up, rather than a handout. Lily needs to build up a set of skills and find the confidence to use them. That as well as employment, of course. So, yes, I agree that what you propose is the best way to help the young lady to help herself and ultimately her family.

I understand a certain hardship, though not as difficult as Lily's, I assume. My father was a good, hard-working, God-fearing man. He died when I was ten years old and my sister, Jane barely eighteen months. The following ten years were very difficult for my mother and keeping our

Goose Gate shop open was a necessity as it was the income that kept our family with a roof over our heads and food in our bellies.

She was helped by the support of chapel friends and my father's connections, and I recall many days where the two of us walked miles, our feet bare to save our shoes. We collected herbs to dry around our small parlour to then use in an herbal recipe to sell in our shop. I learnt from that young age the sense of fear that my family could lose our home at any moment and the need to work hard to retain what little we had to sustain ourselves.

Have you broached your father about the matter yet? If so, was he compliant? Please let me know if not. I am unsure right now what I could do to help, but I will do my best to come up with some way of assisting you.

I was thinking that to offer her a uniform might be helpful. If Miss Buttons does not have suitable clothing for shop assistant work, then to offer her an alternative item of clothing to her own might be the best option. Learning to wear smarter clothes is also something that she might need practice in doing. People shouldn't but do judge others by their clothing. Those of us who have always been blessed enough to wear good clothing know nothing of how it must feel to wear clothes that others might look down upon.

You are very kind and thoughtful, Florence. I feel certain that Miss Buttons will make the most of your support and hopefully will use what she learns from to you achieve all that she hopes to in her own future.

My warmest thoughts and admiration for your efforts.
As always,
Jesse

Florence was bolstered by his confidence that she was doing the right thing. His advice was excellent as she had known it would be. He didn't mock her idea, which so many men might have done, but she was realising more each day that Jesse wasn't like other men. When he said that he valued her thoughts about a matter, he told the truth. He was never threatened by her intelligence but encouraged her in everything that she pursued.

She folded his letter and slipped it back into the envelope. Now she needed to approach her father and put her ideas into action.

Chapter 20

That evening, as she locked the shop door and closed up for the night, Florence felt happier than she had in weeks. She still hadn't found the right time to speak to her father, preferring to do so when he was alone. Helping Lily out, even in the small way that she and Amy had already done, had raised her spirits. She locked the shop door and walked out the back door leading to the hallway at the bottom of their flat stairs, eager to get to her bedroom and reply to Jesse's latest letter.

27 Queen Street
St Helier
Jersey
21 October 1885

Mr J Boot
16–20 Goose Gate
Nottingham

Dearest Jesse,
    Thank you for your assistance in the matter regarding

Lily Buttons. I will take your advice and am certain that between Amy and me, we will be able to source a uniform for Lily.

I haven't, as yet, spoken to Father, partly because he always seems to be either busy with customers, or with Mother, or out with friends. I have one concern though that I would also like to write to you for counselling on. It is this. Father has always insisted that W. H. Rowe is a family-run business. He doesn't believe there is ever any reason to employ others when we have enough members of our family to call upon to carry out the work. Ordinarily, I agree with him. However, in the case of Lily, I need to find a way to persuade him that she will be worth the expense of a wage.

My issue is how to broach that subject. I feel the need to have answers ready before he asks the questions that I am certain he will put to me.

Can you help me, do you think?

I look forward to reading your thoughts on the matter.

I must add that I continue to miss you, terribly. I thought it would be easier as time passed, but it somehow is more difficult to be without you.

My love, as always,
Florence

She waited impatiently for Jesse's reply. She knew with confidence that he would have a solution to her problem and, once she had heard from him and had all the answers she needed, she would face her father. How had she been lucky enough to find a man who followed her own passions and beliefs? She was truly blessed, of that she was certain. She had always assumed that the only way to live a satisfying life of her choosing was to remain unmarried, but having met and fell in love with Jesse, she realised she had been wrong to be so determined not to marry. Then again, she reasoned, Jesse was unlike most men. She was exceptionally lucky that he had chosen her to be his wife; the thought made her heart swell with joy.

She knew without doubt that she and Jesse would be in agreement about finding ways to help the people nearest to them in what every way they could, and it made her long for their future together to finally begin.

A few days later, Florence received Jesse's reply. It was short but gave her the answer she needed.

> 16–20 Goose Gate
> *Nottingham*
> *26 October 1885*

Miss Florence Rowe
27 Queen Street
St Helier
Jersey

Dearest Florence,

I have given your suggestion about offering work to Lily much thought. It is a very thoughtful thing for you to do. I believe she will agree to come and work at Rowe's Stationers; however, as you say, your biggest barrier to making this happen will be your father's belief that as a family business, only members of the family be employed there. A solution is definitely needed to counteract this.

Have you considered offering to relinquish a portion of your wages to partially cover those that will be needed to pay for Lily's time? You have no need to save your money. I have more than enough for both of our futures, and when we are married, I will support you fully.

I'm sorry that this letter is brief, but I hope it holds the answer that you were waiting for. I must hurry, the carriage is waiting outside to take me to a meeting at the factory and I cannot be late. Let me know what you think and how your suggestion is received by your father.

As ever, your loving,

Jesse

'Yes, of course,' Florence said, reading the rest of Jesse's letter to make sure she didn't miss any other suggestions of his. She could train Lily up to be her replacement, so she could work under Amy and then, when she married Jesse and left, they would not feel her loss in the shop. It made good sense.

She sighed contentedly, aware that by what he'd said in his letter, Jesse was confirming, once again, his commitment for their marriage. She folded the letter and pushed it into her writing slope. Not wishing to speak to her father in front of her mother, she decided she would speak to him the next morning, before she lost her nerve.

* * *

The following morning, Florence waited for a lull between customers and went up to stand behind the counter with him. She needed to put her idea about Lily to him and there was no time to waste if she was to help the girl.

'Father?'

'Florence?' he replied, a glint of amusement in his eyes.

She cleared her throat and took a deep breath. 'I've been thinking.' She clasped her hands together in front of her skirts, to hide the fact that they were trembling slightly.

He finished writing down the sale in his book. Then, screwing the lid back on to his fountain pen, he placed it on the wooden counter and stared at her.

'I can tell by the tone in your voice that this is important.' He narrowed his eyes, all amusement vanishing. 'This isn't another issue with Mr Boot, I hope?'

His question irked her, but wanting to help Lily, she hid any reaction. 'No, it's nothing to do with him.'

He sighed. 'I'm relieved to hear it. Go on then, tell me. Whatever it is that's playing on your mind must be dealt with.'

She told him about her idea to help Lily. 'We're bound to need extra help in the lead up to Christmas and it's only a few weeks away now.' When he didn't reply immediately, she added. 'I'm happy to take a reduction in my own wages, if you wish,' she explained, playing her ace card and hoping it worked. 'I want to help her but I'm unsure how else to do it without it appearing to be giving her charity. I know she wouldn't accept that from me, or anyone else. She's a very proud girl.'

He stared at her thoughtfully while he digested her suggestion. She wished he would stop staring at her so intently. His dark eyes seemed to bore into her mind and she was concerned that he would somehow be able to work out what she was thinking. When he finally looked away, she closed her eyes briefly, relieved to watch him pick up his pen. He unscrewed the lid and began making calculations on a notepad he kept under the counter. He worked silently until he had finished his workings.

'You care that much for this girl you've only met a handful of times that you would forgo part of your wages?' He seemed concerned.

'Yes,' she answered, aware that he knew she had always saved since starting to earn a wage. She had never made a secret of wanting to open her own business. She supposed he must be surprised, but she didn't understand why. Surely, he must know that when she and Jesse married, she wouldn't need to open her own business, but could work with him in his.

'I don't need very much,' she explained. 'I have a roof over my head, plenty to eat and even my own bedroom now. Honestly, Father, I believe it's the very least I should do.'

He patted her arm. 'You are a good and caring girl, Florence. I've always knew you cared a lot for others; however you know I've only ever employed family members to work with me here,' he said thoughtfully.

Florence didn't answer. She knew he was only thinking out loud and wasn't asking her a question. She was relieved he hadn't rebuffed her suggestion instantly. She waited patiently for him to decide, aware that if she interrupted his thoughts his first reaction would be to say no.

He tapped his moustache with the end of his fountain pen.

Eventually, after what seemed like several minutes, but was probably only one, or two, he looked at her. 'I will give her a chance.' Florence gasped. 'Only the one, mind. She may start work here on Saturday from eight-thirty until one p.m. If she behaves herself and there's no light-fingered nonsense, then she can come back the following Monday. We'll do it on a week-by-week basis at first. I don't want to commit myself until I see what she's like and also how quickly she picks things up.'

Florence beamed at him. 'Thank you very much, Father. I promise you won't regret giving her this chance.'

He mumbled something and then went back to scrutinising to his sales book and began working through the day's takings so far. 'I'd better not. You're the one who's going to see a deduction in your wages, so I'll make her your responsibility. Is that fair?'

'Yes, absolutely,' she said, excitement coursing through her.

He had agreed. She could barely believe it and couldn't wait to share her news with Jesse. She was certain he would have done the same as her in her position. She gazed out of the window and, seeing a young girl about Lily's age, Florence wished she was able to tell Lily now; however, she would have to wait until she next came to see them at the shop.

Chapter 21

If Florence had been hoping to see Lily immediately, she was disappointed. Several days passed and she was beginning to think that her great plan would come to nothing if she didn't speak to Lily soon. She hadn't been to see them at the shop at all and Florence couldn't help wondering if she was all right. If only she knew where to find her. Even if she did know, Florence was well aware that to visit their home could not only incite a violent reaction from Lily's dad, or his friends, but would almost certainly cause trouble for Lily. She couldn't be responsible for causing more issues in the girl's life and decided that she would have to wait for Lily to visit her.

Florence was on her way back from visiting friends with her parents and Amy one evening in late October, when she spotted a girl coming from the opposite direction, turning into Waterloo Street. She was sure she recognised the shawl and hoped it was Lily.

'Was that Lily?' she asked, interrupting Amy's flow of words.

'Where?' Amy looked around and obviously hadn't seen her.

'Sorry,' Florence said, not wanting to miss the opportunity of catching up with the girl while she had the chance. 'Tell

Mother and Father I won't be long. I must go after her. I need to know that she's all right.'

She didn't wait to hear her sister's answer and hurried ahead of them, hearing her parents' voices as they stopped to ask Amy where she was going.

She walked as fast as she could without breaking into a run. It would not do to be seen acting in such an unladylike way, however much she was desperate to catch up with Lily. She was grateful for her long legs and lengthy stride as it helped her cover the ground and soon catch up with the girl. She didn't want to call out to Lily again, in case she ran off.

She was one step behind her when Florence reached out and gently tapped Lily on her right shoulder.

She spun round, eyes wide with fright and her mouth open. 'Oh, it's you, Miss Rowe,' she said, her hand going to her chest. 'You gave me such a fright.'

Florence was mortified to have shocked her. 'I'm so sorry Lily. That wasn't my intention at all.'

'It's fine. I didn't hear you coming up behind me, that's all,' Lily said, panting slightly.

Florence assumed her breathlessness was due to the fright she had just given her. 'I didn't mean to . . . it's just that I've been concerned about you,' she admitted. 'We haven't seen you at the shop for a couple of weeks and I had been hoping to speak to you about something.'

Lily frowned and refolded the green shawl Florence had given her over her chest. 'Nothing's wrong, is it?'

Florence shook her head, feeling her hat wobble. She must

have rushed the pinning of it earlier, she thought momentarily. 'Not at all.'

'I'm wearing the shawl you lent me.' Lily rested her hand on the hem of the woollen garment. 'I've really been grateful for it, thank you.'

'I'm glad you like it. In fact, it's how I recognised that it was you,' Florence said, smiling. She knew she had little time before having to go and catch up with her parents. She didn't want to upset them, today of all days. 'I wanted to speak to you about some work, at Rowe's Stationers.'

Lily stared at her silently for a few seconds. Florence wasn't sure if she was trying to think of an answer, or merely confused and thought she had better explain further.

'When you were last at the shop you mentioned that you had ambitions to be a shop assistant.'

Lily nodded slowly. 'I did.'

'Well, I spoke to my father soon after and he said he would be willing to give you several days' work each week. Starting this Saturday morning, if you're interested. For a trial period, of course.'

Florence was aware that when the Christmas rush was over there would be fewer customers in the shop and her father might wish for things to return to there only being family members working in the shop. However, a few weeks might make all the difference to the Buttons family. She could see by the pinched look in her pale cheeks that she was desperate to make money to help her family.

'Tomorrow? Are you sure, Miss Rowe?' Lily asked, brightening immediately.

'Yes, absolutely certain. Do you think you'll want to come along and see if you like it?'

Lily's face lit up and eyes glistened. 'I would, Miss Rowe,' she said quietly. 'Very much. Me dad has been in Newgate Street again. He's still there, in fact.'

'It might only be for several weeks during the run up to Christmas,' she said, not wishing Lily to bank on the job lasting forever.

'Any time at all would be grand,' Lily said. 'I've never worked in a shop before, though, and don't know what to do.'

'You will report to me and I'll show you all that you need to do.'

'That would be wonderful, Miss. Truly wonderful.'

'Good. Come to the shop tomorrow at eight-thirty,' Florence said cheerfully, relieved that it was a Saturday. She gave Lily the times and smiled. 'I look forward to showing you how everything works.'

Lily seemed to gather herself. 'Thank you, Miss Rowe. You don't know what this will mean to me. Ma will be cheered to think that I'm working in such a posh place.'

Rowe's was hardly posh, Florence thought, but it did have good standing in the town, and she was happy to hear that Lily was delighted with her offer.

'Then I'll wish you good day and see you in the morning. I'd better be on my way, or my parents will wonder where I've gone.'

Lily smiled at her. 'Thanks very much, Miss Rowe. You really are very kind to look out for me in this way. I wish I'd gone back to see you before now, but I'll be very happy to come and work for your family. I promise I won't let you down.'

'I know you won't, Lily,' she said, feeling like she had been given a gift.

Florence's thoughts immediately turned to Jesse and how he would react to this good news. The pain in his joints worsened in colder damp weather and so far it had already snowed in Nottingham. She was concerned about him and had been dreading having to celebrate Christmas without him. Now, though, she had Lily coming to work with her and she could focus all her attention on training her.

Chapter 22

'Yes, I know you'll look after her, but I felt that as I had persuaded her to come and work here, then the very least I could do is be here to welcome her and show her what Father will be expecting of her.'

'Well, I'd also like to help her sometimes, that's all I'm saying,' Amy argued. 'I know it was your idea, but I'm looking forward to seeing her again. She's a dear girl and I hope she can get the hang of working here to the level Father will expect.'

At that moment the brass bell jangled. Florence looked over to the door to see Lily step into the shop.

Florence could see that she seemed terrified. It must have taken a lot of courage for her to come here today, she mused, hurrying over to her.

'Good morning, Lily,' she said, a wide welcoming smile on her face. 'We've been looking forward to you working here with us.' She waved Amy over.

'Have you?' Lily asked, looking surprised. 'I've been really scared about this morning, but excited too.'

'Good morning, Lily,' Amy said as she joined them.

'You mustn't be worried,' Florence reassured her. 'This is your first day and both Amy and I will be here to show you anything you need to know. We only expect you to get a feel of what we do here at first. Then as the days go on, you'll find everything will start to feel a little more familiar.'

'Yes,' Amy assured her. 'We want you to enjoy working here at W. H. Rowe.'

Florence could see Lily visibly relax at their words. 'Now, if you'll follow me, I can take you to the back of the shop. You can hang up your things, they'll be safe in there.'

Lily followed her and took off the shawl. Florence noticed how bedraggled the girl's dress was and as Lily gazed at Florence's dress and then back at her own, she realised how ashamed Lily was to be wearing such a dress to work. Florence wanted to put her out of her misery instantly, thanking Jesse silently for his suggestion that they offer her a uniform. Florence hadn't wanted Lily to be offended by the offer. She was concerned about the girl's father's reaction when he was released from jail, if he insisted on knowing where the dress had come from. She and Amy had discussed which dress to offer her and decided on one from Amy's wardrobe as she was smaller than Florence and more Lily's size.

She could see Lily pulling at her sleeves.

'We have a dress,' she said, smiling with as much reassurance as she could muster. 'We thought it would be like a uniform for you working here. Do you want me to fetch it for you?' She waited for Lily's reaction, willing her not to be offended and to take the offer in the way it was meant.

Lily thought for a moment. A range of emotions passed

across her face and Florence's heart pounded heavily as she became more concerned about what she had just said the longer she had to wait for Lily to reply.

'Um, it will be yours, so you'd be entitled to wear it home if you'd rather.'

Lily shook her head. 'Oh no, I couldn't do that,' she said. 'Me dad would have a fit if he saw me wearing anythin' smart. He'd know I had been given it and he doesn't accept charity.'

Florence smiled. 'It's not charity, though, Lily; it's your shop assistant's uniform. But if you'd rather not wear it home then that is perfectly fine. What do you think?'

Lily's eyes widened. She glanced at the doorway back into the shop. 'If you wouldn't mind, I'd love to change into the dress, but I think it would be best if I kept it here for when I'm working. Would that be all right?'

'Yes, it would be perfectly fine. Wait here and I'll fetch it for you.'

Relieved, Florence left the shop and ran upstairs to Amy's room where the dress was hanging on the outside of her wardrobe. It was plain and dark grey, but it was a smart dress. She hoped Lily would like it and that it would fit her well enough.

Going back to the shop, she hurried into the storeroom, closing the door behind her.

'Here it is. What do you think?'

Lily's mouth dropped open in surprise. 'It's beautiful! Are you sure I can wear it?'

'Yes, it's yours to do with as you wish. And, if you do ever change your mind about wearing it home, then that's fine too.' Florence hooked the hanger on a hook on the back of the door. 'Will you need any help changing, or shall I leave you to it and see you in the shop?'

'I'll be fine, thank you, Miss Rowe.'

Florence smiled at her and left her to it.

She joined Amy restocking some shelves, and quietly told her of the conversation she'd just had with Lily.

'I noticed you taking the dress into the storeroom. I'm glad Lily decided to wear it.'

Florence nodded. 'I'm pleased. I want her to take more away from this job than just the wages,' she whispered. 'I want her to gain confidence. She needs to discover how bright she is and know that there is more out in the world just waiting for her to find it.'

Amy stopped what she was doing and frowned thoughtfully at her.

'What?' Florence asked, unsure what she might have said for her sister to react in such a way.

Amy shrugged. 'I knew you wanted to help her, but I didn't realise quite how important it was for you to do so.'

Florence couldn't understand why her sister was surprised. 'If we don't give Lily a helping hand, I can't see that she has anyone else in her life that might be able to do it. I simply want her to experience some of what we're lucky enough to have by birth.'

Amy took Florence's hand in hers, her eyes awash with unshed tears. 'You're right. I'm glad we're doing this for her.'

They heard the storeroom door opening. Amy quickly wiped her eyes as they heard the door open and saw Lily walking slowly into the shop. She looked around for them, but both of them were so taken aback by the sight of how different the girl appeared that it took a moment for one of them to move. She seemed to have grown in stature already. Her head was held high and already there was a hint of the confidence to come.

Florence walked over to her, closely followed by Amy.

'It's a little big,' Lily said, her voice quavering slightly. 'But I think I'll grow into it, don't you?'

'It suits you very well,' Florence said, delighted and relieved at the same time. 'I'll take it in at the seams slightly, so that it fits you better the next time you wear it. Are you happy wearing it though, that's the most important thing? We don't want you to feel you have to do this.'

Lily's eyes watered slightly and Florence realised she was trying to hold back tears.'

'I love it,' she murmured. 'Thank you both so much. I've never worn anything this beautiful before.'

The brass bell jangled, and they turned in unison to see a customer entering the shop.

'I'll serve her,' Amy said quietly, walking off to greet the elderly woman.

'Now,' Florence said, wanting distract Lily from her emotions before they got the better of her, 'you're not to worry about Father. He's out meeting with a representative who provides us with stock for the shop, so probably won't be back by the time you finish. He can be a little abrasive, but as long as you're on time and not caught slacking at any time, you'll be fine.'

Lily chewed her lower lip.

'Don't be concerned. If he didn't want you here, he would not have let me ask you to come and work here.'

'I will do my very best, Miss Rowe.'

'I'm sure you will,' Florence said, relieved her father was out and would not be looking over Lily's shoulder to ensure everything she did was correct. At least the girl would have a chance to learn some of the duties expected of her before having to work with him questioning her. It would make them both anxious, Florence knew.

'Right,' she said cheerily, 'let's begin by me showing you around the shop properly. What do you say?'

'Yes, that would be lovely.'

Later that afternoon, after closing the shop and going to her room, Florence sat at her small table by the window and wrote to Jesse about the excitement of Lily's first day working at Rowe's Stationers.

27 Queen Street
St Helier
Jersey
31 October 1885

Mr J Boot
16–20 Goose Gate
Nottingham

Dearest Jesse,
I hope that you're keeping well and not working too hard.
I know how you sometimes forget to take time to relax.

It was Lily Buttons' first Saturday morning working at Rowe's today and I believe it went well. She is a hard-working girl, as I presumed she would be, and conscientious. I hope that when I leave and come to live in Nottingham that Father will be happy enough and used to Lily to ask her to take over my role in the shop. If she carries on the way that she did during the morning today, then I'm almost certain he will. Although it is always an uncertainty. I think the only reason Mother agreed to Lily working part-time in the shop was because she met her that time Mr Buttons was chasing Lily and Mother took her up to the flat to feed her while she was hiding up there.

Honestly, Jesse, it was wonderful to see how much Lily grew in stature over the morning. By the time she left just after 1 p.m., her head was held higher and I could see much more confidence in her walk. I'm so happy. She is a dear girl and I am only relieved that I have the means to make a tiny difference to her life. I just hope that her father doesn't go back to their home too soon and take umbrage against us at Rowe's and insist that she leave. It would be too cruel for Lily to see that she could have a future doing something she enjoys, only for her hopes to be dashed.

My only other news, apart from the fact that I'm missing you terribly, but you know that already, is that it's raining here, again. I can't help my thoughts drifting to Lily and her family. I wish I could give her a pair of boots that Amy doesn't use any more, but I fear that to offer them so soon after offering her a dress for the shop, would be going too far and I'm terrified of upsetting her. I also doubt they'll *be the right size, as Lily's feet seem rather small. I'll see how things go.*

Mother is calling, so I shall sign off now. Please, do take care of yourself in this weather. If it is icy here, then it must be far worse further north where you are.

Until next time,

My love,

As always,

Florence.

She folded the letter and, hearing her mother call her and Amy to supper for the second time, rushed to go to the kitchen to offer any help in serving.

Chapter 23

16–20 Goose Gate
Nottingham
5 November 1885

Miss Florence Rowe
27 Queen Street
St Helier
Jersey

Dearest Florence,

Reading your letters always makes me smile. I enjoy the happiness you feel seeing Miss Buttons growing in pride. I believe that we gain more from being able to help others. Those of us who are fortunate to have the means to give help girls like Lily in this way are, I believe, truly lucky. While we restore their faith in others, they in turn allow us to feel our own sense of pride in witnessing their growth.

I think you should find a way to give Miss Buttons a pair of boots. I mentioned in an earlier letter about walking for miles with my mother to collect herbs, both of us *barefoot. This is because the wet grass would have ruined the leather and we needed to protect our shoes so that they were in the best condition to enable us to be presentable in the shop for serving our customers. We also did not wish to humiliate ourselves by not having decent shoes to wear at chapel on Sundays.*

I feel certain that with a pair of decent boots to go with her smart attire, you will be giving Lily a great deal. I understand that it can be difficult at times to gift something to someone without them being embarrassed by the action, but I know that you will manage this somehow.

I am well. My joints tend to hurt more in colder weather like we are experiencing now, but I am luckier than most others, in that my home is warm and offers me much comfort. I spend many of my evenings sitting in front of the fire and imagining how perfect it will be when we are married. I picture you relaxing in the chair next to me and think of all the conversations we will have, instead of needing to put our thoughts and feelings into letters and then wait for the other's reply. Those evenings, I know, will be worth waiting for, but still I find myself impatient for that time to come.

I must sign off now, as I must soon leave to attend a meeting at the Town Hall. Good night, sweet Florence.

As always,

Your Jesse

If Florence was concerned that Lily had found working at Rowe's too overwhelming the previous Saturday and wouldn't return the following week, her fears were dispelled ten minutes before opening time. She spotted Lily waiting at the shop door to be let in, this time her face was lit with a wide smile. Florence's mood lifted immediately. It was satisfying to know that she was making a difference in Lily's life.

Florence hurried over and unlocked the shop door, called Lily inside and then quickly locked it again so that no customers followed her in before they were due to be open.

'Ooh, it's getting very cold out there, isn't it?' she said, rubbing her arms.

'It is,' Lily said, her teeth chattering as she spoke. She took off her green shawl and smoothed down her hair.

'How are you, Lily?' Florence asked, delighted to see that she carried a look of confidence that hadn't been there prior to the previous Saturday morning.

'I'm well, thank you, Miss Rowe. I thought I'd come a little early so that I have time to change into my uniform before the shop opens. I hope that's acceptable.'

'Of course, it is. In fact, it's a good idea,' Florence said, before adding, 'How did you find your first day here?'

Lily beamed at her. 'Oh, it was everything I expected and much more,' she said, clapping her hands together. 'I told my ma all about it and she said she knew I'd be happy working here with you.'

Florence was delighted to hear such praise. 'I've taken your dress in slightly at the sides for you and shortened the sleeves so that you don't have to fold them at the wrists. I think you'll find it fits better.'

'Thanks very much. That's very kind of you.'

'Not at all,' she said, 'Amy is due down in a moment and when she gets here, I'll pop upstairs and make us all a cup of tea. Would you like one?'

'Yes please,' Lily said, disappearing into the storeroom, oblivious to the fact that drinking tea wasn't usually something they did before opening the shop.

Amy arrived shortly after, and Florence told her what she was about to do.

'I'd love one, too,' Amy said. 'I had a bad night's sleep last night and didn't have time for a cup of tea before coming downstairs. 'You go and I'll get Lily started on what we need her to do today. Remember Father will be watching everything Lily does; you know what he's like only trusting family working here.'

'I know,' Florence said, wishing Amy would keep her voice down. The last thing she wanted was for Lily to overhear and get a fright. 'She did well on Saturday; I was pleased for her that she seemed to take to working here so easily.'

'I was too. I was relieved for you also. Anyway, don't fret. We'll both keep an eye on your little protégé.'

Florence pursed her lips at her sister's teasing and ran upstairs to make the tea. She was relieved they had been able to spend Lily's first day at work without their father worrying over every little thing that she did. Florence wanted him to be pleased with Lily and, although she had confidence in the girl's abilities, she was going to try and remove any chance of him being upset or anxious about her being there. She couldn't bear to think of letting him have any reason to fire her. The thought of giving Lily hope to then have it dashed worried

Florence immensely. She would have to make this work, for all of them.

If Lily did well at Rowe's, it would give her new prospects. Florence knew that she would then being able to leave her job at the shop after her marriage to Jesse without having any qualms about letting her father down. It also might help persuade her mother that everything didn't have to change too much when she and Jesse did marry and go to live in Nottingham. Especially as far as the running of Rowe's was concerned.

This idea of hers that she and Amy had put underway was working so far. Now they simply had to ensure that it continued to do so until their father became as comfortable with Lily working at Rowe's as they already were. Florence hoped it didn't take too long. Jesse was due to come back to Jersey at the beginning of summer, so that only gave her six months to make this project a successful one.

She made the tea and took three cups and saucers downstairs on a tray, together with a small plate of biscuits. She suspected that Lily might not have had much breakfast before walking here in the cold, if indeed she had eaten anything. She reached the shop, happy to see Lily chatting to Amy and looking anything but the timid skinny girl she'd spoken to last week. She was still skinny, of course, but her thin arms were hidden by the dark grey sleeves. She also appeared older and more relaxed.

'Here we are,' Florence said, placing the tray on the counter. 'I've bought a few biscuits, too. Help yourself Lily, don't be shy,' she said, noticing how Lily was staring at the butter shortbread circles her mother had baked the previous day. 'Help yourself. We need to be quick before Father gets here in five minutes.'

As soon as they had all finished their drinks and the biscuits were gone, Florence returned the tray of crockery quickly upstairs and washed everything up. Their parents were out visiting Adelaide, whose health was improving, but their mother wanted to see her for herself and take her a batch of biscuits. Their father hadn't wanted her to go out on the icy pavements alone, so had begrudgingly accompanied her when she had insisted going early rather than waiting until the end of the working day.

They had been working for several hours. The shop was busier than Florence and Amy had expected on such a miserable day, and their father had just gone upstairs to eat his lunch.

As soon as he had left, Florence turned her attention to Lily; she was reading one of the new books that had arrived that morning.

'What do you think?'

Lily gasped and slammed the book closed. 'I'm so sorry, Miss Rowe,' she said, looking terrified.

Florence was shocked that she had frightened Lily. She hadn't meant to. She would have to be a little more careful with her, she decided. It was no good treating her like Amy when Lily didn't know her well enough yet to understand that Florence only had the best intentions and would never wish her harm or be intentionally cruel to her.

'I'm sorry I gave you a shock.' She rested a hand on Lily's forearm. 'I hadn't meant to. I only wanted to know what you thought of the book you've just been reading.'

'Reading?' Lily stared down at the floor. 'I wasn't reading, Miss Rowe.' She lowered her voice as if confiding a dreadful secret. 'I'm ashamed to admit that I cannot read.'

'You have nothing to be ashamed about,' Florence insisted, stunned to discover this information about her assistant. 'I don't understand, though; haven't I seen you noting things down?'

'Yes. Well, I can read, a little,' Lily explained quietly. 'But not well enough to enjoy a book such as this.' She held up the copy of *Treasure Island*.

Florence was devastated that no one had taught Lily to read well enough to enjoy one of the many books they had in stock. She decided that she should be the one to rectify this omission as soon as possible.

'Then we shall see that you can.' She smiled, hoping to reassure the girl. 'I can teach you during quiet moments here and if you wish you may come to the shop either before we open for lessons or stay back afterwards. I shall ensure that you are reading in no time.'

Lily's eyes widened and her full lips drew back into a smile. 'You will? For me?'

'Yes. We will start immediately.'

'And I'm happy to stay back after the shop closes for as long as you need me to.'

Florence was touched by the girl's enthusiasm. 'I think an hour each time will be long enough. You'll be tired after working here for a full day and your mother will be expecting you home to help her with chores, I assume.'

'Of course. Thank you, Miss Rowe.'

'It will be my pleasure,' she assured her, deciding that if she was unable to get the desired result from her teachings that she would ask Adelaide to step in and help Lily. After all, Adelaide already taught in a school and knew how best to encourage students. First, though, she would do her best to help Lily obtain the reading skills she so desired. She couldn't wait to get started. 'There's no one in here now, so shall we find a book that you do feel comfortable with and begin there?'

The next couple of hours passed quickly and, happy with Lily's immediate progress, Florence lent her the book that they had been working on. Now, she thought, we need to build her experience in the shop. 'How do you feel about serving your first customer?' she asked.

'I'd like that.' Lily beamed at her, her cheeks flushed with excitement.

'Good. Then the next customer who comes here can be yours.' She checked that Amy had heard. 'In the meantime, you can straighten the items on the display at the front of the shop, please.'

Lily would then be in the perfect place for the customer to notice her, so that she could ask them how she could help.

Lily walked away happily, leaving Florence to rearrange a larger display at the side of the shop so that she could include stock that she thought to be perfect Christmas gifts.

A few minutes later Florence groaned.

'Whatever is the matter?' Amy asked. 'Are you unwell?'

Florence shook her head. 'No, look,' she said, pointing out of the window.

Mrs Wolstenholm was about to open the shop door.

'Oh no,' Amy grimaced. 'Shall we go and help Lily?'

Florence wanted to, but saw Mrs Wolstenholm – her father's most valued, yet annoying customer – tap her silver-topped walking stick noisily on the wooden floorboards near to the counter. Lily, her cheeks flushed, smiled and offered her help to the short, rotund woman.

'And who might you be?' Mrs Wolstenholm demanded.

'I'm Miss Lily Buttons,' she said, her voice trembling a little with nerves.

Florence was pleased to note that Lily stood up straight. If she didn't know better, Florence would have thought Lily far more confident than she knew her to be. Florence wanted to assist Lily, but didn't want to usurp her control of the situation.

'I'm Mrs Wolstenholm,' she said, her tone clipped. 'You must be new.' She tapped her stick against the maid's skirt Florence had just noticed had come in behind her. The poor girl was carrying several parcels, which, judging by the redness in her face, must be heavy. 'Stand out of my way.'

The woman waited for Lily to come directly in front of her before looking her slowly up and down as if she had never seen a specimen quite like her before. 'You don't look as if you're one of those modern women,' she sniffed, scanning the shop until her focus landed on Florence. 'All those ruffles and draping material, it's too fanciful if you ask me. I believe unmarried women should wear plainer clothing.'

Florence was used to this rudeness, so wasn't offended by her. 'Good afternoon, Mrs Wolstenholm,' she waved.

'Delightful to see you again.' She was determined not to give the woman satisfaction of letting her know she had annoyed her.

'Is there anything I can help you with today?' she heard Lily ask.

Mrs Wolstenholm rested both hands on the top of her walking stick and glowered at her. 'I will not be served by a mere girl.' She looked across at Florence and bellowed. 'Where is your father. He always serves me and I do not have time to dawdle.' She raised her chin and glowered down at her maid. 'Do stop fidgeting, Martha.'

Not wishing to leave Lily alone with the cantankerous woman, Florence said, 'Lily, please will go you and ask my father to come and speak to Mrs Wolstenholm?'

Lily was stumped for a second and then quickly went out the back of the shop to the stairs.

'May I take those from you?' Florence asked the maid.

'She's perfectly capable of holding them.' Mrs Wolstenholm began pacing back and forth in front of the counter.

'Place them here, if you like,' Florence whispered to the poor girl, who after a brief consideration of the offer, placed the parcels quietly down on the wooden surface next to her and mouthed a thanks to Florence.

Too irritated to notice what was happening behind her back, the older woman tutted loudly. 'For heaven's sake, what's keeping the man?'

'I'm sure he'll be here presently.' Florence willed her father to hurry, aware that he would come to the shop as soon as he possibly could.

She heard footsteps and stared at the back door, relieved to see her father coming to join them in the shop.

'My apologies for keeping you waiting, Mrs Wolstenholm,' he said. 'Florence, why don't you help Lily to unpack that order that arrived earlier.'

She could tell her father wanted Lily out of the way so that he could appease his customer for him not being there to greet her. The woman was a dragon and well known for her nastiness, but unfortunately, her father, like most of the shopkeepers whose shops the woman frequented, were not in a position to refuse to serve her. She had money and, for all her rudeness, did spend a lot on herself.

Florence reached the doorway at the back of the shop leading to the storeroom. She couldn't help feeling angry on her father's behalf to hear the woman address him so rudely.

'She's not very nice, is she?' Lily whispered so quietly Florence could barely hear her.

'No, but she comes here often and buys a lot, so we have to pander to her, unfortunately.'

Leaving her father to serve the woman, Florence went back to the storeroom just as her sister Amy arrived from the family's flat above the shop.

'Poor Lily,' Florence said, giving Lily an apologetic glance. 'I let her serve Mrs Wolstenholm. She was to be her first customer.'

'Don't mind her,' Amy said, keeping her voice very low. 'She might act all grand and look down on the rest of us, but she's only a shopkeeper's daughter herself.'

'Which means, she's no better than we are,' Florence explained to Lily. She couldn't imagine ever taking on airs like that vile woman she could hear talking down to her father. She folded her arms across her chest, stunned.

'You wouldn't think so by looking at her, or listening to her posh voice,' Lily said, eyes wide.

'I was surprised when I found out too, Lily,' Florence admitted. 'I never would have guessed it by her superior behaviour.'

'Nor me. She's nothing like you two kind ladies,' Lily said quietly.

Florence smiled at her. 'I'm glad you think so.'

Amy wasn't finished yet though, it seemed. 'Apparently, she met a wealthy Colonel in Torquay when she went there on holiday as a young woman and they married very quickly. She only came back to the island after she had been widowed a few years ago.'

They were all relieved when Mrs Wolstenholm finally departed, her maid carrying her books and some new ink for her fountain pen.

At the end of the day, Florence changed for bed and sat down to write to Jesse.

27 Queen Street
St Helier
Jersey
12 November 1885

Mr J Boot
16–20 Goose Gate
Nottingham

Mrs Boots

Dearest Jesse,

It seems that the closer we get to Christmas the more I'm missing you. However, I shall try my best to remain positive, and on that note will tell you about my day at father's shop.

Lily seems to be enjoying working with us at the shop. She looks well in her uniform and she appears to grow in confidence with every hour she's with us. She loves her uniform and I've decided that I shall buy her a pair of boots to wear. I hope she accepts them.

Today was to be Lily's first experience of serving a customer. She was nervous but excited and unfortunately the person she encountered was the unfriendliest customer we have at Rowe's. Lily dealt with the situation well, despite the woman demanding to speak to my father instead. I was concerned the experience might put her off trying again later, but I've come to realise that she has encountered far worse from others. Thankfully, Lily later served a sweet lady and her niece and sold her first Christmas presents to a customer. She was very proud of herself, as was I of her.

Usually when we begin displaying our Christmas stock, I find that the spirit of this time of year raises my own spirits. I can't, however, believe that the same will happen this year. I miss you and can't help thinking that if my parents hadn't refused your proposal to me that I would be with you in Nottingham and not still here in Jersey. I sometimes find it difficult not to feel resentful of them, even though I know their intentions were for the best.

However, as far as Lily is concerned, she is doing well and that is something for which I am happy.
My dearest love,
As always,
Florence

She was also proud to think that she had a part to play in Lily's growth of confidence. Florence closed her eyes briefly and pictured the younger woman cheerfully holding the shop door open for the first customer that she had served. Florence thought back to saying goodbye to Lily as she left the shop that evening and hearing the girl humming happily to herself as she walked down the street. Yes, she had definitely done the right thing asking her father to give Lily a chance. Just as she had suspected, Lily was making the most of this unexpected opportunity.

Chapter 24

The weeks passed more quickly in the run up to Christmas. Lily was becoming more confident in her work each day, but Florence still missed Jesse terribly.

'You could think of it as celebrating your last Christmas with your family,' Amy suggested, and Florence knew her sister was only trying to help her manage the day. She watched Amy hand the end of a string of coloured paper chain up to Lily who was standing on a wooden stepladder in the corner of the shop.

The women had spent hours the previous afternoon whenever they had an opportunity, to make up the bright chains. It was something Florence and Amy usually did with their mother each year. This time they had Lily to help.

They made up the chains not only because their father believed customers would buy more if they were cheered by the Christmas spirit, but also because he sold the packets of coloured paper. He told them that if young people accompanied their parents into the shop, they would see the paper chains and wish to emulate the display in their own living rooms. It made sense and she knew from experience over the years that he was right.

'Here,' he had said to Lily the previous afternoon handing her a packet, 'take this home and ask your younger brothers and sisters to make up a couple of chains for your living room.'

Lily gasped. 'Oh, thank you Mr Rowe,' she exclaimed. 'That is very kind of you. Mother and the kids will love them.'

Florence could see that Lily was almost overwhelmed by the thoughtful gift. She hoped that the boots she had bought for her weren't going to upset her in any way.

She watched as Lily pressed a drawing pin through the end ring and pressed it into the cornicing, then climbed down the ladder and carried it diagonally across the shop floor, with Amy carrying the end of the coloured paper chain. She then did the same in that corner.

'You are right, I know that,' Florence said, aware that she hadn't responded to her sister's suggestion about Christmas.

'Try to think of it from Mother and Father's point of view,' Amy said, following Lily to the next corner and waiting for her to step up the ladder. She reached up to hand the other end to her. 'This is the last time our parents will have the two of us together with them in the flat on Christmas Day. We can all go to chapel together first and then open the gifts we have for each other in front of the fire in the living room after our grand lunch.'

Florence pictured the scene that had traditionally been followed by her family since she could remember. In the last few years first Adelaide had married and although they would both visit over Christmas and Boxing days, she had chosen to spend her time with her spouse and then her brother, Willie had married and moved out into his own flat.

'You're making me feel rather selfish,' Florence said, pushing a drawing pin up into the cornicing and wincing as she hurt her thumb doing it. 'I hadn't thought about it from their point of view, only mine and Jesse's.'

She had been thoughtless, she realised. She and Jesse had been so caught up in their sadness at missing each other that neither of them had thought to consider her parent's feelings.

'I'll make an effort to celebrate the day with them. Thanks, Amy, I'm glad you pointed this out to me. I would hate to have realised it after the event.'

'It's fine,' Amy said, going to pick up the second paper chain and taking it to the next corner with Lily. 'If I was in love with someone I would probably be just as caught up in my feelings for him as you are with Mr Boot. It's understandable.'

'Please, refer to him as Jesse when we're alone,' Florence said quietly. 'I like being able to speak about him using his name and you're the only person I can do that with.'

She felt excitement well up inside her. To think that this time next year she would be Mrs Boot and share her own home with Jesse. It felt like she was dreaming. Would it be as perfect as she hoped? she wondered. She had nothing to compare married life to, after all. Only that of her parents. They seemed happy enough, Florence mused. What would her life with Jesse be like in reality? On the one hand she couldn't wait to find out, but on the other, she was frightened that everything wouldn't be as perfect as she had hoped and that she would have to deal with her dreams being crushed. She realised her sister was talking to her.

'If you wish,' Amy said. 'As I was saying though, I just didn't want you to miss the chance of making this last Christmas in Jersey a special one, for Mother and Father mainly, but also as something for you to look back on fondly when you have your own smart Christmases with your husband.'

Florence smiled at her sister and placed the stepladder down, opening it. 'Next year is going to be the start of a whole new life for me,' she said, almost to herself. 'I'm so excited.' She was determined to look on the bright side. 'And to think that I never wanted to be married.'

As soon as Amy and Lily had finished pinning the final chain, Lily put the stepladder away in their small stock room.

Amy straightened the receipt book thoughtfully before saying, 'When you first told me about you and Mr Boot – sorry, Jesse – getting married, I couldn't quite envisage it.'

Concerned at her sister's words, Florence asked, 'Why not? Do you think the match won't be a good one?'

Amy shook her head and laughed. 'Not at all. I suppose because of your insistence that you would never marry meant that I had never thought of you with a husband, that's all.'

'How did you think of me then?' Florence asked, intrigued to find out her sister's thoughts.

'Well, as you are now, I suppose,' Amy said, a perplexed expression on her face.

'What? Here, in this shop?' She loved working here but if she was to spend the rest of her life being someone else's shop assistant she would be thoroughly disheartened. She knew that now more than ever before. Now that she had had a chance to dream of bigger things with Jesse by her side.'

'Behind the counter, yes, but not in this shop. I picture

you running your own establishment, and I know that, with or without Mr, err, Jesse, you would have brought that vision to life.'

Lily went and stood in front of the counter looking a little awkward when she realised Florence and Amy were chatting.

Florence was soothed by her younger sister's words. It felt reassuring to know that the person who knew her best in the world, and who was most aware of her capabilities and ambitions, believed in her and in her ability to bring those ambitions to fruition.

She decided that if the worst happened and for some reason she could not marry Jesse, then she would focus all her energy on obtaining her own shop selling everything from inexpensive ribbons and hairpins to handbags, and silver photo frames that could be bought as a present for a woman in which to keep the photograph of her beloved. She would build her business and give girls like Lily jobs and help them realise their worth in the world.

She could see that Lily's confidence, if she'd ever had any, had been diminished by her bully of a father. Lily deserved to have expectations, just like she and Amy did. Yes, she would make certain to employ girls who deserved a chance in life and who hadn't been lucky enough to have come across any yet.

A customer entered the shop and handed Florence her dripping umbrella to prop up in the stand by the door kept especially for keeping drops of rain off the wooden shop floor.

'It's shocking out there,' the woman said, glancing around the displays in the shop. 'I need to buy Christmas gifts for three nephews. They're six, eight and nine years old, and I have no idea what they will like.'

'We'll definitely find something they'll like here,' Florence reassured her. 'If you want to take a seat then I'll bring you over a few choices.'

Florence had been worrying about what to buy Jesse for Christmas and despite searching all the shops in St Helier that she supposed might stock something to his liking, she still had not found anything suitable. It was only when she was serving the older lady that it dawned on her. She would buy him the most exquisite leather letter-writing case. Jesse enjoyed writing letters and travelled from factory to shop constantly. If she bought this for him, and had it engraved with his initials, then he could write to her from anywhere.

Satisfied that she had finally thought of something suitable, she settled and focused her attention on the customer.

'How about a thaumatrope set?'

The woman frowned. 'I don't know if I've heard of such a thing. Do you think it suitable for all three of the boys?'

Florence reassured her that she did and asked Lily to fetch one, pointing to the picture on the box. 'You see? It's a disc with a picture on either side. Then they attach two pieces of string, in some sets a stick is attached. The boys then spin the disc and it makes the two pictures appear to merge into one.' She took out the example and showed the woman how it worked.

'The three of them can make their own thaumatropes and colour or paint them, then they can do a show for their parents.'

Florence noticed that Lily was still standing nearby rather

than having returned to her work. She wondered if maybe she hadn't seen a thaumatrope set before, but sensed that Lily wanted to say something.

'Lily, is there something the matter?' she whispered as the customer focused her attention on the toy.

'I . . . well . . . I was wondering if I could make a suggestion about the boys' gifts?'

'Oh, please do,' the lady said, overhearing. 'Any suggestions will be most welcome.'

Lily's face reddened. She caught Florence's eye and seemed unsure what to do. Florence realised she was worried about speaking out of turn and smiled at her.

'What did you have in mind?'

'I have little brothers of similar ages to your nephews,' she said, her confidence rising with every word she spoke. 'I was thinking what they might like if they could choose anything from here, and I think they'd enjoy.'

'Go on,' the lady said, beaming at Lily.

'Well, the oldest of my brothers would like one of the Kaleidoscopes that we have.' She glanced at Florence who gave her an encouraging nod. 'The middle one, I think would like a box of tin soldiers, and my youngest brother would probably enjoy the hobby horse.'

'What a clever woman you are,' the lady said, perking up and clapping her hands together gleefully. 'I was beginning to think I'd fail to find anything for the boys. Such dear children, too, but rather a handful for their mother. If I buy them the gift that you suggested, Miss Rowe, for them to share. Then,' she said, focusing her attention on Lily, 'I could also buy them individual gifts. They should then be kept entertained for several hours, if not days. I'm sure their mother will be delighted.'

'I can imagine she will be.' She took a cheaper example from a nearby cupboard. 'Let me show you this one. It will give you the idea, without breaking open your box. Your nephews might be different ages, but most children enjoy painting and it's something they can do indoors in the winter and outdoors in the summer.'

She and Lily waited patiently while the woman inspected the toy.

'Splendid,' she said finally. 'That looks perfect and I can imagine that none of the other relations will have come up with this idea,' she said, as if the suggestion had been her own.

Florence smiled at Lily, satisfied that between them they had helped solve the lady's problem. She gazed out of the window. The weather had worsened, and it was going to be nasty enough for the woman to walk home without having to carry an awkward box.

'It's still raining, and I doubt you want the box to get wet. If you want, Lily can take down your address and we'll have it delivered to you first thing tomorrow.'

'Thank you, my dears. You were both exceedingly helpful. I shall tell all my friends to visit you here if they need help buying presents. Now, do you have a piece of paper and a pen for my address?'

As soon as the customer had left, Florence turned to Lily. 'Thank you,' she said, her happiness at the excellent sale, aware that she and Lily working so well together had bene-fitted the business, she watched Lily's delight that her suggestions had been so well received.

'I hope you don't think I overstepped the mark?' Lily said thoughtfully seconds later. 'I hadn't meant to offend.'

Florence took her friend by the shoulders and shook her head, smiling. 'Not at all. You were a wonderful help. It goes to show that with your experience of younger siblings you know a great deal about what children would choose given the choice. That knowledge is invaluable. Well done for step-ping forward with your ideas.'

Lily's mouth drew back in a wide smile. 'I'm so pleased that you're not cross with me.'

'Cross? Why would I be? You've taught me to make the most of your talents, as well as my own.' She pulled Lily into a hug. 'Thank you, and well done.'

Later, satisfied that she and Lily had learnt something valuable from each other, Florence left her to keep an eye on the shop and went to find the latest delivery of writing folders. She wanted the most impressive one Rowe's stocked for Jesse.

She could hear Lily speaking to a couple about gifts, happy that she had a free few minutes to source the best present she could think of for Jesse. She opened each box, carefully peeling back the tissue paper inside to check which one she favoured most. She was about to open the next box when something caught her eye. It was a larger box. She couldn't recall seeing this box before. There seemed to be only one in this size.

Florence lifted it from the chest and carefully lifted the lid, gasping at the magnificent oxblood-red embossed leather cover. She folded back the two ornate brass clasps holding the book shut and lifted the top cover to display the most exquisite photograph album she had ever seen. This was what she would buy for Jesse for their first Christmas.

They might not be together, but this gift would express the hope that she held for their future together and over time they would slowly fill each of the empty framed spaces with photographs of themselves and, God willing, their family when it arrived.

Florence ran a fingertip around the edge of one of the empty framed areas, then, closing the cover lightly, ran her fingers across the embossed leather. She felt certain that Jesse would love this as she did.

She did not mind how much it cost, the gesture meant too much to scrimp and hopefully this gift would last their entire lives together.

She painstakingly wrapped the album in the tissue paper once again and placed it into the box, closing the lid very slowly.

She would package it carefully and send it to him first thing in the morning, together with the carefully chosen Christmas card she had found for him earlier in the week.

It was Christmas Eve. After a day filled with one customer after the other coming to the shop panicking over what last-minute gifts to buy people, their father, Amy, Lily and Florence were finally able to lock the door.

'I'd like to give you a little Christmas box, Lily,' their father said. He had spoken to Florence and Amy a few days earlier about his idea of giving Lily a small bonus as a Christmas gift.

'I beg your pardon?' Lily's eyes widened as she glanced from one of them to the other. 'But I've only been working here a few weeks.'

'Yes,' Mr Rowe said, handing her a small brown envelope with her wages inside. 'And you've been a little gem. You've learned quickly and worked hard. You're always on time, and we've thoroughly enjoyed having you working here at W. H. Rowe.'

Her expression changed immediately, and she seemed as if she was on the brink of tears. 'You want me to leave now?'

'What?' he frowned. 'No. I'm simply praising you for your work. And wishing you a happy Christmas. I expect to see you back here bright and early on the twenty-seventh. We'll have a lot of work to do after the next few days. People wanting to change items and the like.'

'Oh,' she said, her cheerful expression reappearing on her pretty face, 'that's very kind of you. Thank you.'

'It's a Christmas box for your family,' Florence explained.

Lily stiffened. She could see that she wanted to refuse but wasn't in the position to do so.

'For your younger siblings, too,' she added. 'I don't have children, but I recall how excited I was for Christmas. We thought that maybe you could give them a little treat.'

She knew the treat would probably be by way of food and hoped that it would be the case. If Lily's skinny appearance was anything to go by her siblings and mother would need a bit of a boost.

After a little hesitation, Lily shrugged. 'As long as it's not charity. Father won't let us accept any charity.'

Florence's father shook his head. 'No, it isn't that,' he insisted. 'Not at all. We give a Christmas box to some of the people that deliver to us. We wanted to include you in the group of people to whom we share this token gift.'

Lily's pride restored, she smiled. 'Then I'd be very happy to be one of your people. Thanks, Miss Florence, Miss Amy, Mr Rowe.'

'You'll also find an extra two shillings in your wage packet,' her father said proudly.

Lily stared at the brown envelope in her hand. 'Two bob! Thanks very much.'

Florence wondered if they could have got away with giving Lily more. 'See you after Christmas, Lily, and have a lovely time with your family.'

She was visibly brighter now, Florence was relieved to see. Lily's right hand clasped shut around the envelope. 'I'm looking forward to it. Happy Christmas to you all.'

Now Florence really did feel like she had the Christmas spirit, she thought, as she watched Lily leave. She hoped Lily hadn't realised that they had made up the story about the Christmas box. Either way, she thought they had managed to give Lily a little money, which Florence knew she would use to make this Christmas slightly special for her mother and siblings.

'And I have a small gift for you, too,' Florence said, going behind the counter and taking the wrapped boot box and handing it to Lily.

Her eyes glistened with unshed tears. 'Thank you,' she sniffed.

'Have a lovely Christmas,' Florence said, giving Lily a hug.

'You, too,' Lily said before leaving the shop.

Florence went upstairs to the flat, feeling emotionally drained. Her mother pointed out a package that had arrived addressed in Jesse's handwriting for Florence. Unlike the one she had posted to him the day before, this package was very small.

'I imagine it's jewellery,' Amy whispered as Florence studied the brown paper surrounding the gift. 'Why don't you take that off? I would imagine he has had the gift itself wrapped prettily for you. At least, I should hope so?'

Florence was certain that Jesse would have done. He was such a thoughtful man and always took note of the details with anything he did. She untied the string surrounding the package and peeled off the brown paper to reveal a card box. She lifted the lid off it carefully to reveal a beautiful pale crushed rose paper tied neatly around her present and tied with a silver ribbon.

A small label attached to it said simply, *To Florence, may this be the one and only Christmas that we celebrate alone. My love, Jesse x*

Amy gasped. 'You'd better hide that from Father. He won't be pleased to see Jesse's affections for you demonstrated quite so openly.'

Her sister was right. Now she knew why Jesse had taken such care to add an outer layer of wrapping. She placed the gift back into the box, closed the lid and re-wrapped it, tying the ends of the string in a tight knot so that it would need cutting to remove it.

'There, that's better,' she said happily knowing what was inside. 'Now no one will be able to open it but me.'

Chapter 25

Florence woke and silently wished Jesse a happy Christmas. Soon the world would be celebrating 1886 and then she could count down the months until Jesse's return to the island.

Her thoughts turned to Lily. Her reading had come on exceedingly well and Florence could not be more proud of her protégé. She pictured her and wondered what Lily's Christmas was going to be like? She hoped the family's circumstances had improved. Maybe Lily would have a celebratory day with her closest ones, she hoped so.

Florence stretched and, swinging her legs over the side of the bed, got up. She yawned as she brushed her hair; parting her hair into sections, she expertly twisted and pinned it in place and in moments her hair was presentable. She washed and dressed and, wanting to be alone to open Jesse's gift, crept into the living room and retrieved his present from under the Christmas tree.

She went to her bedroom and taking a small pair of manicure scissors, snipped the string holding the brown paper around the box. She removed the dull paper and held the beautifully wrapped box in her hand, marvelling at the

265

intricate Christmas paper with the lace motif that had been used to wrap her gift. Florence carefully untied the silver ribbon and folded it gently.

Then taking her time so as not to tear the paper, she finally removed it and opened the box. Within it was a letter and a smaller leather box. She unfolded the single sheet of paper and pictured Jesse saying the words to her.

> *16–20 Goose Gate*
> *Nottingham*
> *16 December 1885*

Miss Florence Rowe
27 Queen Street
St Helier
Jersey

My dearest Florence,

I hope this small gift that I commissioned a jeweller to make for you is to your taste. I am painfully aware that I have not been allowed to present you with a promise ring and wanted to give you something that symbolised our love without offending your parents. I therefore thought of a love knot. To me it not only symbolises our love but the eternity that we will share once we are married. I believe that despite our enforced separation we have a bond that no other can break and so, my love, I give you this to wear until I am able to present you with the engagement ring you deserve. The ruby is the deepest red the jeweller could

*source and this, as well as the embossed roses, represents
my love for you.*

*I shall miss you on Christmas Day, more than I do on the
other days we are apart, but I know in my heart that this
will be the last time anyone has the power to keep us apart.*

*So, my dearest Florence, Happy Christmas. Think of me
and know that summer will soon be here.*

Your ever loving,

Jesse

Her heart fluttered as she pressed lightly on the metal clasp
of the box and it opened to reveal an exquisite brooch. She
gasped at the intricate love knot with tiny roses embossed
over it and in the middle was the deepest, reddest ruby she
had ever seen.

With trembling hands she carefully removed the brooch
from its protective casing and pinned it onto her dress. She
walked over to the small mirror at her dressing table and
stared, admiring the perfect gift that Jesse had sent her. He
might not be here today, she thought, but his sentiments had
come across with this present. She didn't need reminding that
he loved her, but he had ensured that all the love he held for
her was displayed in this precious gift.

'Thank you, Jesse,' she whispered, longing to be with him,
even if for one moment, to kiss him and wish him a very
happy Christmas.

'Florence?' It was her mother calling from the hallway. 'Amy?
Hurry along, girls; we need to be at chapel in fifteen minutes.'

'Coming, Mother,' Florence replied, surprised at how long she must have been sitting thinking about Jesse and wondering what he was doing at that precise moment. Probably leaving for chapel, too. She wished they were going to the same one together.

'Never mind,' she murmured. 'This time next year things will be very different.'

Hopefully different in the way that she hoped. Although she was determined to marry him regardless of the opposition against her by her mother and maybe even her father, she did still live in their home and wasn't in a position just yet to be able to afford to move out and rent a place of her own.

It was a cold but sunny day, and everyone they passed on the way to Halkett Place seemed more cheerful than usual. They walked past the home where she had been born and stopped while her parents chatted briefly with their previous neighbours. Amy and Florence left their parents talking to their friends and walked the last few yards to the steps of the impressive church that she had known all her life.

Amy nudged her gently. 'Look,' she whispered, indicating a small group of people standing slightly apart from everyone else.

'Isn't that the Buttons family?'

'Yes,' Amy said. 'Look, doesn't Lily look well.'

Florence noticed how Lily's skin glowed. It was such a change from the pinched, anxious expression she had borne that day Florence had spoken to her in Waterloo Street about the job at Rowe's. She seemed to have filled out slightly too. Florence's sadness at missing Jesse lifted slightly. She couldn't wait to tell him about the Buttons family. She presumed their cheerfulness and the children's rosy cheeks had come about by Lily buying extra food for them. Lily's clothes seemed newer too.

'Let's go and speak to them,' Florence said, not wishing them to feel out of place, which, judging by the nervous looks on the face of Lily's mother as she kept scanning the crowd outside the church, they did.

'Mrs Buttons,' Florence said when she reached them, closely followed by Amy. 'Hello, Lily. We thought it was you.'

'Florence, Amy,' Lily said, beaming from ear to ear. 'Mum, these are the kind ladies who I work with. Florence, who arranged for me to have my job at W. H. Rowe.' Florence put her hand out to shake Lily's mother's. 'And her sister Amy.' Amy did the same as Florence. 'They've both been very kind to me.'

'You've been very hard-working,' Florence said, smiling first at Mrs Buttons, who, she noticed gazed at Lily with pride, and then at Lily. 'I don't know what we would have done without your assistance at the shop these past few weeks.'

'Yes,' Amy agreed. 'You've picked everything up very quickly, Lily. Father was saying so only this morning.'

Mrs Buttons placed a hand on Lily's left arm. 'She's a good girl, is my Lily. She's been a Godsend to this family, always looking after us and goin' without to make sure her brothers and sisters are cared for.'

'She bought these new clothes for us,' a little boy of about four announced.

'And we've got dinner,' a little girl not much older than him said.

'That's enough, you two,' Lily said, her face reddening.

'You do all look very well,' Florence said. 'It's good to see you at chapel today. Have you been here before?'

'No,' Mrs Buttons murmured. 'Lily mentioned that your family come 'ere and we thought, as it's Christmas, we should be here to offer our thanks.'

'Mum,' Lily whispered. 'Please.'

Her mother raised her chin and Florence could see that she was determined to have her say. 'We're very grateful about how you've helped our Lily. It's made all the difference to us this winter.' She seemed at a loss for words for a moment. Florence opened her mouth to say something to fill the silence, when Lily's mother added, 'It's good to see my girl being treated so well. So, thank you.'

Florence didn't know what to say. She felt certain that the satisfaction she felt having helped Lily far outweighed the difference the job had made to Lily's family, but didn't want to demean Mrs Button's kind words by trying to explain her thoughts.

'Thank you,' she said simply. 'We've been very happy to have Lily working at our shop.'

'Yes,' Amy said, 'and it's very pleasant to meet Lily's family today and on such a perfect occasion.'

Florence noticed their father waving at them discreetly. 'We're going to have to go now, I'm afraid. It was lovely to see you all here today though.' She could not help wondering where Mr Buttons was and presumed he must still be away.

'Miss Rowe, one moment please,' Lily said. 'I have a small gift for you, to thank you for everything you've done for me.'

Florence couldn't speak. She watched in silence as Lily took a small bag from her middle sister's hand that she hadn't noticed before. 'This is for you. It's just something small, but when I saw it in the Central Market the other day, I knew I should buy it for you. I hope you like it.'

Florence's throat constricted with unshed tears. She opened the small cotton bag that Lily had handed to her and took out a woven silk picture bookmark. She held it up and gazed at it, taking in the greens of the holly and red of the berries on the beautiful fabric that said, *Christmas wishes to a friend*.

'It is beautiful,' Florence said, her voice cracking with emotion. 'So thoughtful and such a perfect gift.'

'You like it?' Lily asked.

'I do, very much indeed. Thank you, Lily. Truly, this is a perfect gift.'

'I'm afraid there was only one in the shop,' Lily said quietly to Amy.

'That is perfectly fine. I know my sister is very touched by your thoughtfulness, Lily,' Florence reassured her. 'Now, we really must go and take our place inside or we'll miss the start of the sermon. Merry Christmas, Mrs Buttons, Lily, Buttons family.'

'Yes,' Florence said, shaking herself out of her stupor. 'Thank you again, Lily. Nice to meet you, Mrs Buttons. I hope you all have a wonderful remainder of your day.'

After speaking with their own friends, all of them dressed in their best clothes for the occasion, they made their way up the wide stone stairs and in through one of the two huge doorways to the chapel inside.

It was an uplifting sermon. Florence enjoyed singing along

to the hymns and, as she scanned the high ceiling, she couldn't help wondering what the chapel Jesse attended would be like. She couldn't imagine she would find it as magnificent as this place.

Afterwards the congregation filed outside, chatting and exchanging good wishes. She supposed that most of them would go on their way to family lunches later. She was glad that Jesse had planned to spend the day with his sister and a few friends and hoped he had a pleasant time.

They strolled home, she and Amy following her parents along the pavement.

Florence opened the black painted front door and walked into the tiled hallway, smiling to herself. She had made a difference, not only to Lily's life, but also to her family's. Seeing them at chapel today, dressed in better clothes and genuinely happy, with Lily looking so proud, made Florence want to help more girls like Lily. There were so many girls in her predicament, young women who simply needed a helping hand. A hand up, not a handout, as Jesse had said to her in one of his letters.

She loved feeling like she was achieving something in her life and these women were the same. The only difference between them, Florence mused, was that she had been lucky enough to be born into a family where she was given the means to earn a living.

She had so much to look forward to next year. Being married to someone as kind as Jesse and with the means behind him meant that they could help many girls like Lily. It really did feel like Christmas could begin in earnest now.

Chapter 26

The delicious smell of cooking filled the hallway as Florence closed the door behind her. She unwrapped her scarf and thought of Jesse as she strode up the stairs to the flat. 'Happy Christmas, my love,' she whispered, before opening the door and stepping inside to join her family.

'You will be joining us after all, then,' her mother said, giving her a sideways glance.

Florence could see that breaking ranks from the family to go and speak to Lily that morning was not the best way to be in her mother's good books. She wanted the day to go well, so forced a smile and apologised.

'I'm sorry, Mother,' she said. 'I hope you didn't mind me going to speak to the Buttons family earlier outside the chapel?'

'No, of course not. She's a hard-working girl and your father is very happy with the way she's fitting in with you and Amy in the shop.'

'The food smells delicious. I've been looking forward to spending the rest of the day with my family.'

This had the desired effect, she noted, as her mother's face lit up. 'Good. It will be an enjoyable day. I will have all my children around me at one time or another, and your father is ready to carve the goose his cousin gave to us especially for today.'

'It smells heavenly,' Florence said, taking a deep breath. She could almost taste the delicious meat and realised for the first time how hungry she was. 'I'll take off my coat and hat and come back to help you.'

'There's no need,' her mother said, softening slightly. 'You go and read for a while; I'm quite content to carry on here. All the hard work has been done and I'll only need a little help to serve it when Adelaide and Francis have arrived.'

Happy for some time alone before the family meal got underway, Florence went to her room. She unpinned her hat, bending to check her hair in the mirror. The prospect of the tasty meal ahead of her made her stomach rumble and her thoughts drifted to Lily. She gave thanks that she had been able to speak to Lily and give her just a little something to make her family's Christmas slightly better. Florence couldn't help wondering what the Buttons family would be eating this lunchtime.

She took off her coat and hung it up in her wardrobe. Then she gazed at the brooch Jesse had had made especially for her, and her heart seemed to expand. She lifted the bottom of it and gazed lovingly at it, awed by having been given something so beautiful. She loved the gift and knew that, each time she wore the exquisite gold love knot, it would serve as a visual reminder of his adoration that would help keep her going during their separation.

She sat down to write to him and tell him all about her chat with Lily. She pictured Jesse sitting in his favourite armchair that she presumed he must have, while he opened her present to him. She hoped he liked it. She knew that the heavy leather photo album had reached him safely because he had written her a note to let her know, curious as to what her gift could possibly be.

She heard Amy welcoming Adelaide

She went out of her room to join her them. 'Adelaide, Francis,' she said beaming at them. 'Merry Christmas to you both.'

'Thank you,' Adelaide said, giving her a brief hug. 'We've been looking forward to this today and by the smell of Mother's cooking, we're in for a treat.'

Their mother blushed and waved the compliment away. 'It's nothing more than you would expect,' she said as their father linked arms with her.

'We're all very lucky to have such a talented cook treating us to our food,' her father said, kissing their mother quickly on her pink cheek. 'Come, let's go into the living room. I have the fire going and it's much warmer in there.'

Florence and Amy exchanged glances. They knew their father was right, the small living room was much warmer than the hallway, but they both also knew that he was looking forward to showing off the tree that he had helped decorate.

The living room and dining room were usually kept separate to keep the heat in the one where they sat, but today, as with all extra-special days, the connecting doors had been folded back and the splendour of their Christmas table – with its creamy white candles circled at the bottom with holly their father had bought from the market the day before, and the crystal jug, given to them by a grateful client – was on display.

'It's splendid,' Francis said, looking, Florence decided, suitably impressed.

Their parents beamed. 'It was a joint effort between Margaret, Amy and Florence,' he said proudly. 'You girls have done an excellent job here. I know we're all going to have a perfect day.'

'Willie is here now.' Their mother's face lit up as announced her son's arrival.

Florence saw her father visibly relax. Her mother would be happy now that she had the entire brood around her.

'Margaret, I know that one day you will have grandchildren to join us for Christmas meals, but we still have to wait a while yet, it seems.' He turned to the rest of them. They knew he was teasing but was also trying to reassure their mother. 'Now, I suggest we all take our places at the table. There's fresh orange juice and a jug of lemonade for us all. Girls,' he said, addressing Amy and Florence, 'please help your mother in the kitchen with the final preparations for our lunch.'

Lunch, as expected, was delicious. After Grace was led by their father, he carved the goose and everyone was served. Francis kept them amused with memories and anecdotes of when he was an apprentice shipwright. Florence had thought the work sounded hard and difficult for a boy. Adelaide then shared stories about her teaching. Some Florence had heard before, several times, but were still amusing in the way that Adelaide portrayed them.

There was a lull in the conversation and her mother seemed to notice Florence's brooch for the first time.

'Is that from Mr Boot?' she asked, her lips pursed as she waited for Florence to answer.

The relaxed atmosphere shifted slightly, and Florence had to concentrate on keeping her voice light as she answered. 'Yes, isn't it beautiful?'

Adelaide leant forward to inspect it. 'It's delightful.'

'He's quite a romantic on the quiet, I think,' Amy whispered, but not quietly enough for her mother to miss.

'That's enough of that language,' their mother snapped, placing her fork onto her plate. 'How dare you refer to such things at the dinner table?'

Everyone kept silent, not wishing to be the next person to receive their mother's wrath. Eventually their father said, 'Dearest, I don't think Amy intended to upset you. If you think about it, the gift is very much a gesture of romance. And should we be surprised? Truly?'

Florence watched her mother pick up her fork, chewing slowly as she considered her husband's questions. No one moved. Everyone waited for her to speak.

Florence noticed Adelaide glance at her husband and fidget slightly in her chair. She could tell her sister was trying to hold back from speaking. Florence knew she couldn't do it for long and, to avoid the day deteriorating into an argumentative disaster, she willed her mother to hurry up and speak.

Adelaide got there first. 'I sense you have an issue with Florence being married to Mr Boot,' she said, fully aware that was the case as Amy had confided in Florence that she had spoken to their older sister about it some weeks before.

When their mother didn't answer, Adelaide took her husband's hand in her own and said, 'If it is because of Mr Boot being what, fifteen years older than Florence . . .'

'It's twelve,' Florence heard herself saying.

'Twelve then. If it is because of that, then surely knowing that Francis and I have been happily married these past five years, should put your mind at ease. Don't you think, Mother?'

Florence tensed. She knew her sister had her best interests at heart, but was also aware that their mother was not one to change her mind once it had been made up. Their mother's gaze moved slowly from her plate to Frances and then finally rested on Adelaide.

'If you believe that I am insulting your marriage to your husband by way of my refusal to allow Florence to marry Mr Boot, then you are mistaken. I am perfectly aware that your marriage has been a success as far as the pair of you are concerned.'

'Then I don't understand what reasons you could have against Florence being married to a man a few years older than her?'

'Neither do I,' Willie said. 'I didn't get to meet him, but he sounds very pleasant.'

'It is not something I wish to discuss. Florence is aware of my concerns and I believe that is all that matters.' She looked at Francis, who had pulled his hand from Adelaide's and was reaching for his glass of lemonade. 'I do not mean to cause offence to you, Francis.'

'None taken.'

'Now,' she said, picking up her cutlery once again, 'I think we should continue with our meal.'

'Yes,' their father said, before anyone else had a second to react. 'It is Christmas Day and we should be grateful for this feast in front of us. Very grateful indeed.'

Florence waited for the conversation to begin again, this time with Amy sharing anecdotes about some of their snobbier customers, like Mrs Wolstenholm. 'She must be a tyrant to work for,' she giggled. 'I noticed she was accompanied by yet another maid last week. You would think she'd realise that if she was only a little nicer to her servants that maybe they wouldn't keep leaving her.'

'Maybe she's firing them,' their father suggested. 'Had you thought of that?'

Amy paused. 'No, it hadn't occurred to me.'

Florence took the opportunity of her parent's attention being kept by Amy's stories to give Adelaide a grateful smile. She knew her sister was frustrated by their parents' resistance to her being with Jesse, and, even though her attempt to change her mother's mind hadn't been remotely successful, it was comforting to know that both her sisters were on her side over this matter.

She decided that when she next wrote to Jesse she would leave this conversation out of her description of their day's celebrations. It would only concern him and that was the last thing she wanted to do.

She struggled to remain cheerful and not drift off into a daydream where she and Jesse were sitting, hand in hand in front of a roaring fire. What was he doing right now? she wondered as Amy chatted to their mother about the deliciousness of the goose.

She pictured his handsome face as he smiled at her. Was he thinking about her now, too?

'Florence.' Her father's voice snapped her out of her reverie.

'She's away with the fairies,' her mother teased. 'Florence, dear. Do try to eat something. I've spent hours preparing this meal and I'd rather you ate it while it was hot.'

'Sorry, Mother,' she replied, embarrassed to have been caught daydreaming about Jesse. She took a mouthful of the crispy roast potatoes her mother always insisted tasted best cooked in the goose fat that had drained from the bird she was cooking. 'It really is delicious,' she said honestly. 'Even more so this year than usual.'

Her mother beamed at her. 'I'm glad you think so.'

'She's right, Margaret. Don't you think so girls?' he asked, addressing Adelaide and Amy.

They both nodded enthusiastically. 'Heavenly,' Adelaide said. She ate a mouthful of food and then turned her attention to Florence and Amy. 'That young girl I saw you speaking to earlier at chapel. She's the one who's been working at the shop with you for the past few weeks, isn't she?'

'Yes,' Amy agreed. 'She's very good, too.'

'I'm sure she is.' Adelaide grinned at their father. 'I can't imagine Father employing someone who wasn't. Do you intend keeping her on after Christmas?'

'Yes, why?' Their father frowned. Florence knew he hated having his authority questioned. She also knew that they hadn't discussed how long Lily was to work for at Rowe's. Did her father realise that she was hoping for Lily to be there long enough to take over from her when she left to marry Jesse?

For the first time it dawned on her that he had probably seen through her plan all along. Florence's eyes locked with her father's and without him saying anything, she realised that he hadn't been fooled for a moment.

'She is a very good worker and I will employ her at Rowe's for as long as I choose,' he said simply. 'How long that will be, I haven't as yet decided.'

Had Florence imagined it, or did he just give her the faintest hint of a smile?

She glanced at her mother, happy with most of her brood sitting around the table eating their sumptuous meal, and couldn't help picturing her own home next year with her sitting at one end of a shiny mahogany table eyes locked with Jesse's sitting opposite her. And she could invite her parents to stay with them, she decided.

Her mother could have a break from cooking Christmas lunch and have it cooked for her. Florence wasn't sure if her mother would appreciate the thought or resent it. After all she had been cooking this meal for her family for over two decades now. Now wasn't the time to suggest it, but Florence thought that it was something for her to mull over closer to the time. Their mother finally finished eating her pudding and the three sisters cleared away the plates, washing them up while their parents and Francis moved into the living room and settled down ready for the present opening to begin.

That night as Florence lay in bed, she thought over the

day's events. All in all, she considered it to have been a successful one, with the only awkward moment being when Adelaide had questioned their mother about Jesse's age and her unwillingness for their father to agree to them being married straight away.

She closed her eyes, trying to picture how her life would be one year from now. She didn't really mind how it was, as long as she was spending it with Jesse.

Chapter 27

16–20 Goose Gate
Nottingham
3 January 1886

Miss Florence Rowe
27 Queen Street
St Helier
Jersey

*D*earest *Florence,*
    Happy New Year to you and your family.

I hadn't received three of your letters and then they were delivered on the same day. I believe it was an issue with one of the postmen, but I'm not certain what happened exactly. I was glad to hear that you had a joyful Christmas. Mine was pleasant enough, and Jane and I spent much of Christmas Day discussing you and how much I'm looking forward to bringing you home to Nottingham and intro- ducing you to everyone here.

Jane is impatiently awaiting your arrival and is certain

that you will settle in well in Nottingham and feel at home in no time. I sincerely hope that she's right. Nottingham is wonderful, to me, but I worry that you will miss your pretty island and all that you know there, the charming lanes with their French names and the delicious milk and potatoes that I became so fond of during my visits. I will do my level best to see that you want for nothing when you are finally living here, but still I can't help worrying.

I was relieved to read that your father is pleased with Lily Buttons and how she's getting on at the shop. It must have been a surprise to see her and meet her family at chapel on Christmas Day, too. I know how much you fret about the poor girl. It really is too cruel to see how difficult some people's lives are. You are such a compassionate woman, Florence. You think of others continually, but rather than just think of them, you do something about helping make their lives a little easier and it only serves to make me love you more.

It has started snowing again here and I have two meetings that I need to attend after breakfast today. I hope the snow ceases soon and that it doesn't cause issues with travelling.

I have just noticed the time and must sign off if I want this letter to catch today's post before I leave.

My dear, I think of you always and trust you to take the very best care of the person I love most in the world.

As always, your,

Jesse

It was cold and the pavements icy in Jersey, too, and Florence wrapped up well to go out to take leftover mince pies, nuts and fruit to Adelaide and Francis. The pair of them had been suffering from colds since Boxing Day and their mother had wanted to help them in some small way. Nervous that she had to go out in such dire weather, and risk the chance of slipping and hurting herself, Florence had offered to go instead.

She pinned her hat to her hair and wrapped the thick scarf and gloves her mother had made her for Christmas, grateful to have them as soon as she stepped out of the door.

That morning even their kitchen windows had ice on the insides, and, being someone who favoured the spring and autumn season, Florence was already tired of the cold and damp.

'Be careful out there,' her father said as she left. 'Try not to be too long; Lily Buttons starts today at eight this morning.'

'Yes, Father,' she said, raising the scarf slightly at the back of her neck to keep it as covered as possible. 'I'm just dropping this basket of food to Adelaide. Mother was going to go, but it's terribly slippery out there and I didn't think she should go.'

'Right, of course. Well done.'

She heard him mumble something to himself that sounded remarkably like wishing her mother could wait until the end of the working day to be delivering food to her sister, but set off. Adelaide didn't live far away and Florence wanted to be back at the shop to welcome Lily. Lily tried to give off an air of someone confident and capable, but it didn't work nearly as well as she probably hoped.

Her foot skidded on some ice as she rushed around the

corner and for a split second she expected to fall, relieved when someone grabbed hold of her and helped ensure she didn't completely lose her footing.

She smoothed down her coat and went to thank the person, only to see it was the postman she had told off several weeks before when he had been rude to Lily.

'Thank you,' she said, clearing her throat. 'I'm relieved you were here and have such quick reactions.'

'It was my pleasure, Miss Rowe.' Realising what he had said, the man's face reddened. 'That is to say . . .'

She couldn't bear to witness the poor man stumbling around his words. 'Please, it's no matter, but I am grateful. Thank you.' She indicated her basket of goodies, surprised to note that none of them had spilled out. 'I must be getting on my way, so that I can be back in the shop before opening time.'

'Of course. Bye, Miss Rowe.'

'Goodbye.'

She would have to take more care, she decided, as she walked slowly. She wouldn't be any use to her father if she did fall and break an ankle or a wrist, and, although she would be leaving his employment later in the summer he needed her at the shop working, at least until Lily had been trained up to take her place.

She was shivering by the time she reached Adelaide's cottage. She knocked twice. The sound of her sister coughing inside worried her. She was glad she'd come after all.

The door opened and Adelaide's husband welcomed her inside.

'Quick, come in before you let in all the cold,' Francis said, sniffing. 'It's perishing out there and I wish I didn't have to go out to work.'

'But you do,' Adelaide teased, coming to join them from the scullery. The inglenook fireplace held a small stove on which their maid Abigail was stirring a pot of food.

'Would you like to join us for a bowl of porridge?' she asked, noticing for the first time that Florence was carrying a basket.

'No, thank you,' Florence said. 'I've only popped by to deliver these. Mother thought you might want them.'

She handed the basket to Abigail, who placed it cheerfully on the worn kitchen table. 'What have we here?' she said happily, stopping to pull a handkerchief from her sleeve and blowing her nose several times.

'Should you not be in bed?' Florence asked, frowning.

'No, I've been in bed for the past few days and I'm feeling much better now. Anyway, I have chores to do.'

Knowing that her sister, like their mother, was not one to be persuaded to do something she didn't want to do, Florence didn't argue.

Adelaide took out the first packet and unfolding the top peaked inside. 'Nuts, thank you.'

'There's some fruit and half a dozen mince pies that Mother cooked yesterday. We won't eat it all and she felt sure that you would enjoy the rest. There are a few other bits in there too.'

'We'll enjoy all of this,' Adelaide said, wiping her nose again.

'I'd better get back. There's someone new starting work at the shop this morning and I want to be there to greet her.'

'Please thank Mother for us?' Adelaide said. 'And thanks to you, too. It was kind of you to come out on such a bitter day.'

'I wanted to see if you were any better than the last time I saw you,' Florence said, relieved to see that she was.

'Yes, thanks,' Francis said, taking one of the nuts from the packet and reaching for a metal nutcracker Florence recognised as being an old one of her mother's.

'I was surprised to hear Father extolling Lily Buttons' virtues and how well she's doing in the shop,' Adelaide whispered. 'I'm pleased that she works so hard and is proving your suggestion that she work there right.'

'She is a fast learner,' Florence said, certain she could confide in her sister and that Adelaide would never mention anything about it to Lily should she ever bump into her at the shop. She explained about Lily's circumstances and that she was trying to help her in some small way.

'I think that's very generous of you, Florence.' Adelaide smiled at her. 'I'm not surprised though. You've always felt the need to help the underdog. You've always been extremely thoughtful and kind. Well done. I hope this girl is worthy of your trust and good nature.'

Florence didn't like to think of Lily being described as an underdog. She was a dear girl who could make something of herself if only she was given the chance to do so.

'Thank you,' she said simply. 'Now, I really must get back.'

'Please tell Mother I'll return her basket later today, or maybe tomorrow morning.'

'Yes, all right,' Florence said, aware that the time was

passing, and she needed to get going. 'She said not to rush it back to her if the weather doesn't improve.'

She kissed her sister on her upturned cheek and braced herself for the cold as she stepped outside. Her sister shouted a goodbye and quickly closed the front door. Florence didn't blame her; it was freezing.

She made her way carefully, watching every step. Several minutes later she arrived back at the shop. She stamped her feet outside the door to remove any ice, and stepped inside.

'It's freezing out there,' she said, unwinding the long scarf from around her neck and pulling off her gloves, pushing them into her coat pocket. 'I almost fell just past that corner,' she said, unbuttoning her coat and hanging it, along with her scarf, onto the wooden coat stand to the left of the entrance. Unpinning her hat, she did the same.

'Did you fall?' Amy asked, looking concerned.

'No, thankfully. That postman that I had a go at about Lily not so long ago saved me.' She rubbed her hands together, hoping the friction would warm them and went to stand behind the counter.

'He did?'

'Yes. One minute I was slipping and the next he had grabbed hold of me and placed me firmly on my feet again. I don't mind telling you I was very relieved he was there.'

Amy gave her a knowing look. 'I presume you were hurrying, as usual.'

'I have to admit I was. It's so cold out there, I wanted to get back here.' She rubbed her hands together to warm them up. 'Adelaide was asking about Lily. She told me Father has been saying how happy he is with Lily's work and how she's fitting in at the shop. It was good to hear.'

'I can imagine,' Amy said, smiling. 'I'm pleased her working here is going well.'

Florence spent the next few days in anxious anticipation. News had broken of the collapse of the Jersey Banking Company where many of hers and her father's friends banked.

'What is to become of their businesses,' her father said mid-morning when he returned from meeting an acquaintance in the next-door tea shop.

'Is W. H. Rowe safe, Father?' Florence asked nervously.

'Yes, thankfully,' he said, wringing his hands. 'I did bank there for many years but moved my money only last year. I keep imagining what would happen to us if I hadn't done so.'

She didn't like to think of the consequences and that night wrote to Jesse about the situation.

27 Queen Street
St Helier
Jersey
12 January 1886

Mr J Boot
16–20 Goose Gate
Nottingham

Dearest Jesse,
The most dreadful thing has happened on our island. The

Jersey Banking Company, where so many people we know have kept their savings, has collapsed. There is talk of a court case and many rumours are circulating, but all I can think of are the people who've worked hard and saved hard and who have now lost everything. It's all too distressing.

Thankfully, Father's money is safe, for now. I, too, have savings but they are in a different bank, and for that I'm grateful. To think of the families who have now lost everything is heartbreaking. It only goes to show that you cannot be too careful about the wealth that you do have.

I'm sorry to write with such sad news, but I needed to share my thoughts with someone and didn't like to speak of it with Father, because any mention sends his mood into a downward spiral. How our lives can change in a moment; the thought terrifies me, but I know that I must push all negative thoughts aside, and instead find a way to help these people when they need our help most.

Sending you my love,
As always, your dearest,
Florence

Florence felt much better having shared her thoughts with Jesse. Her family were lucky not to have been immediately affected by the economic tragedy and for that she was grateful. Now, though, she needed to listen out for any families who were in dire straits and to find ways to help them, with food parcels, or anything else she might be able to offer.

* * *

Two days later she received Jesse's reply.

16–20 Goose Gate
Nottingham
16 January 1886

Miss Florence Rowe
27 Queen Street
St Helier
Jersey

Dearest love,

I am dreadfully sorry to hear of the shocking situation on your island and if there is anything you feel I can do to assist you in helping your friends, please do let me know.

You are right in saying that life is precarious and that is why I am grateful every day for all that I have. It is also why I cannot wait to be able to begin our life together and make the most of whatever time we are blessed enough to enjoy.

You are good and kind, and I know you will help your friends now that they need you the most. Please do take care and look after yourself. You are, to me, the most precious jewel and I need to know that you are above all other things, safe and well.

My love to you,
As always,
Jesse

Chapter 28

Florence was busy serving a customer, so didn't take any notice when the postman delivered the mail that morning. She was glad it was Friday and looked forward to seeing Lily the following day to discover how her week had been. It would be her sixth week working for Rowe's, and even Florence's father had to admit that she was a hard-working and conscientious employee. It was a relief to Florence, and no doubt to Lily too, to see how happy he had been with her work.

She took the money from the gentleman and wrapped the leather-bound notebook he had just purchased, handing it to him and bidding him a good day. As soon as the front door closed behind him, Amy came up to her and handed her an envelope with Jesse's writing on it.

'It feels like a card,' Amy teased. 'Are you going to open it now, or wait until Sunday?'

'Sunday?'

'Valentine's Day. It's in two days. Did you not think to send him one?'

'No,' she admitted. She had considered doing so, of course,

but wasn't entirely sure that Jesse would go with that sort of thing. He was more romantic than she had ever initially expected he would be but she wasn't certain if Valentine cards might be just that bit too frivolous for him. She studied the envelope in her hand, turning it over and then back again.

'Why not?' Amy said, pursing her lips and teasing her.

She didn't like to admit her true reasons, feeling like it might make her seem as if she didn't know Jesse as well as she hoped others would think. 'I meant to, but have been so tied up with the shop and training Lily that it must have slipped my mind.'

Florence knew that her sister wouldn't believe that for a moment. She rarely forgot things, especially not something as important as a token of love for Jesse. However, Amy said nothing.

'Watch the shop for a moment, will you?' she asked, hurrying to the back of the shop and into the storeroom.

Once alone, she carefully opened the envelope and withdrew the dainty, lace-patterned card with two love birds each with one side of a heart in their beaks. The cover simply read, *To my Valentine.* Florence opened the card to see, *To Florence, my perfect Valentine, my love. J*

She pushed the card back into the envelope and into her pocket and went back to speak to Amy, grateful that their father was out meeting a friend.

'Do you think if I post one now that it will reach Jesse in time?'

'You can but try. Look, we have some over there.'

Florence had seen the ones they had in stock. Some were very pretty, but it had felt odd sending one from Rowe's, especially if her father had known that she had done so. However, he was out and had no way of knowing that she had been the one to purchase a particular card, not if she did it right now, before his return.

'I won't be long,' she said, going over to the display of cards and working through the ones she liked best until she fell upon one that she thought most suited Jesse. It was a puppy holding a heart in his mouth saying the words, *Valentine Greeting*. She opened it and fetching her fountain pen from behind the counter, quickly wrote inside, *Jesse, my one and only Valentine. Sending my love to you, F*

She hurriedly wrote his address on the envelope. 'I'll be as quick as I can,' she said, as she pinned on her hat and pulled on her coat and scarf, hoping to catch the post that would take this card with her love to Jesse.

Fifteen minutes later she was back at the shop, blowing on her cold hands. 'I made it,' she said to Amy glancing around to shop relieved to find her father had still not come back. 'Shall I make us some tea?'

'Good idea.'

The following week she received a letter from Jesse.

> *16–20 Goose Gate*
> *Nottingham*
> *15 February 1886*

Miss Florence Boot
27 Queen Street
St Helier
Jersey

My dearest Florence,

Thank you for my touching Valentine card. I have to admit that the one I sent to you was the first one I have ever bought. Up until meeting you it had never occurred to me to take part in this romantic occasion. I had thought it an occasion for young people only. However, now I find myself of a different mindset and this, my love, is entirely down to you.

The days and weeks are passing slowly, but very surely, and soon our time will come when we can be together and in charge of our own destinies.

My love, As ever,
Jesse

Florence could sense his delight at the card she had hurriedly sent to him and was relieved that she had given into her instincts and finally sent him the Valentine card. How guilty she would have felt not do have done so, especially when he took the time to choose such a perfect card for her.

After supper she retired to her room to reply to his brief letter with one of her own.

Mrs Boots

27 Queen Street
St Helier
Jersey
19 February 1886

Mr J Boot
16–20 Goose Gate
Nottingham

Dearest Jesse,

    I am delighted that you liked my Valentine card to you. To be honest, I wasn't certain that you would appreciate a card, but am now happy that I thought to send one to you. I was thrilled with mine and once the time is right and I need to take it down from my bedroom mantelpiece, I'll place it together with your other letters in my wooden writing slope.

    The time is certainly passing, not as quickly as I would like, but soon it will be spring and then summer.

    It'll soon be time to harvest the delicious Jersey Royal potatoes that you mentioned during your stay here last summer. My brother Willie assures me that he will buy a batch of the tastiest ones to be found on the island, so that I may post them over to you in Nottingham. They taste buttery without the addition of any butter and I look forward to hearing from you, once you have sampled the batch that I will send to you, for your thoughts.

    My love to you,
    As ever,
    Florence

Chapter 29

'I've bought you that batch of Jersey Royals,' Florence's brother Willie shouted as he strode up the hall stairs one afternoon in early April. 'I'm assured that they're the very best on the island, but all the farmers say that about their spuds.'

'Thanks for fetching these for me,' she said, taking the box of potatoes from him. 'I can't wait for Jesse to receive them and have them for supper. I'll send a note with strict instructions not to add mint, or butter. I believe they must be eaten with as little added to them as possible.'

'I agree,' Willie said. 'You can't improve on perfection, so why try.'

Florence laughed. Her brother was right. She was yet to eat a creamier, tastier vegetable than the Jersey Royals her island was so famous for. A thought came to her.

'Do you think it would be a nice touch to include Jersey Royals in our wedding breakfast menu?' she wondered out loud.

Her brother screwed up his face as he thought through her idea. 'I don't see why not. In fact, I think it would be odd if you didn't. You should take the opportunity of having your first meal together as husband and wife to introduce local delicacies.'

'Like Jersey cream, butter and milk, you mean?' she asked, liking the idea very much.

'Exactly.'

She noticed the time on the mantel clock and gasped. 'Do you think I have time to take them to the post office before it closes?'

He shrugged. 'Maybe. If you do manage it, they might get them to the harbour in time for tonight's boat. It's worth a try.'

It was. She quickly pulled on her jacket and, grabbing her purse, picked up the box and hurried down to the post office, making it with minutes to spare.

She had to wait several days for a letter back from Jesse regarding her gift to him.

16–20 Goose Gate
Nottingham
9th April 1886

Miss Florence Rowe
27 Queen Street
St Helier
Jersey

Dearest,

I have not only received your delightful food parcel, but after giving Cook your strict instructions about how to prepare them, have eaten a sumptuous meal with them as the only added vegetable. I have to admit that I am unable to imagine ever tasting any other potato that would come up to the taste of those that you have sent me.

Initially Cook was unimpressed to be given advice on how to prepare the meal, but, having insisted she try one and receiving her assurance that she now has a new favourite potato, she has confirmed that you were right to send them with your note.

Once you are living here, I believe that Cook will want to impress you with her knowledge on specialities of her own making. It is not often that someone is able to teach her something new about cooking or baking. I think she found the whole experience quite refreshing.

Thank you again. You were right; the Jersey Royal potatoes were delicious.

My love, as ever,
Jesse

Florence was thrilled to have made such an impression on Jesse's cook and relieved that the woman had not been insulted in any way by her instructions for the Jersey Royals. Knowing how particular her own mother was about the produce she bought and how she prepared it and also how upset she could be if anyone was to question anything that she had prepared for them, Florence had been a little concerned that she might upset one of the people she would have to deal with once she married Jesse.

Thinking of her mother and cooking, it occurred to Florence that maybe if she included her mother in some of her wedding plans that maybe she might soften towards Jesse and the thought of him being her husband.

That night, when her mother was boiling a pan of milk to make them all a cup of cocoa, Florence went to join her in the kitchen.

'Let me get those for you,' she said, seeing her mother about to reach for four cups and saucers from the wooden rack and hooks on the wall beside her. She took the tin of cocoa from the small larder and spooned in some of the powder into each of the cups.

Her mother continued to stir the warm milk with her wooden spoon. She narrowed her eyes at Florence. 'Is there something you wanted to speak to me about? Is something wrong?'

'Yes and no.' Florence smiled, trying to lighten the atmosphere in the kitchen. Her mother was wary; she could see that much. She doubted she had come around to accepting Jesse as her husband, but Florence was going to try and make things between her mother and her future husband as amicable as possible. 'I wanted to ask your advice about my wedding breakfast menu. Do you mind?'

Her mother blinked rapidly a few times and Florence could see that her mother was taken aback by her question. She forgot to stir for a moment.

'I would be very happy to help you. I've been waiting for you to ask me.'

Florence couldn't hide her surprise. 'You have? Even though you are against me marrying Jesse?'

Her mother lifted the pan from the heat and stirring slowly, she poured an even amount into each cup. She placed the pan into the sink and sighed.

'I don't have anything against Mr Boot as a person. I've discovered more about him in the past few months and, apart from being a hard-working man, he seems loyal and thoughtful to his staff. It's you that I worry for, but we've had this conversation several times now.'

'We have,' Florence agreed, wishing the outcome of the conversation changed.

'You might think me strange, but I've made my decision and I stick by it. However, if you insist on going through with the wedding, then I would like to ensure that everything is perfectly arranged for you.'

'Thank you.' Florence wished her mother would change her mind, but knew better than to rely on it happening. She was a proud woman who, when she decided something, felt the need, more often than not, to stick to her decision. However, if she had softened towards the wedding to the point of helping arrange certain areas that was very welcome to Florence.

'What were you thinking of including?' Her mother wiped a drop of spilt milk with a damp cloth.

Florence told her mother about wanting to include Jersey Royals, butter, cream and milk. 'I thought it was a good way of bringing Jersey into my first meal as a married woman.'

'I like that idea.' Her mother rested a hand on Florence's. 'I'll make your wedding cake, if you wish.'

This was far more than Florence had dared hope her mother might do. 'That would be incredible,' she said, hugging her mother. 'Thank you.'

They parted and Florence didn't care that she still had a grin on her face.

Her mother stared at her momentarily. 'I know that you can cook certain meals and assume that Mr Boot has his own cook?'

'He does.'

'Pass me a tray,' her mother said, lifting each cup and saucer and placing them on to the tray Florence now held. 'I will go through a few more recipes with you before your wedding,' she said. 'Now, let's take these cups of cocoa through to your father and sister before they cool.'

Florence carried the tray out to the living room where her sister and father were chatting quietly. Both stopped the instant Florence and her mother walked in and she couldn't help thinking that they had been swapping guesses as to what she and her mother had been discussing in the kitchen.

'Cocoa's ready,' she said, giving her sister a knowing smile.

Chapter 30

Florence was relieved to be putting on a lighter jacket for her walk to walk to the post office. She couldn't believe it was already nearing the end of May. Jesse's thirty-sixth birthday was on the second of June and she had no idea what to buy him. She thought back to his most recent letter to her, which she had received the previous day.

16–20 Goose Gate
Nottingham
19 May 1886

Miss Florence Rowe
27 Queen Street
St Helier
Jersey

Dearest Florence,

You are as thoughtful as ever thinking about my birthday. However, and I mean this, I do not wish for you to fret about what to buy me. I am scolded each Christmas and birthday *by Jane about how impossible I am to buy gifts for. She tells me that I need to read more widely, then she could buy me a book. She also admonishes me, telling me that in the months preceding Christmas or my birthday that should I discover a book, or item that I wish to purchase, I am not to. I am instead, she insists, to write down whatever it is and pass it to her, so that when the time comes she will know what gift to purchase for me. I am yet to do as she asks.*

So, my dearest love, I am well aware how difficult the act of buying gifts for me is and, to be perfectly honest, the only thing that I truly wish for in this world is for you to be my wife. Hopefully I only have to wait for another couple of months for this to happen. Until then, please, do not worry to buy me anything. A card, if you wish, from you will be a delight.

As always, your loving,
Jesse

Florence could not let the occasion of his birthday pass without her sending him something to commemorate the occasion. She was still, however, at a loss as to what that gift should be. She had found the perfect birthday card, so that was something at least.

The months had passed slowly, she mused, as she picked up her bag from the table in her bedroom and checked it contained her change purse. At least now the weather was warm.

She was lost in thought, imagining the summer months that would soon be here and Jesse's arrival, when she walked out of her bedroom and slammed into her mother coming along the hallway.

'For pity's sake, Florence,' her mother cried, grabbing hold of the doorframe to steady herself. 'Why don't you look where you are going? You always seem to have your mind elsewhere these days.'

Florence apologised, noticing the letter she had been holding in her hand had fallen and landed on the wooden floorboards at her feet. She had been posting letters to Jesse as quietly as possible, not wishing to antagonise her mother.

Her mother glanced down seconds later, her expression darkening.

'I know you think I was being unkind about Mr Boot and not wishing you to marry him?'

Florence wasn't sure if her mother was asking a question or merely making a statement. 'I understand that we all see people differently.' She bent to pick up the envelope and took a deep breath to steady her temper as she stood back up to face her mother.

'I'm sure you know that I don't dislike him, Florence,' she insisted, looking hurt. 'You are my priority, as is your happiness, and I had to do what I believed right for you.'

'I know, Mother,' she said, feeling guilty for snapping. 'Sorry, I didn't mean to be mean. But I assumed that when you agreed to help with my wedding breakfast and make the cake for the occasion that you had changed your mind, almost.'

'I want you to be happy, but I haven't changed my mind about the wedding itself.' She appeared to be as sad as Florence suspected she felt. 'You're still writing to each other,' her mother said thoughtfully, almost to herself. 'And we've discussed your wedding breakfast. I'm aware you still intend to marry him this summer.'

Florence was confused by her mother's words. Then it occurred to her for the first time that her mother still held out a little hope that she and Jesse would grow tired of each other and cease their correspondence and with it their plans to marry. The realisation shocked her.

'I do and I would love you to feel happy for me.'

'I would love nothing more than that and for my reservations to be proved wrong. 'Don't forget though,' her mother said quietly, 'he still needs to ask your father's permission for your hand.'

Panic coursed through Florence. She wished her father was there with them right now. She would ask him to reassure her that he would not go back on his word. Could he ever be persuaded to? she wondered nervously. Her mother had, after all, persuaded him to retract his approval of she and Jesse marrying the previous year. Surely though, he would stand by his compromise that should they still wish to do so after these long months of keeping apart, he would grant them permission to marry. Wouldn't he?

'I trust Father to do as he promised,' she said more assuredly than she felt. 'Now, if you are all right after our collision, I need to hurry to the post office and mail this letter to Mr Boot.'

Florence waited for her mother to move. Eventually she went to leave, stopping before she entered the next room, and turned to Florence.

'You can stop off at John Cory's on Snow Hill on your way home and bring half a dozen of his best pork sausages,' she said, as if their conversation about Jesse had never happened, before continuing on her way into the living room.

'Yes, Mother,' Florence called before leaving the flat.

She wasn't sure if it was her imagination, but the people she passed in the streets seemed much more cheerful than they did during the winter. Florence stopped to chat to several people and for a while she almost forgot how strained her relationship was becoming with her mother.

As she exited the post office, she crossed the road to walk a little way along Bond Street, deciding that on such a lovely day, she would walk through the Town Church and admire the flowers. As she reached the metal railings, she saw a young girl selling bunches of daffodils and decided to buy some for her mother, her sister Amy and for her own bedroom. They were the perfect pick-me-up, and might go some way to cheer up her mother, she thought hopefully.

'Three bunches, please,' she said to the young girl whose face immediately brightened at the thought of a sale. 'How much are they?' The girl told her and, taking her change purse from her handbag, Florence took out a few coins and handed them to her. 'Thank you,' she said smiling. 'These are delightful.'

'They remind me of sunshine,' said the little girl, who, Florence thought, could not be much older than ten. For a split second she wanted to ask her why she was not at school, then, thinking how difficult it was for Lily to care for her family, decided to mind her business.

She held up the bunches and studied them. They were the brightest yellows. 'They remind me of that, too,' Florence said, wistfully. 'Goodbye.'

She stepped up through the open gate and into the church yard. Despite this being in the middle of several roads, she always found this place to be more peaceful than most other places in town. She desperately tried to think of a suitable gift for Jesse as she walked slowly around the side of the granite church to the lawn. She gazed at the flowerbeds with their primulas and primroses giving a colourful creamy yellow, purple and pink display, the sight cheering her slightly.

She stared at the delightful display as two women walked nearby in conversation.

'He was very good, I thought,' the older woman said. 'Your father's family will be very happy with the cartes de visite when we send it to them.'

The younger woman laughed. 'Father only had the photograph done to show off to them.'

'Hush now. You shouldn't say such things.'

'Well, it's true. He's always wanting them to know how well he's doing since we all came to live on the island.'

A photograph. Florence had to hold back from laughing. It was the perfect gift to send Jesse for his birthday. He had said he didn't want a present; well, this was not one, exactly. She walked up to the two women.

'Excuse me for interrupting your conversation,' she said, 'but I heard you mention a cartes de visite. Would you mind telling me which establishment you chose to attend to have it done?'

She thought the mother seemed a little embarrassed that she'd overheard their conversation, but the younger one, who Florence now assumed to be the daughter, nodded. 'We went to T. Price and Son at number two Peter Street,' she said. 'Mr Price was ever so accommodating, as was his son.' She smiled. 'There are so many studios to choose from now, but it's difficult to know which is the best one to use.'

'It is,' Florence agreed. She thanked them for their assistance and walked on, thrilled at the prospect of now knowing what she would do for Jesse's birthday.

Recalling the pork sausages that her mother wanted her to buy, she set off out of the opposite gate and onto La Rue Trousse Cotillons, turning right for a little way until she reached Mulcaster Street and then left past the back of the Judicial Greffe towards Snow Hill. She was looking forward to the new library opening later; then it dawned on her that by then she would be a married woman and living in Nottingham. The thought made her smile.

Mr Price was very helpful and booked her in later that afternoon for her studio session. She had enough time to go back to the flat and hand the sausages to her mother, before quickly changing into her favourite summer dress and hat, and hurrying back to Peter Street to have her photograph taken.

Afterwards, she held the photograph lightly in her hands, surprised at how impressed she was by her own reflection. She had stood next to a table, her right hand resting lightly on the dark wood as she stared straight at the camera. Mr Price had asked her to gaze into the distance, but Florence had wanted it to seem as if she was staring straight into Jesse's eyes when he gazed at her photograph. She was delighted with the result.

She addressed an envelope and inserted the photograph into it. Then taking a piece of her writing paper, wrote a note to accompany her gift.

27 Queen Street
St Helier
Jersey
25 May 1886

Mr J Boot
16–20 Goose Gate
Nottingham

Dearest Jesse,

I hope you are pleased with my small but personal birthday gift for you. I wanted to give you something that you could not buy for yourself, so thought of arranging for a portrait photograph to be taken of me, gazing into your eyes, albeit from a distance.

Imagine when you look at my image that I am thinking of you, thinking of being with you and sending you all my love.

One day soon there will be no further need for you to look at my face in a photograph and I cannot wait for that day to come. Until then though, this photograph of me will have to suffice and I hope you like it.

My love, as ever,
Florence

* * *

The following week, she received the letter from Jesse that she had been waiting for.

16–20 Goose Gate
Nottingham
2 June 1886

Miss Florence Rowe
27 Queen Street
St Helier
Jersey

Sweetest and most thoughtful Florence,

You are too clever. I could not have asked for a better present from you and your portrait has now been framed and has pride of place on my desk. I adore being able to look into your eyes whenever I choose. In the few months since last I saw you, you have grown into a more beautiful woman than even you were before. I am so excited that soon I will be able to call you my wife.

Your portrait makes me smile and reminds me daily of all that happiness that we have to look forward to in our future together. You watch over me from my desk now and I feel closer to you than ever before. I can never feel lonely now I have this picture to remind me of the love we share and that very soon we will constantly be together. I can hardly wait.

I am beginning to realise that it doesn't matter what I say, you will do as you see fit in any situation. This time,

313

I am most grateful for your determination to do as you wish and, as I mentioned, was overwhelmed with delight at receiving the splendid photograph of you.

I can't believe that I had not thought to ask for a photograph of you before now and feel remiss that I have not had one taken of myself to send to you. I have arranged for a studio sitting in two days' time so that I may rectify this omission.

Well, my dearest one, it will not be long now. An hour apart is too long, but the weeks, days and hours tick by and soon, very soon, my love, I will travel back to your jewel of an island and, most delightful of all, to you. I find that I am becoming more impatient with each passing day and long to be married to you.

Until the next time.

My love, as ever,

Jesse

Chapter 31

Finally, it was the day before Jesse's arrival back in Jersey, and Florence could barely think straight. Her mood swung from heightened excitement to nervousness. What if he met her again and decided that she wasn't how he remembered her? What if they had no conversation when they were together again? What if her father didn't stand by his word and grant Jesse permission to marry her? What if Jesse decided not to ask for her hand? So many what ifs.

She could hear Lily chatting to Amy as they walked from the storeroom back to the front of the shop, just as the brass bell above the front door announced someone's arrival.

Florence looked up to see who was entering, a smile already on her face. The man stopped walking, his hand still on the door handle as he stared at her. She heard a gasp behind her and it took a moment for Florence to realise that this scowling person standing in front of her was Lily's father.

After a moment's hesitation, she unscrambled her wits and walked over to him. If he was going to cause trouble for Lily, she would insist on him listening to her first. After all, she had been the one to persuade Lily to come and work at W.

H. Rowe, so if anyone was to be shouted at, it would be her.

'Mr Buttons,' she said, her smile fixed on her face as she went to greet him. 'Please, come in.' The last thing her father would want was trouble on his doorstep where the neighbouring shops and their customers could hear. She was grateful that no other customers were presently in the shop. 'Have you come to see Lily?'

'Dad?' Lily said, her voice timid. 'You're—'

'Yes,' he interrupted, 'they've let me out.'

'Dad, please don't be cross.' Her voice was low, as she hurried to pacify him. 'The Misses Rowe have been very kind to me.'

Florence tensed and could sense Amy doing the same as she came to stand next to her. She wondered if together the two of them could defend Lily should her father have come here to admonish her for working at the shop without his permission or knowledge. Without looking at Amy she knew that her sister was staring at the man and preparing to defend their assistant.

'Mr Buttons,' Florence began, 'Lily . . .'

He took his cap off and held it tightly in his hands, wringing it between them slightly. 'Please, Misses Rowe. I ain't come 'ere to cause trouble for my girl.'

Florence stared at Lily, whose mouth fell open at his unexpected words.

'My wife tells me that you give 'er a job and she's done well.' He looked Lily up and down, taking in her smart appearance, her hair neatly tied in at ribbon that Amy had given her recently. 'She looks right grown up and I'm told she's supported my family when I 'aven't bin 'ere to do so.'

'I only wanted to do something to help, Dad,' Lily said, a quaver in her voice as she spoke.

Florence was sorry to see that Lily's confidence gained over the last few months working at the shop had almost evaporated. How easily her father's presence had diminished the girl and that was when he was being pleasant. She couldn't stand by and not try to boost her in some way.

Florence stepped forward. 'Lily has worked hard and been an asset to the shop,' she said, bracing herself . . . for what, she wasn't sure. 'My father is very pleased with how much she's learnt and how reliable she is. We hope you are happy with her working here. We would hate for her to leave us.'

Florence waited for him to mull over her words. She hated to think of all Lily's hard work and time settling in at W. H. Rowe to go to waste. She also hoped that Mr Buttons would not expect her to leave, especially so near to Jesse's return and her hoped for departure.

'Oh, Miss,' he said, stepping forward so that they were almost toe-to-toe, 'I ain't come to cause no bother. Mrs Buttons told me all about Lily working 'ere and that she would 'ave no trouble caused for her by me.' He shrugged. 'Not that I was goin' to cause trouble.' He turned his head to look at Lily, who was staring at him, her mouth agape. 'I'm proud of my girl. Truly, an' I want her to keep workin' 'ere for as long as she can.'

'You do?' Amy grabbed Florence's arm. 'Why that's wonderful, isn't it, Lily?'

Lily gave a little cry and immediately covered her mouth

with her right hand. Recovering slightly, she finally gave a high-pitched, 'Yes, it is.'

Florence's throat tightened. The relief that Lily's father now knew of her employment with W. H. Rowe and had seen her smart dress, and hadn't minded at all, was massive for her and, she knew, for Lily, too.

'Thank you, Mr Buttons.' She wasn't sure what to say next.

He placed his cap back on his head and went to leave, stopping as soon as he had opened the shop door. 'I'll leave you be. I don't wish to intrude on your day.' He scrutinised Lily for a few seconds. 'I'll see you back 'ome later then.'

'Yes, all right.'

The three women watched him leave and stood in silence as they watched him walk down Queen Street.

'You must be very relieved, Lily, that your father was happy for you to stay working here,' Amy said. 'I know we are.'

'Yes, I am.'

Florence noticed Lily was trembling and realised, not for the first time, how lucky she was not only to have such a reasonable father, but also that Jesse was such a kind man, too. How difficult must it be to live in fear of a man every day of your life?

The following day finally arrived. Florence gazed at herself in her bedroom mirror. She had wanted to look her very best for Jesse's arrival, but three nights with barely any sleep had taken their toll on her skin. She appeared peaky and sallow, and the dark circles under her eyes added nothing to her looks.

'Damn.' She pinched her cheeks to try and give them a bit

of colour, but only succeeded in pinching too hard and looking as if she had hurt herself.

She gazed at the new cotton dress with fine lace cuffs and collar that she had had made specially to wear to greet Jesse and hoped that by the time she had changed into it she might look a little less peaky. She went down to the shop to work, needing to keep her mind busy.

An hour later her father called her over to him. 'I want you to take this message to the minister at chapel. He's expecting it.'

'Can't Amy or Lily go?' She knew how much the minister liked to chat and always found it difficult to find a way to end a conversation with him. The last thing she needed today was to be late back home and not have time to change to go and meet Jesse off the mailboat.

'No. You need something to take your mind off Mr Boot's arrival. You've been fidgety all morning and it's getting a little tiresome for the rest of us.'

Florence doubted her sister or Lily were bothered, but knew how much her father disliked it when she wasn't focused on her work.

'Yes, Father,' she said, taking the note and fetching her hat. 'You will recall that I'll need to leave early today to change before going and meeting Jesse from the mailboat, don't you?'

'How could I possibly forget,' he sighed. 'Now, go.'

She walked out of the shop, stopping to chat briefly to Albert who was standing in the doorway next door, before retracing her steps to the opposite corner where Queen Street met Halkett Place. She turned right and walked hurriedly all the way down to the end before crossing over Burrard Street.

She was stopped at the other side of the road by one of her father's regular customers to answer a question about an order the woman had made and then continued past Grove Place where her family had once lived to the Methodist church where they still worshipped.

The whole time she was thinking about what she would say to Jesse when he first stepped off the boat. She walked up the wide steps and into the left of the two enormous double doors to find the minister waiting for her.

'I'm sorry if I'm late,' she said, disliking it when she wasn't punctual. 'I was stopped on my way by one of father's customers who had a query about an order.'

'No matter,' he said, waving away her concern with his hand. 'You have a message for me?' She nodded and handed him the note. 'Good. Now you must come and take tea with me. I have a few things I wish to discuss with you.'

She had feared this might happen, but hid her concern and tried to look as cheerful as she could manage as she went with him into the vestry.

An hour and a half later, Florence finally left the church and was walking along Grove Place when she observed the tall mast standing over Fort Regent and noticed the signals. Seeing the flags announcing that the mailboat was approaching La Corbière, her heart pounded to know that Jesse's boat would be docking in about one hour. She had to rush home to freshen up and change into her new dress, if she was to arrive at the harbour in a calm manner to await his arrival. She could not bear to be late to see him having waited so many months for the moment to finally arrive.

Chapter 32

Florence hurried down Mulcaster Street, arriving at Victoria Pier with moments to spare. She had seen the two masts of the steamer, *Laura*, as she reached Weighbridge, and for a moment had thought that she was too late. She noticed with relief that the ship was docking and that she had time to gather herself before Jesse would be able to disembark.

Her stomach fluttered anxiously. Over the past months she only had the photograph he had sent of himself to look at whenever she was in her bedroom. And she worried that she had forgotten the sound of his voice, his accent that she had loved to hear as he spoke and the twinkle in his hazel eyes that wasn't obvious in the photograph.

She hoped that when he saw her again, he wouldn't be disappointed in any way. They might have become much closer through their months of correspondence, but she couldn't help worrying that maybe one or both of them might have built the other up in their mind's eye somewhat. What if either of them were disappointed by the other? The thought terrified her.

Florence was so lost in thought that she had missed the

passengers walking along the harbour towards her and others waiting to meet people. She scanned the people making their way from the boat and, unable to see Jesse, panic welled up inside her. She focused on the people around her, wondering if maybe he had not recognised her and walked past. She tried to quell her increasing nerves, when a voice that she recognised only too well spoke behind her.

'Dearest Florence, I can't believe the time has finally arrived when I am in your company once more.'

She spun around to face him, a wide smile already on her face. 'Jesse,' she said, her throat constricted by emotion, 'you're here.'

She stared at him in awe. It was hard to imagine that he was finally here. Florence reached out and placed her right hand lightly against his cheek, the side of his moustache tickled her hand. 'You are real.'

He took her hand from his face and kissed her palm lightly. 'I am and this time I will not be leaving without you.'

Any anxiety about seeing him again, or concern that his feelings towards her, or hers to him had changed, vanished.

'Good,' she said, knowing that she had been right to wait for him. He was the man she remembered. She might know him better through his letters now, but he was still the Jesse she had fallen in love with.

'Where are your bags?' she asked gazing around him.

'They are being delivered to my hotel room. I've booked in at the same hotel as last time. They treat me well there and I find the rooms very comfortable. I also like to be able to see the harbour from my bedroom window and they assured me that I shall have a room overlooking the water again this time.'

'I'll accompany you there then.'

He took her hand and linked his arm around hers. It felt right to be with him again.

They began walking. Florence noticed several acquaintances giving her inquisitive stares as they passed.

'We'll be the talk of the town now we've been seen together like this,' she laughed.

'We have much to do,' he said. 'I thought I would visit your parents this evening, if they are happy for me to do so, and then tomorrow, or maybe the next day, I shall approach your father again to ask for your hand.'

The mention of his approach to her father sparked off Florence's nerves once more. Could she rely on her father to stick to his word and accept Jesse's offer? She hoped so. Florence loved and trusted her father; he was an honourable man, after all. However, she had assumed he would accept Jesse's request the previous year and look what had happened then. She took a calming breath. She would be positive. They would find a way to be together this time. She would not stand for anything less and, she guessed, neither would Jesse.

They arrived at the Pomme d'Or Hotel.

'Shall we take tea?' he asked, as a porter walked up to greet them.

'Yes, that would be most welcome.' It was hot outside and Florence realised that now she was in the cool of the reception, her throat was parched. She was feeling the effects of too little sleep and too much excitement.

'We'll find you somewhere to sit and then I can go and check in and arrange for some tea and biscuits to be brought to us. Or, would you rather sandwiches? You must be hungry by now?'

She was starving, she realised. In fact, she felt hungrier than she remembered for such a long time. 'Sandwiches, please. We might sit in the shade in the garden, do you think?' she suggested.

Jesse smiled at her, taking her left hand and giving it a gentle squeeze. 'A good idea, as always.'

He spoke to the porter and moments later a waiter came up to them and showed them out to the garden. He led them to a table shaded by the building and held a chair out for Florence to take a seat.

Jesse remained standing as he gave their order. 'I shall be a few minutes, while I sort out my accommodation. Then I'll be back, and we can catch up with everything that needs to happen this month.' He took her hand once more. 'Our wedding, Florence. Not long to wait now.'

Florence beamed at him. Excitement welled up inside her and she had to use all her resolve to remain calm and not let it show. She sat quietly, as she knew a lady should, pretending to enjoy the peace of the garden, while all the time she was bubbling with joy at the thought of her upcoming wedding. Only a few tables had people sitting at them and they were all far enough away so that she could only hear their voices very slightly. It allowed her to think of the preparations she still had to do.

If her father agreed to their marriage, which she hoped he

would, then she needed to arrange for her wedding dress to be made. She hadn't even begun to collect her trousseau, not wishing to tempt fate by presuming to do so prior to her father giving his blessing.

If they were to be married in weeks rather than months, then she would not intend collecting too many items, merely the essentials. The rest could follow once she was ensconced in Jesse's home. Their home. The thought gave her a warm feeling.

She thought of what she should wear on her wedding night. A negligee? What would happen between them? She was eager to discover what happened between a husband and wife when they were finally alone in their marriage bed. The thought excited her, although she couldn't help feeling nervous. Whatever happened, she trusted Jesse to show her all she needed to know.

Realising she was flushing slightly, she turned her thoughts to her clothing. She would need several chemises, a couple more elaborate than the others that she would use for everyday use. Drawers for every day of the week with trimming to match the chemises and several night dresses. Corsets, she would need new corset covers for her corsets, as well as maybe two more. What about hose, she mused; she needed a couple of fine thread and several of heavy cotton, as well as new skirts, wraps, collars and cuffs, both in linen and lace. She also needed new handkerchiefs, gloves and footwear suitable for the colder weather in the more northerly areas of England.

She groaned. Why hadn't she begun collating these items already. Even if she had not wished to presume that her father would accept Jesse as her husband, she could have still bought half these items without needing to use them simply as a married woman.

Jesse sat opposite her, a look of concern on his sweet face. 'You are all right?'

'Yes,' she answered, unsure why he should ask.

'It's just that I thought I heard you groan when I returned to the table. I wasn't sure if you were unwell.'

She shook her head. 'I'm perfectly well, especially now you are here.' He took her hands in his, waiting for her to elaborate. 'It's simply that I haven't begun organising my trousseau, or indeed a wedding dress.'

'You are superstitious?' he asked, amused.

'A little.'

'As am I.' He raised her left hand and kissed the back of it. 'We'll have no more waiting now, though, my love. I will arrange to see your father and speak with him, and you must set about arranging for whatever clothes you'll need to bring with you to our home.'

'Our home,' she repeated. The words had a magical quality.

Chapter 33

That night Florence went with Jesse to meet her parents. 'You're looking well, Mr Boot.' her father said, while her mother sat quietly, glancing at Florence a couple of times.

Florence assumed her mother was trying to gauge her reaction, but refused to give her any reason to think that she wasn't assured of her father complying with his intentions from the previous year.

'Thank you. It is good to be back on your beautiful island once again,' he said. 'I am pleased to find you all well and gather from Miss Boot that the shop is going from strength to strength.'

Florence wondered if maybe she should not have been so open with him about the state of affairs in her letters. He was such a brilliant businessman, though, that she had assumed her father could benefit from Jesse's business knowledge as she had done with his suggestions when wanting to help Lily.

The four of them made small talk for about an hour. She noticed Jesse clasp his hands together. He seemed slightly nervous.

A few moments later when there was a lull in the conversation, he said, 'Mr Rowe, I wonder if I could trouble you for a private moment of your time?'

Her father glanced at her and then at her mother, before replying to Jesse. 'Yes, of course. My dear, do you think you and Florence could leave us for a few minutes?'

Her mother stood and Florence waited for her to leave the room before following her. She reached the door, but before closing it locked eyes with Jesse, willing him to be successful this time. Then she closed the door, leaving the two men closest to her to talk.

'Come out to the kitchen, Florence,' her mother said. 'I wish to speak to you.'

Her heart pounded noisily in her chest. She had to get through this if she wanted her marriage to Jesse to go ahead. She walked into the kitchen. 'Yes, Mother?'

Her mother smoothed down the sleeves of her dress despite them not needing the attention. 'Your father and I spoke last evening. Knowing that Mr Boot was arriving today, we felt that it was only a matter of time that he came to speak with us.' She stared out of the window briefly as if trying to gather her thoughts. 'Your father will agree to your marriage to Mr Boot.'

Florence hadn't been expecting her to say anything of the sort. 'He will?' she asked wanting to be certain.

'Yes. However, I shan't attend your wedding.'

The words pained Florence as if her mother had stabbed her in the chest. 'But I don't understand . . .?'

'Nor will we agree for you to be married at chapel.'

Florence gasped. 'Why not? I have done all that you asked and this is how you repay an obedient daughter?' How could they stop her from being able to hold her wedding in the place that she had worshipped her entire life. 'How could you be so cruel? I thought you said Father was happy for us to marry.'

Her mother turned her back on her and stared at the sink. 'He will not go back on his word and refuse Mr Boot's request for your hand. However, I am unable to attend a wedding where I don't believe it is the best thing for your future.' She faced her once more and took her by the arms. 'Please don't misunderstand me. I like Mr Boot. I can see that he is a good man with the best of intentions and that you love each other.'

'Surely that's enough,' Florence cried, her throat constricted by unshed tears. 'Why would you tarnish our day by not allowing us to marry in chapel or attending the wedding? It's too cruel.'

'Florence. You believe the right thing to do for your future is to marry Mr Boot. Your father and I disagree. I might like him as a person, but you can't ignore that he is older than you and walks with a stick. I admit that he seems able enough today, but we both know he has days where his health is poor. I don't want a daughter of mine to end up being a nursemaid to her husband. Life is difficult enough. Marriage is difficult enough without an extra problem such as that.'

'And Father . . . will he be attending my wedding?' Florence asked, angrily wiping away a stray tear with the back of her right hand.

'He isn't sure. We have agreed that we must both do as we

see fit. I shall not change my mind about going though, so please don't hold out false hope that I might.'

The door opened and both women looked round to see Florence's father smiling. How could he seem so happy to have given his permission, she thought, when he doesn't even support me marrying Jesse. She hoped that one day their chosen behaviour towards this most important occasion in her life would fade in her memory, but for now it smarted.

'Come and join us, Margaret, Florence.'

Florence followed her mother into the room. 'So you have agreed for me to marry Mr Boot?' she asked just to be certain.

'I have,' he assured her.

She didn't ask about the wedding day, not wishing to spoil the moment for Jesse by letting him know that her parents might not be attending.

'We will now leave you for a few minutes, so that Mr Boot can ask you formally for your hand.'

Florence watched her parents leave the room and turned to Jesse to say something. Before she had a chance to speak, he got down on one knee and taking her left hand in his said, 'My darling girl. Will you do me the honour of becoming my wife?'

'Yes,' she said without a second's hesitation. 'Oh, yes.'

He rose with a little difficulty and, putting his hand in his right pocket, took out a small green leather ring box. Smiling at her briefly, he then focused on the clasp and pressed it. The lid sprung up, revealing a deep red ruby surrounded by smaller diamonds.

Florence's mouth fell open at the exquisite ring being presented to her.

He lifted the ring from its place in the box, and, taking her left hand, slipped the ring on her finger. They both stared at it silently. These shiny gems represented their love, enforced separation and hopefully the life that they had to look forward to together.

'It fits perfectly.'

'Do you like it?'

'I love it,' she whispered honestly.

He pulled her into his arms. His mouth found hers and he kissed her, their passion heightened by their time apart. Eventually he moved away from her.

'We have a lot to do in a short time. First, though, I believe we need to have the Banns read.'

Her heart dipped. 'I'm told that we can't be married at chapel,' she said, explaining part of what her mother had informed her.

His mouth fell open for a second before he closed it again. 'We can't?'

She shook her head. 'No. I'm not sure why, but I am tired of arguments. To be honest with you, I would have loved to be married in the same place I've always worshipped, but as long as we're married in the eyes of God I don't much care where it is. If I argue with my parents about being married in chapel then it could delay our wedding and I think we've lived with enough delays so far, don't you?'

'I do.' The delight in his face after placing the ring on her finger seemed to dissipate. 'If we are not able to marry at chapel, then where?'

She thought of the beautiful Town Church minutes down

the road from where they both stayed. 'The Town Church. It's the seat of the Dean of Jersey, so he will be the one marrying us, if he agrees. It's closer to the Pomme d'Or and we've walked past it several times. Do you remember it?'

He thought briefly. 'I think so.'

'Then if you're happy, I suggest we go there and speak to the vicar,' she said, determined not to let anything get in the way of their plans this time.

He hugged her tightly, kissing her once more. 'We will do as you suggest. First thing tomorrow.'

She beamed at him, happiness once again lifting her heart.

'Then, you need to speak to your dressmaker about your bridal gown and trousseau,' Jesse said. 'I can barely wait to see you in your wedding finery.'

'I long to wear it,' she said, picturing herself walking down the aisle to become his wife.

'You will need to find someone who can make your dress soon. We only have a few weeks.'

'Yes,' she said, deciding to speak to Amy about accompanying her for the first fitting. She had expected her mother would change her mind and offer to be with her for such a special appointment, but was only too aware now that this was nothing more than a dream.

'I thought I would arrange for us to have a betrothal supper to announce our engagement. What do you think?'

Florence agreed. 'I think it a wonderful idea.'

'You can invite your friends and of course the rest of your family. I thought we could hold it on the twenty-ninth of July.'

'My birthday?' she exclaimed.

'Exactly.'

She kissed him again. He thought of everything. Maybe this was why he was such an impressive businessman. 'You are so clever, my darling Jesse.'

'I do my best.' He winked at her and kissed her again. 'You've made me so very happy, Florence. I never expected I would ever meet someone as perfect for me as you are.'

'I feel the same about you,' she said, gripping his hands in hers and staring into his beautiful eyes. 'I always assumed that my perfect future would be as a spinster, running my own business. I never imagined I would want to marry anyone.'

He threw his head back and laughed. 'I'm relieved you've changed your mind.'

'Thank you for thinking of my birthday and linking it to our betrothal supper. It's going to be my most perfect birthday celebration ever, announcing to everyone that we are to be married. I can't wait.'

'Neither can I,' he said, pulling her into his arms once again and kissing her.

Chapter 34

The following morning, Florence walked to meet Jesse. She had arranged a few days off work so that she could make the necessary arrangements for her wedding day. Her father had been happy to give her the time off, which Florence accepted graciously, despite her hurt that her parents had placed such demands on her over her wedding.

She had contemplated speaking to him and asking him to explain his and her mother's reasons for their decisions, but was aware that once they had made a decision, they would not go back on it.

At least she had some time away from the shop. Her father had agreed to this no doubt, she thought, because Lily was now able to stand in for her and cover any of the work Florence would otherwise be needed to do.

She felt breathless even before leaving the flat and knew it was down to her nervousness that the Dean of Jersey might decide not to marry them in the protestant church as both of them were practising Wesleyans.

She stepped into the church yard of the Town Church and

immediately saw Jesse waiting for her. They exchanged smiles when they saw each other and took each other's hand.

'I arranged a meeting with the Dean after leaving you yesterday evening,' he said. 'He seemed most sympathetic to our plight and is waiting to meet with us.'

He pulled open the heavy wooden door and they walked into the coolness of the granite church.

'Look at that incredible stained-glass window,' Florence whispered, astonished by the intricate beauty and workmanship that it must have taken to produce such a beautiful piece.

'Magnificent, indeed.'

They heard footsteps and spotted the Dean of Jersey smiling up at the window. 'We are very lucky to have such splendour in our church,' he said, before walking up to them and shaking first Florence's hand and then Jesse's. 'Miss Rowe and Mr Boot, I presume?'

'Yes,' Jesse said. 'Thank you very much for agreeing to see us at such short notice.'

'It is my pleasure. Please, come through to the vestry and we can make any necessary arrangements.'

They followed him through the peaceful church through to a small office where he indicated they take a seat. 'You advised me in your note, Mr Boot, that neither of you have been married before.' He sat at his desk and pulled a large leather book towards him. 'The Banns will need to be read, naturally.' They murmured their agreement. 'I have studied my diary and can advise that the earliest date on which I am free to conduct your wedding ceremony will be—' he ran his finger down the page, turned it over a few times and eventually tapped the page and smiled at them '—Monday, the thirtieth of August. How does that suit you both?'

Nine weeks away. Florence would have liked to have been married sooner, but it was summer and the time when most brides wished to be married. She also reminded herself that her bridal gown still needed to be made and other arrangements sorted. She gazed up at Jesse who was waiting for her to reply.

'Well, dearest,' he said. 'How does that date suit you as your wedding date?'

Florence wanted to laugh out loud her joy was so great. 'I'd say it's perfect.'

Jesse gave her hand a squeeze and addressed the grinning Dean. 'Thank you, sir. The thirtieth of August will be the perfect day for our wedding.'

'Good,' he said, picking up his fountain pen, unscrewing the lid, and, after requesting their full names, wrote them down in his diary. 'Now, let us go through the formalities, so that we are fully prepared.'

An hour later, Florence walked with Jesse down to the harbour. 'I can't believe it's all arranged,' she said, wishing the weeks away.

'At least we now have a firm date to look forward to.' He turned to smile at her. 'I can see you're impatient, as am I, but we've waited this long, we can wait a little longer. And we still have much to do in order that we are fully prepared.'

They took a train to St Aubin and chatted about how perfect their future together was going to be.

Now that the date of their wedding had been set, Florence

allowed herself to picture her and Jesse with a brood of children. It was going to be wonderful and so very different to what she had ever deemed of for herself. She had never before been obsessed by bearing children, like most of her friends. Now, though, she wanted nothing more than to have children with and for Jesse. He was such a kind, caring and giving man and he deserved to have a family and she thought herself the most honoured of women to be able to give them to him.

That afternoon, Florence left Jesse to meet with Amy at the dressmaker she had booked to visit.

Madame Mallet welcomed Florence and after a brief discussion about the design of the wedding dress Florence wanted, she made a sketch.

'Is this the sort of design you are imaging?' The dressmaker held up a piece of paper showing a dress with a rounded neckline with what appeared to be a pretty lace border. The long sleeves had cuffs of lace and rows of lace frills in the skirt. There was a slight bustle and a train falling from it and pooling on the floor behind.

It was. 'Yes, that's slightly different to what I had in my mind, but it's even better.'

'Good.'

Madame Mallet took her and Amy through to her storeroom and presented her with a selection of white materials.

'They are all so beautiful,' Florence sighed, feeling a little overwhelmed. She picked up and studied the fabrics for a second time. 'It's difficult to choose just one.'

'We can use one for the outer garment, another for the

frills of the underskirt and then we have some Nottingham lace for the neckline and cuffs of your dress. It is the best.'

'Her future husband is from Nottingham,' Amy said. 'And so including lace from there will have a significance too.'

'Ah, I see. Then we must find the very best that I have to complement your dress.'

Florence thought of Jesse and how happy he was going to be to see her in her dress complete with Nottingham lace. She was certain he would love the dress Madame Mallet had designed for her.

They took some time to work through the choices, but finally, Florence was satisfied and so they agreed a cost. The seamstress set about measuring Florence while her young assistant wrote down her measurements in a small notebook.

'You are tall with a slim waist,' Madame Mallet said. 'You will look splendid on your wedding day and I'm certain your husband will be very proud.'

She hoped Madame Mallet was right.

Later that afternoon she met Jesse for tea at the Pomme d'Or.

'I can't believe how much we've already arranged and in only one day.' She sipped her tea happily. This is what she had imagined happening last year, before her parents had insisted on their delay.

Never mind, she thought; at least they were free to make their preparations now. Her parents might have refused them their choice of marrying in the place that they had hoped, and her mother's refusal to attend was still like a pinch to her heart, but she was determined not to let their choices ruin her and Jesse's special day.

Jesse reached out and took one of her hands in his and gave it a gentle squeeze. 'Now we need to decide who will be our witnesses for the ceremony. Do you know who you will ask?'

'I'm asking Amy,' she said, thinking back to how supportive her younger sister had always been of everything she'd done.

'Good choice.' He took a bite from one of the slim cucumber sandwiches.

'How about you?' Florence asked. 'Will you ask a friend from the mainland to travel over?'

After swallowing his food, he sat thoughtfully. 'I am unsure who to ask. All my friends are very busy with their lives. However, there is a man with whom I've become friendly during my stays at the hotel,' he explained. 'He comes to the hotel for morning coffee, most days. We've sat together on quite a few occasions and had many discussions on business and how we see the future panning out both on the mainland and here on the island. His name is John Blampied.'

'Do you think he'll agree to do it?'

Jesse shrugged. 'I don't know, but if the time feels right when we next speak, I'll ask him then.'

Everything was coming together. Now they just needed to hope that nothing happened to disrupt their plans.

Chapter 35

Florence woke to the sound of seagulls outside her window and the sun streaming in through a gap in her floral curtains. She stretched languorously. It was her birthday and only four and a half weeks until she would be marrying Jesse. She would need to get up soon if she was to make the second fitting of her beautiful wedding dress before work.

She sat up and rubbed her eyes gently. Already she could tell that this dress was going to be exactly as she'd hoped. The fabric was perfect and today she would see the folds of the skirt and bustle at the back of her dress and how they appeared on it.

Florence got out of bed and touched the light cotton fabric on the dress that she had chosen to wear for her birthday dinner and betrothal meal at The British Hotel in Library Place, which Jesse had arranged for her family and his new friend John Blampied that evening. She was delighted that Lily had also accepted her invitation. She was now very much becoming part of her family and at sixteen was growing up to be a delightful and self-assured woman.

Florence looked forward to Jesse seeing Lily in a grander

situation than when he had originally met and rescued her from her father. Lily had grown so much since then and, although Jesse had spoken to her once or twice when he popped in to see Florence at the shop, it had only been for the briefest of occasions.

She was relieved her parents had agreed to attend the meal. It wasn't as much as she had hoped from them, but it went a little way to show that despite their reservations about her marriage, their attendance at the meal did prove to her that her mother did not have an issue with Jesse as a person.

She was also looking forward to meeting John Blampied. She had heard a little about him, but if he was Jesse's choice as a witness then that was good enough for Florence.

Jesse understood that she was to be working all day. She didn't mind too much. The shop was busy and she was to be seeing him that evening, so she was fairly happy to wait until then.

Florence was in the middle of showing a customer some of the best fountain pens when she spotted Mrs Wolstenholm arrive and make a bee-line to her father who was handing change to a gentleman.

'Mrs Wolstenholm, how can I assist you today?' her father asked.

'My maid advises me that your daughter, Florence, is to be married.'

'That's correct.'

Florence's heart raced. She couldn't imagine why Mrs Wolstenholm wanted to discuss her forthcoming nuptials, or what business of hers they might be. She smiled at the lady next to her and unscrewed one of the pens to show her the fine gold nib, hoping that she didn't notice how distracted she was by Mrs Wolstenholm's conversation with her father.

'His name is Mr Boot, I gather?'

There was a pause before her father answered. 'Yes, it is.'

'I've never heard of him. He isn't local, I assume?'

Her father cleared his throat and noisily straightened a notepad and pen on the counter. 'He has shops in Nottingham and more recently Sheffield.'

She sniffed. 'He is a shopkeeper?'

Florence tensed and saw that the woman next to her had stopped studying the pens to listen to the conversation.

'He is rather more than that, Mrs Wolstenholm,' her father replied, his tone clipped. 'As well as his increasing number of shops, he also now employs a pharmacist to dispense prescriptions.'

Florence tried to focus on the pens in front of her, but couldn't help wondering why her father was telling Mrs Wolstenholm so much about Jesse. He was never usually one to share information about people and he sounded as if he was trying to impress her, which was not like him at all.

'Does he indeed?' she said. 'It sounds to me as if your daughter has done pretty well for herself, Mr Rowe. You must be relieved that she has finally found a husband?'

There was a long silence before Florence heard her father's footsteps across the wooden flooring as he marched over to the shop door and opened it. She turned to stare at him, his eyes narrowed.

'Good day, Mrs Wolstenholm,' he said holding the door

and waiting for her to leave. 'As far as I'm concerned my daughter's happiness is the most important thing, not your opinion of the husband she has chosen. I'll thank you to take your custom elsewhere.'

Mrs Wolstenholm gasped and shot a steely glare in Florence's direction, as if she had been the one to insult her. 'I will never visit this establishment again,' she said her face flushed as she stomped out of the shop.

Florence couldn't think of a thing to say. She stared at her father as he quietly closed the door and turned to face the customers still in the shop.

'I apologise if any of you feel I spoke out of turn just now and hope that none of you were offended.'

No one spoke. Florence's customer picked up one of the pens and studied it. 'It's about time someone put that harridan in her place,' she whispered.

Florence looked over at her father, but he was already serving someone else.

Later that day she finished serving one of several customers and showed the woman out of the shop. It occurred to her that she hadn't seen Lily for a while.

'Lily? Are you there?' There was no reply.

Florence stopped moving to still the rustling of her skirts and listened intently, certain she had heard something, but unsure what. It was sobbing and it was coming from the storeroom. She hastily locked the shop door and flipped over the sign to say that they were closed before running to the storeroom to see what had happened.

'Lily?' she asked, finding her friend crouched down in a

corner, her hands holding a crumpled handkerchief over her mouth to stifle her sobs.

Florence's chest contracted in horror. What on earth could have happened? She crouched down next to her friend, reaching her arm around Lily's shaking shoulders.

'Whatever's the matter, Lily? Are you hurt?' Her heart raced at the thought of Lily's father returning to his old behaviour. Surely he hadn't come into the shop while Florence was focusing on something else and hurt the girl? She would have noticed, wouldn't she?

Lily took a few gulps of air and seemed to be calming slightly.

'It's all right,' Florence soothed, pulling her own handkerchief from her skirt pocket and wiping Lily's eyes. 'Take your time and then tell me what's happened. I'm sure we'll find a solution to whatever it is.'

Lily blew her nose and slowly calmed down.

'Right,' Florence said, helping her friend to stand, 'tell me.'

'You'll think I'm selfish,' Lily said between shuddering breaths.

Florence doubted it very much. 'Go on.'

When Lily didn't speak, Florence took her face in her hands and smiled at her.

The younger girl took a deep breath. 'It's just that you're leaving Rowes, and even Jersey, and I don't know when I'll ever see you again. You've been so good to me, you and your family, so I've no right to behave like this.' She gave in to a fresh bout of crying and Florence, understanding her sentiments, and her feelings of losing a dear friend, hugged her tightly.

'You're not selfish. You have every right to feel this way.' She held Lily away from her, her own tears now threatening to escape. 'I'm going to miss working here and especially working with you.'

'You are? But you're goin' to have such an exciting life with Mr Boot.'

'I hope so, but that doesn't mean I won't miss you, Lily. You're my friend. I'm used to seeing you every workday here and on Sundays at chapel. It's going to be a big change for me too, and I have to admit that, as excited as I am – and I am – I'm still frightened about all the changes I'm going to have to make.'

Lily's eyes widened in astonishment. 'You are? But you're the bravest woman I know.'

Florence frowned. 'I doubt that very much.'

'You're really going to miss me?'

'I said so, didn't I?' she said, smiling. 'But you're going to stay on here at Rowes and take over from me. You'll do a brilliant job. I'll be back here. Jersey's my home and it's also where my family live. We'll see each other again, I promise.'

'Truly?'

'Yes. Now we've both got to be brave,' Florence insisted, aware that she was trying to persuade herself as well as Lily. 'I'll have to get used to my new home and way of life, and you'll continue to learn everything you can about being a shop assistant. Who knows what you'll achieve in your life, Lily?'

Lily smiled and wiped away a stray tear. 'You're right, Florence. We have to be brave. Who knows, I might even come and visit you one day in Nottingham?'

'Good,' Florence said, honestly, 'I look forward to that day.' She spotted someone at the door peering into the shop. 'I think we should stop talking about this now and serve that poor customer,' Florence said, hugging her dear friend.

They parted and Lily walked away.

After the customer had left, Lily said, 'I wonder what he's bought you for your birthday present?' She straightened two picture frames at the back of the window display. 'If your engagement ring is anything to go by then he will have chosen something very special.'

'I think it will be a necklace,' Amy said, grinning at Lily conspiratorially.

'Neither of you know, so don't insinuate that you do,' Florence said, aware that Amy was almost as excited as she for the evening to begin.

'You can all stop chattering and get on with tidying this place and restocking the shelves,' their father said as soon as the shop was clear of customers. 'We won't have time to stay behind to prepare the shop for opening in the morning, not if we need to leave to get ready for your meal tonight, Florence.'

'If you and Mother can come tonight, Father, don't you think you could persuade her to come to the wedding, too?' she pleaded, determined not to give in to the tears caused by the hurt her mother's decision had caused her. 'It would make my day complete to have her there.'

He smiled at her sadly. 'You know your mother almost as well as I do. She makes her decisions, and, whether we like them, or even understand them, she is not one to change her mind. It's your future she worries about. This meal is about your birthday, and—' he hesitated '—your engagement.' He closed his eyes and shook his head. 'I'm sorry. I have tried to persuade her.'

She forced a tight smile. She didn't want him to have to witness her pain. It wasn't his fault that her mother was still refusing to attend the wedding.

In truth Florence was glad to have work to do to keep her from getting over excited at the thought of the evening ahead. She couldn't wait to sit next to Jesse with all their family present. Jesse had arranged for a carriage to collect them from Queen Street for the short ride to the smart hotel at Library Place. Lily, excited at the opportunity of another ride in a carriage, had offered to meet them outside the shop just before the carriage was due to arrive.

She and Jesse had decided earlier that her father should sit at the opposite end of the table to him with her mother sitting by his side. Lily suggested that she sat Amy next to John Blampied. Jesse had mentioned that he was a widow of two years and she hoped that if he and her sister had a mutual attraction that maybe her sister would then be able to celebrate a wedding of her own.

She had tried to find out more information about Mr Blampied from Jesse, but as with all men, he was hopeless when it came to giving an opinion on the suitability of another man.

Florence and her family stepped outside to find Lily looking very grown up in a new dress. She had confided in Florence that she had bought it second-hand and her mother had helped her make the necessary alterations to get it to fit her.

'You look very beautiful,' Florence whispered as her father locked the front door. 'That navy material suits you.'

'Thank you.' Lily smiled. 'Our neighbour came to help me with my hair. Do you think it looks all right for this evening?'

'It looks perfect,' Amy said, before Florence had a chance to reply.

'It does.'

They settled down in the carriage. It was a bit of a squeeze as Willie was with them too. Adelaide and Francis were making their own way there after Francis had insisted that the short walk would suit them both, especially on such a pleasant evening. She was determined to enjoy these moments as much as possible. This was her birthday and celebration of her and Jesse's engagement. She was determined to enjoy every moment of the evening and not allow herself to think ahead to the wedding and the absence of one of the people closest to her. She was not going to allow that person's choices to take away the joy of her evening.

Jesse was at the hotel awaiting their arrival. She smiled lovingly at him as the carriage stopped.

'You get out first, Florence,' her father said, giving a brief wave to Jesse. 'I see that your future husband is eagerly awaiting your arrival.'

Florence smiled and took Jesse's proffered hand, holding it tightly as she stepped onto the small metal step and onto the pavement.

'How are you?' Jesse asked quietly as they waited for her family and Lily to follow suit.

'Excited and very, very happy,' she said honestly, holding

his hand, aware of the gold band of her engagement ring pressing against her middle and little finger on her left hand

They greeted each other and went through to the restaurant to take their seats. The sommelier came to the table and Jesse explained that none of them drank alcohol, apart from maybe his friend who they were waiting to arrive.

At that moment, a man walked in through the restaurant door and up to their table.

'I believe this is the Boot–Rowe table,' he said loudly. 'I am John Blampied. I'm delighted to meet the lady to whom my good friend is engaged to be married.' He took Florence's hand and raised it towards his lips as he bowed. 'My felicitations to you both.'

Florence stared into the man's kind eyes and liked him immediately. Jesse was a good judge of character and Florence's instincts told her that Jesse had been right about John Blampied.

Jesse then introduced the tall, smart man who Florence gauged to be in his early to mid-forties. She glanced at her sister but saw no interest in her eyes. Never mind, she thought; there was still time.

The meal was delicious, and the conversation flowed.

After their dessert, Jesse stood. He had arranged for their glasses to be filled with a cool elderflower cordial.

'Good evening, good friends and soon-to-be family,' he said, holding Florence's hand with his free one. 'Thank you all for celebrating our upcoming wedding at this betrothal supper. My fiancée and I—' he grinned at Florence and added '—I can never tire of saying that.' Then addressing their guests once more, said, 'We are grateful for your company this evening. As most of you know, it is also Florence's birthday today and I have a gift that I wish to give to her. So, if you don't mind, I'd like to first say a toast to thank you all for being here and for my dearest Florence for agreeing to be my wife and to wish her the happiest of birthdays. To Florence.'

They stood and raised their glasses and Florence couldn't help feeling prouder than she ever had done before. 'Thank you,' she said, beaming at each one of them.

'Please, sit.'

They did as Jesse requested and he turned to Florence and handed her a small box. 'I hope you like them.'

He sat down and watched as she opened the ribbon holding the pretty silver paper in place, then, removing it, she held her breath as she lifted the lid to discover a pair of ruby and diamond earrings. 'They're utterly beautiful,' she said quietly, before looking up at him and smiling. 'You're too generous, Jesse.'

'For you nothing is too generous a gift,' he said quietly, his voice low enough so that only she could hear.

'Thank you.' She kissed his cheek.

'We only have another month to wait now.'

'I know,' she whispered, unable and unwilling to hide the excitement she felt.

'You're very lucky, Florence,' Amy said, without any envy in her voice.

Florence could tell her sister was truly happy for her, despite being aware that her sister would miss her when she left their home and was no longer working at the shop.

'And you deserve it all,' her mother added. 'You are my daughter and all that I do is in an attempt to ensure the best future for you.'

Florence smiled warily at her, wondering if maybe she had softened enough towards her marriage to Jesse to make her want to change her mind about attending their wedding.

She would have liked to hope so, but suspected that she knew her mother well enough to know that she was being a little too ambitious with her dreams.

Chapter 36

The next four weeks during the lead up to their wedding day were filled with fittings, and whispered conversations with Amy about whether they could find a way to persuade their mother to attend the wedding. Florence knew her mother was determined but had hoped she would have changed her mind by now.

'She's adamant,' Amy said, two nights before the wedding, as she sat on the end of Florence's bed. 'I've tried every argument I can think of and even resorted to emotional blackmail, but she won't have any of it.'

Florence chewed her lower lip. 'She isn't going to change her mind, is she?'

'I don't think so.' Amy pursed her lips. 'You mustn't let her decision to tarnish your big day though. You and Jesse have waited far too long to let anyone have the power to make it anything less than the perfect day you've been planning.'

'I won't.'

'Say that again, but this time with more gusto.'

Florence laughed, determined to hide the hurt at her mother's rejection that she still felt. Amy had a way with words that usually managed to cheer her up. 'I won't,' she announced, loud enough to disturb her parents, but hoping she hadn't done so.

'Show me that beautiful ring again,' Amy said, reaching out to take Florence's hand. 'You are lucky. He has great taste and is generous too.'

'I am incredibly grateful to Jesse for making me see that marriage can be a partnership, rather than a woman being nothing more than a chattel to be dictated to.'

Amy was silent for a moment. 'Let's hope that he doesn't change when you have the next ring on your finger then.'

Florence gasped. 'Don't say that!' She thought of Jesse and, try as she might, she couldn't imagine him becoming one of those dictatorial husbands she had seen many times in the shop, bossing their wives around and telling them, rather than asking them, what they should buy.

'I'm joking,' Amy said, letting go of her hand. 'I believe I know him well enough now to trust that he'll never change. I'm sure he can be tough,' she said. 'He is a successful businessman, after all, and has had to work hard all his life, but he is fundamentally kind and certainly a good person.'

'He is.' How many men would have waited this long to be married, she wondered. Or take the news calmly that he was unable to marry in his chosen church, simply because his mother-in-law to be had insisted that their marriage not be conducted there. 'I can't imagine Jesse ever being anything other than the lovely man I know him to be.'

'At least Father will still be there.'

The thought comforted Florence.

'But Adelaide won't be,' Amy said, sad to think of her sister missing such an important day. 'She's staying here at the flat to be with Mother.'

'No! Not Adelaide. She can't miss my wedding too, surely?' She felt as if Amy had just punched her in the stomach.

'She doesn't mean to hurt you, Florence,' Amy insisted. 'I suspect Adelaide is intending on being with Mother to try and persuade her to go to your wedding. She will then be there to help Mother get ready. She thinks she's doing the right thing. She wants to be there for you but feels it's her responsibility to stay with Mother.'

Her final day as a single woman saw her accompany Jesse to chapel for morning service. She persuaded him that, despite them not being able to be married there, she had no intention of not attending her church on her final Sunday living in Jersey.

They walked to chapel, taking their time and enjoying being together.

'I can't believe your mother has not changed her mind about attending our wedding,' he said through gritted teeth. 'I was certain she would relent and be there for you.'

Florence didn't want to spoil their day by getting upset about something she knew she had little power over. 'Tell me a little about our life in Nottingham,' Florence asked as they strolled along the busy pavement.

'After we're married, we'll take the ferry to Southampton, then travel over the next three days by train, stopping off to stay in pretty hotels along the way to break up our journey and give us some time together before arriving at our home. Do you like the sound of that?'

She nodded, excited to think of the adventure ahead of them.

'Once we arrive at our home, I'll introduce you to the staff. We only have a small staff, so there's nothing to worry about, and you can decide how you would like things to be run in the household.'

She gave his arm a gentle squeeze to show her approval. 'And how soon will you take me to the shops and factories?'

He laughed. 'Ever the businesswoman, eh?'

'Yes. It's who I am.' She smiled up at him. 'Well, how soon?'

'As soon as you like.'

She was about to tell him that she would want to travel with him to work as soon as possible, when she spotted the Buttons family at the bottom of the wide chapel steps. Florence was delighted to see them all there again, and this time Mr Buttons was with them, an unusual occurrence but one that, by the look on her beaming face, pleased Mrs Buttons very much.

'I can't believe I'm going to church two days running,' Lily said quietly to Florence. 'I'm that excited about going to your wedding tomorrow morning that I don't quite know what to do with meself.'

'You're not the only one,' Florence giggled, gripping Jesse's hand.

'It was good of your father to close the shop for the morning, don't you think?' Lily asked.

'I don't think he had much choice,' Jesse said, amused.

'Especially when one of his employees is getting married and the rest are either at the wedding or, well, sitting with others.'

Florence felt Jesse tense. She could tell by the muscle working in his cheek that he was angry and holding back from saying more. She knew he meant well and gave his hand a gentle squeeze. 'Shall we all go in?'

After chapel, Florence and Jesse went off by themselves to spend the afternoon alone. 'We have nothing else to do before tomorrow,' she said, gazing lovingly at Jesse.

'You don't think your family would rather you spend the day with them?' he asked, as they made their way along the promenade on their way to the Esplanade.

'I think they'd be calmer to know there wasn't any chance of me trying to persuade Mother, yet again, to come to our wedding,' she said, refusing to let her mother's determination to miss her wedding sour her day. There was nothing to be done to change her mind now; Florence was almost certain of that. 'They can rest easy if they know that I'm out walking with you.'

They walked, arms linked, stopping every so often to look down at the families eating picnics on the beach, children splashing in the sea, watched by parents enjoying the warm summer day.

'That will be us in a couple of years hopefully,' Jesse remarked, putting his arm around her waist and pulling her gently to him. 'If we're lucky enough to have a family together.'

She watched the young family closest to them on the beach,

the two youngest children screaming in laughter as the father chased them round in circles on the golden sand.

'I do hope so.'

They watched in silence for a few minutes before walking on again.

'I've arranged for us to stay in the honeymoon suite at the hotel for one night and then thought that the following day we could catch the mailboat and sail to England.' Jesse stopped walking to watch her reaction. 'If you'd rather we stay here longer then I'm happy to do that instead.'

'No.' She smiled, happy to think that she only had a couple of days until she could see her new home for the very first time. 'I can't wait to move to Nottingham and get settled in our new life there.'

'That's settled then. I still need to arrange a honeymoon for us, but wasn't sure where you might want to go.'

'I'm happy to wait,' she said, suspecting that he must be wishing to get back to his shops and factory to see how everything was fairing in his absence.

'You are too good to me, Florence. I don't know that I deserve to be married to such a gem as you are.'

'Nonsense,' she said, kissing his cheek. 'We are lucky to have found each other. We are a perfect match.'

'Despite our age difference and my—'

'I said we are a perfect match.' She kissed him quickly on his mouth. 'And I meant it.'

After an hour walking and chatting, they reached St Aubin. Jesse took her hands in his. 'I think it's time we made our way back, don't you?'

'I suppose so,' Florence said, looking back at the way they'd come and then across the pale sands where the sun shone on the glistening waves.

'Aren't you going to miss your life here in Jersey?' he asked. 'It's such a beautiful place.'

She thought for a moment. 'Yes, of course,' she said honestly. 'I love it here, but I can always come back with you. I'll miss not being ten minutes away from the sea, but then I will have so much to distract me in Nottingham. I'm excited to look forward, Jesse. I don't want to think about the things I'll miss, only the excitement of what lies ahead for us both.'

They strolled in silence for a few minutes, each lost in their own thoughts.

'This time tomorrow you'll be Mrs Boot,' he said, kissing her cheek lightly. 'It seems like a dream to me.'

'A dream that by this time tomorrow will have become a reality.'

'Nothing can go wrong now,' he said, determination filling his voice. 'I simply won't let anything come between us and our wedding.'

Chapter 37

Florence sat in front of the mirror, the sun streaming through her open bedroom window. This was the last time she would leave this room as a spinster, and she couldn't wait. Already a small crowd had accumulated outside the shop, and she could hear the excited chatter and the horse's hoof slamming down on the cobble stones as he waited impatiently for her to set off in the carriage.

'Thank you, Mother,' she said, staring at her reflection and moving her head from one side to the other. 'You've dressed my hair beautifully.'

She knew this was her mother's way of creating a memory for them both on her wedding day. It was a shame, Florence thought, that it happened to be one that didn't include her Mother being in the church with her.

'I'm glad you like it,' she said, resting her hands on Florence's shoulders and smiling at her through the mirror. 'Your day will go well, I know it.'

'Are you nearly ready?' Amy called from the hallway before entering the room. 'Father is waiting for you by the carriage and says to tell you that you're going to be late if you don't leave immediately.'

'I'm coming now,' Florence reassured her.

She pinched her cheeks lightly and took a deep breath. 'I wish you'd change your mind,' she said quietly to her mother as soon as Amy had gone.

'I can't,' she said simply. 'I do wish you a wonderful future, though.' She gave Florence a brief hug and then stepped back. 'Right, you must go.'

Florence swallowed tears, determined not to give in to them on her happy day. She walked carefully down the stairs and outside to the carriage. She waved at the acquaintances and neighbours she spotted waiting to see her in her finery, smiling at the oohs and ahhs, as she took her father's hand and stepped up into the carriage.

He helped Amy up and then climbed in after her, sitting next to Florence.

'You look delightful, Florence,' he said quietly, waving to his friends who stood in the crowd.

'Thank you,' she said, amazed not to feel any nerves at all.

They waited while her brother Willie stepped up into the carriage and sat opposite them next to Amy and the carriage moved on. 'You're certain you want to do this?' her father asked, smiling. He knew as well as Florence did that she had no intention of changing her mind.

'Absolutely,' she said with conviction.

'I am sorry I didn't manage to persuade your mother to come today,' he said quietly. 'And that we wouldn't let you marry at chapel. That was the wrong thing to do and I'm ashamed of my part in it.'

'It's fine, Father,' she said, surprised to hear him admit such things. 'Despite everything, I'm happy to be marrying the man I love. Nothing will ruin today for me.'

'You look very beautiful,' Amy said, wiping away a stray tear with her fingertips. 'I'm so happy for you.'

Florence took her sister's gloved hand in her own for a moment. 'Thank you, Amy. You look wonderful, too. I'm going to miss you.'

'You won't miss me?' Willie teased.

'Not as much as me, she won't.' Amy giggled.

'Behave yourselves, you two. People are watching.'

Ten minutes later, after a slow carriage ride through the streets, they stopped at the Town Church. Florence was helped down by her father and walked silently with him to the open church doors.

She could hear Amy whisper something to Willie and him giggle, and assumed it was because they were both happy to be able to attend the wedding when their mother had been so adamant not to.

As Florence walked with her father into the darkness of the church, the candlelight flickered and coloured sunrays in reds, blues and yellows from where the sun poured through the stained-glass window brightened the aisle.

She spotted Lily first, grinning at her and looking very smart in the pretty dress she'd worn to her birthday meal, a small corsage pinned to the front of her dress.

Then she saw Jesse. He had his back to her, but hearing

their footsteps, he glanced around and their eyes met. Finally, it was their time.

Seconds later she was standing next to him, exchanging glances. She wondered if her happiness shone through her eyes as Jesse's did through his.

Her father nodded to Jesse and stepped away to sit next to Amy and Willie.

The Dean of Jersey, resplendent in his robes, welcomed the congregation and began the sermon.

It was all a bit of a blur for Florence. She remembered Jesse beaming at her, his hazel eyes twinkling as he said, 'I do.' Then it was her turn.

The next thing she knew they were walking back down the aisle, her arm linked through his and this time she had a gold wedding band on the third finger on her left hand.

They had overcome her mother's trepidations about them marrying, her father's enforced separation of them and now, after all that, they were joined in holy matrimony and no one could to anything to part them. They had made it.

Florence walked out of the church, squinting slightly in the bright sunlight. Amy and Willie stood either side of Adelaide. Her older sister had come to her wedding after all. Florence beamed at her and mouthed a thank you.

Her three siblings giggled as they showered Florence and Jesse with dried rice. As the tiny grains showered down over their heads, Florence didn't think she could ever be happier than she was right at that moment.

She spotted Mrs Wolstenholm peering at her, a sour

expression on her face, no doubt due to her lack of an invitation to the wedding.

'There she is,' someone cheered. 'Florence Rowe is now Mrs Boot.'

'Mrs Boots, more like,' Mrs Wolstenholm sniffed, snatching her parasol from her current lady's maid. 'There'll be no stopping that girl now, you mark my words.'

THE END

Author Note

Florence Boot (née Rowe) is a woman who has fascinated me for many years. Naturally I'd heard of *Boots the Chemist*, I often shop at one of four local stores here in Jersey. I now know that within the large shop I visit in Queens Street, St Helier, lies the original stationers owned by Florence's father William Rowe at number 27, where she worked as a shop assistant in the 1880s and where she, her sister, Amy, and parents were living above the shop when she met Jesse Boot.

I was stunned to discover St Matthew's church at Millbrook, known locally as The Glass Church, with its Lalique crystal windows, christening font, exquisite three metres tall cross covered with Jersey lilies, and other features, was commissioned by Florence. She lived across the road for many years and paid for the renovation of the church and commissioned unique pieces from her friend Réne Lalique in the early thirties in memory of her beloved husband, Jesse Boot, then 1st Baron Trent, who died in 1931. She also created Coronation Park, a beautiful park with a large pavilion facing the sea and a pond for children to paddle in and sail their boats, situated right next to St Matthew's church.

These are just two places on the island that Florence is responsible for creating. Most school children still enjoy their sports days at FB Playing Fields, there are workers' cottages, maisonettes and even the bay of Beauport, once bought by Jesse for Florence, was gifted to the island. We are very lucky here to have such a generous benefactor and if you come to the island on holiday you can also visit these places. Florence and Jesse lived most of their married life in Nottingham, where Jesse had been born and where his empire began, but Florence never forgot her roots on the island of Jersey, or its people.

When Charlotte Ledger, Editorial Director at HarperCollins and One More Chapter thought of writing about Florence Boot, she discovered that Florence was from Jersey. I had just finished working on *The Poppy Field*, a novel to commemorate the centenary of the end of the First World War, and was delighted when Charlotte thought of me to write *Mrs Boots*. It was a joy to spend time delving into Florence's life, from her younger years working as a shop assistant in Jersey, to becoming the philanthropic wife of a baron, who, despite being the mother of three children, still insisted on continuing to work when women of her means did not do so.

Florence was so much more than I had realised. She cared deeply about her staff and the lives of the women who worked for her, and saw to it that they had both nutritional and educational support believing that it helped her 'Dear Girls' to achieve more in their lives. From the creation of the Boots Lending Libraries to the inclusion of cafés in the shops, Florence's foresight and care for others was inspirational and far-reaching. There is so much more about Florence that I want to share with you, but maybe those stories will have to wait for another time.

I am doubly lucky not only to have been asked to write this novel based on such a strong, inspirational woman, but also to live on an island where her legacy is enjoyed daily by so many people.

Acknowledgements

I'd like to thank the following people who have helped in some way to the research/writing of *Mrs Boots*:

First, I'd like to thank Charlotte Ledger, another inspirational woman and Editorial Director at HarperCollins/One More Chapter. I'm massively grateful for Charlotte's confidence in me and for giving me this opportunity to research and write about Florence Boot, a Jersey woman who has long held my interest.

Mrs Boots would not be the book it is without the support and suggestions of my brilliant editor, Emily Ruston. This is a far better book thanks to her input.

Also, I'd like to thank Donna Hillyer for her thorough copy-edits.

My agent Kate Nash has been a huge support, not just as my agent, but for the information she discovered about Florence and Jesse Boot and sent on to me.

Alison Barrington, Florence and Jesse Boot's great-granddaughter, who, together with her daughter, Heidi Lewis and granddaughter, Lara Lewis kindly met up with me, showed me personal photos of her grandparents and shared private family anecdotes that helped me visualise Florence and Jesse's life together.

Sophie Clapp and Judith Wright, Boots Archivists in Nottingham for the wonderful welcome they gave to me and Claire Fenby when we visited them and I was given access to a treasure trove of documents, including letters written by Florence, personal photos and other exquisite items that helped me to truly discover the breadth of Florence Boot's generosity and care for her staff, especially her 'Dear Girls'.

Claire Fenby, Digital Marketing and Publicity Assistant at One More Chapter for accompanying me to the Boots Archive and helping make the day so memorable.

Michele Leerson at Jersey Archive for connecting me to Alison Barrington and her family, and for meeting with me and giving me fascinating information about Florence. Also, Toni Wolstenholme, Linda Romeril and Stuart Nicolle from the Jersey Archive for their assistance with my research.

Nigel Sweeny, for the loan of his book on The Jersey Eastern Railway by Peter Paye, and further information on Grouville Station that was very useful when writing outings for Florence and Jesse.

The Jerripedia website, a wealth of information and a useful source that helped me visualise life in 1880s Jersey.

My large family for allowing me to share my excitement about discoveries I had made about Florence, Jesse and their intriguing life, and who all kept this project a secret when I asked them to.

My supportive husband, Rob and my son, James, who, if they

tire of hearing about my writing and grumbling when a writing day hasn't gone as well as I'd hoped, don't ever show it.

My daughter Saskia, another woman who is strong, kind and determined to help others, and of whom I'm very proud.

Finally, to you, the reader. Thank you for choosing to read *Mrs Boots*. I hope you enjoy getting to know Florence and Jesse as much as I did.